Along

the

Rio Grande

Books by Tracie Peterson

*with Kimberley Woodhouse

**with Karen Witemeyer, Regina Jennings, and Jen Turano

For a complete list of Tracie's books, visit her website www.traciepeterson.com

LOVE ON THE SANTA FE

Along the Rio Grande

TRACIE PETERSON

BETHANYHOUSE
a division of Baker Publishing Group
Minneapolis, Minnesota

© 2022 by Peterson Ink, Inc.

Published by Bethany House Publishers
11400 Hampshire Avenue South
Minneapolis, Minnesota 55438
www.bethanyhouse.com

Bethany House Publishers is a division of
Baker Publishing Group, Grand Rapids, Michigan

Printed in the United States of America

Library of Congress Cataloging-in-Publication Data
Names: Peterson, Tracie, author.
Title: Along the Rio Grande / Tracie Peterson.
Description: Minneapolis, Minnesota : Bethany House Publishers, a division of
    Baker Publishing Group, [2022] | Series: Love on the Santa Fe
Identifiers: LCCN 2021042632 | ISBN 9780764237294 (trade paperback) |
    ISBN 9780764237300 (cloth) | ISBN 9780764237317 (large print) | ISBN
    9781493435968 (ebook)
Subjects: LCGFT: Romance fiction. | Novels.
Classification: LCC PS3566.E7717 A797 2022 | DDC 813/.54—dc23
LC record available at https://lccn.loc.gov/2021042632

Scripture quotations are from the King James Version of the Bible.

Cover design by LOOK Design Studio

Cover photography by Aimee Christenson

Baker Publishing Group publications use paper produced from sustainable forestry practices and post-consumer waste whenever possible.

22 23 24 25 26 27 28   7 6 5 4 3 2 1

Dedicated to the men and women of
the Santa Fe Railway and all of its divisions.
With special thanks to those members
of the Horny Toad Division.

1

Susanna Ragsdale Jenkins stepped off the Santa Fe passenger train and sighed. The breeze outside was only mildly helpful. Inside the stuffy cars of the train, women had actually fainted from the heat. Susanna's mother had to be revived no fewer than ten times. Of course, that was typical for her overly dramatic mother. Gladys Ragsdale did love attention.

Susanna looked around as her father assisted Mother from the train. Her brother, Gary, was already hailing a porter for their bags. At eighteen, nothing seemed to deter him. He was energetic and impressionable, as well as foolish and thoughtless. He'd barely made it through school, and as the spoiled and pampered son of wealthy parents, no one really cared. Susanna had watched her parents try to manage him, but Gary had no respect for either of them. All they had taught him was how to live a life of privilege and the expectation that someone, somewhere, would provide the means for his desires. With that no longer the case, Gary had become even more headstrong and impatient. It was one of the reasons Susanna had agreed to accompany her family to New Mexico.

That, and she saw it as the easiest way to avoid the promise she'd made her dying husband.

She buried that thought deep as Gary approached.

"I'm going to see what kind of fun is to be had in this town." Beneath his stylish straw hat, his golden-brown hair was dripping sweat.

Susanna fixed him with a stern look and shook her head. "No, you will help Father get Mother settled at the hotel. Then you will make certain our bags are delivered to the hotel."

He looked at her for a moment as if trying to decide whether he'd go along with this new order. For a full minute, Susanna wondered if there was going to be trouble, but when

Mother cried out and began to crumple to her knees, Gary went to help her.

What was Uncle Harrison thinking, sending a pair like her parents to manage a hotel in the middle-of-nowhere New Mexico? Susanna was appalled. San Marcial was a railroad town—a headquarters for the Rio Grande Division of the Santa Fe Railway.

"You have wasted your inheritance by investing in schemes that you were warned against. Time and again you put your family in a state of diminished financial security, always relying on me to straighten out the situation. Well, no more," Uncle Harrison had said on their last night in Topeka. *"I have no choice but to cut you off from further financial support and make you work for a living."*

Susanna could still hear her mother's shriek of distaste. *"I wasn't born to be married to a man who has to do physical labor! How embarrassing! Oh, the thought of it is enough to give me apoplexy."*

"Well, have your fits somewhere besides my hotel sitting room," Harrison Ragsdale had demanded.

Susanna had been invited to the meeting only because her uncle knew she could help keep some sense of order. Having lived her first year of mourning with her in-laws, she had agreed to move with her parents to

New Mexico and see them settled at the hotel her uncle had built. But her years living with her husband had helped her forget just how bad her family could be. Now that they were broke, it was bound to be even worse.

Susanna swept pieces of soot and ash from her black gown. She had already determined that this would be her last day of full mourning. It had been over a year, after all, and she hated black. The constant reminder of what she'd lost—what she would never have again.

"Where is this supposed hotel?" her mother asked as Father and Gary supported her on either side.

"Uncle Harrison said it was two blocks from the train. Easy walking." Susanna motioned for the porter Gary had given up on securing.

A black man came to her immediately. "Yes, ma'am, how may I help you?"

"We're the Ragsdale family, and I need to arrange for the delivery of our luggage. We are staying at the Grand Hotel. It's new, and my family has come here to open it."

"Yes, ma'am. We saw it bein' built. Mighty fine place just over yonder." He pointed to the northeast. There, clearly visible from the train station, was a large, white-washed two-story building with a huge sign that read *Grand Hotel*.

She studied it for a moment, then nodded. It looked just as Uncle Harrison had described. A regal, clean, and very welcoming sight.

She turned back to the porter and smiled. "Would you arrange for our things?" She reached into her purse, pulled out fifty cents, and handed it to him. "Have the baggageman bring them to the hotel's front desk, please."

He gave her a slight bow. "I'll see to it."

"Thank you." She left him to manage the situation and caught up with her folks and brother. "The bags are handled and should be delivered shortly. There is the hotel."

"I cannot live in a hotel as the wife of a . . . *manager*," her mother declared. "The shame is too great."

"Mother, we've already discussed this in Topeka, on the train, and now upon our arrival. The fact of the matter is that you have no choice. Now, let us at least go and see what the accommodations are like." Susanna looked at her father. Sweat poured from his head and had already soaked the neckline of his shirt. None of them looked like anything special. Just a bedraggled crew of travelers who had lost their way.

Susanna led their parade, crossing Railroad Avenue at Zimmerman Street and then walking up to First Street. She raised her parasol for the short walk. The sun was merciless, and she knew she would burn to a crisp otherwise. Her fair skin had always freckled easily, much to her mother's disgust. A proper lady simply did not have freckles.

She reached the hotel well ahead of the others and tried the door. It was locked, and Father had both sets of keys. By the time her family joined her, Mother was sobbing softly into her handkerchief, and Gary was itching to take off and explore.

"I just want to see what's available. We're going to need food no matter what." He started to leave, and Susanna called him back.

"We'll eat at the Harvey House once we get settled. Stay here and help when the bags come. We don't know what to expect. There will be plenty of time to explore later."

Gary pulled off his hat, giving an exaggerated sigh. He wiped the sweat from his forehead. "You aren't happy unless you're bossing me around."

Susanna ignored him. "Father, the door is locked, and you have the only keys. I suggest you give me one set so that we each have one, since I'm going to be helping you keep the front desk." She closed her parasol and gave him a smile.

"Of course. Of course."

Father produced the two keys and handed

one to her. He didn't seem to know what to do with the other one. Susanna finally rolled her eyes and opened the door herself.

The smell of new paint wafted out the door as she walked inside. Everything was pristine and bright, painted in yellow with white trim. She made her way to the front desk. Uncle Harrison had told them they'd find the family living quarters behind it.

She tried the door to the right and found a closet with supplies and bedding. The door on the left, however, opened onto a living area.

"Here we are." She looked around the room. There was ample space for two people, to be certain. Less for the four who had arrived.

"This will not do," Mother declared. "There is only one large room that combines everything. We would have to have the cook in here, working in the kitchen, while we tried our best to relax . . . or worse, entertain."

"Mother, I do not believe we have the budget either for a cook or to entertain." Susanna knew this change of financial solvency had wounded her mother dearly. Gladys Ragsdale had always believed herself to be upper society, and the fact that her husband had lost all of their money was something she could not reconcile.

"You are determined to kill me." Her

mother collapsed onto a cushioned chair. "This isn't even comfortable, and this town is in the middle of nowhere. It feels like a furnace in here."

"I'm sure once we get things organized," Susanna's father began, "it will be better. The nights will cool off surprisingly fast. Everyone says so."

Mother's disgruntled huff suggested otherwise. "We don't even have electricity."

"But they are putting it in very soon."

"There are two bedrooms in the back," Gary announced. "They're very small. Both have two little beds."

"I told Uncle I would pay for a separate hotel room, but he wouldn't hear of it." Susanna began taking off her black gloves. "I'm to have room 101."

"A room to yourself? How very spoiled." Her mother's tone was accusing.

"I suppose you and I could share one of these bedrooms and Father and Gary the other, but it's hardly appropriate for Gary and me to share a room at our age." Susanna wondered what her mother would say to that idea.

She didn't have long to wait.

"This is uncalled for, Herbert. We cannot live this way. I won't live this way!"

"And where will you go?" Father asked, finally reaching the end of his patience.

Everyone looked at Mother, which only increased her discomfort. She burst into tears and made a dash for one of the bedrooms.

"Oh, look, we have a private bath," Gary announced, opening the final door.

"Yes, Uncle Harrison said there would be one," Susanna replied. She set her purse and gloves aside and began to unpin her hat. With that accomplished, she put it with her other things and went to the windows. "We need to open these and get a bit of air in here. That's bound to help our moods."

The baggageman arrived, and Gary hurried off to help with that. Susanna raised the first window and moved on to the next.

"Your mother is very upset, and I cannot blame her," Father said. "She had the best of everything in Topeka."

"And perhaps one day she'll have the best of everything again," Susanna declared. "For now, however, we must be patient and work hard. She has never had to do that, and it will not come easy to her."

Her father shook his head. "I was so sure of that investment. If I hadn't been, I never would have risked the house and everything else. You must understand. It was a sure thing."

Susanna straightened. "What I understand is that it *wasn't* a sure thing. Had it been, you wouldn't have lost everything and be standing here now in San Marcial, New Mexico."

"No, that's for sure. Your mother is right—it is a godforsaken place."

"I don't think so."

Susanna moved on to the next window as Gary carried in the first three bags. They all belonged to her parents, as would most of the next ten. Mother had crammed as much of their Topeka life into those cases as she could, knowing that everything else would have to be sold to cover their embarrassing losses. Thankfully, Uncle Harrison was handling the sale of their things so that Mother needn't be completely covered in shame.

"I should help Gary," her father said, looking to Susanna as if she might correct him.

"Yes, I think that would be good, since most of the luggage belongs to you and Mother. You'll need to give the baggageman a gratuity."

Her father grumbled something, but Susanna couldn't make it out.

By the time Susanna had all the windows open, Gary and Father had moved all of the bags into the living quarters except the two small bags and large trunk that belonged to Susanna. Those they'd left by the front desk.

"Should we unpack?" Father asked, seeming confused.

"No," Susanna said. "It's getting late. I think we should gather Mother and go for dinner. Getting some food in our stomachs will help us think more clearly. Then we can decide what to do first."

It was easier said than done. Mother wanted no part in leaving the hotel, but at the same time, Susanna knew she was famished. They had enjoyed Harvey House food all along the railroad from Topeka. It had been the one thing with which Mother hadn't found fault. Each table was elegantly set with fine linen and crystal. The men were made to wear suit jackets in the dining rooms, and the service was that of an elegant restaurant, even in the smallest Kansas town.

When they finally had Mother on her feet and willing to walk to the Harvey House, Susanna was ready to be done with all of them. Their selfishness and unwillingness to take responsibility for their own actions was more than she could bear. She knew they were more than a little embarrassed at their reduced status, but it was ridiculous to pretend it was all a mistake. Susanna's father had been mismanaging his inheritance since it had been in his possession. He thought himself something of a grand entrepreneur—a financial baron who was able to turn pennies into dollars, lead into gold. But instead, all Susanna had seen was her father continually making poor choices that his brother had to cover and make good on. Now Uncle Harrison had put a stop to his protection and had given his brother an honest-to-goodness job running a hotel. It was quite the departure.

Susanna had no idea what had transpired between the brothers in discussion, but she knew her uncle had reached his limit of understanding and sympathy. He had called Susanna to a private meeting, where he talked to her at length about what had happened to her parents. Susanna had been living with her in-laws and knew very little. Her parents were never ones to discuss money.

News of her family's crisis, however, was rapidly spreading all over town. Her father had heavily invested in a railroad that turned out to be nothing but paper and the imagination of a conman who was now long gone. Father had given everything and was left with nothing. Even the deed to the house had been sold. Uncle Harrison had tried to advise him, as had others, but Father wouldn't listen, and perhaps that was the reason her uncle was ready to wash his hands of the entire matter.

Who could blame him? Since they'd been boys, her father had the reputation of listening to no one. He loved to find what he thought to be lucrative deals, and from time to time they actually worked out. Of course, this only encouraged him to seek out more arrangements, and usually those fell apart. Still, he maintained a reputation of being a man capable of great risk.

Seated in the Harvey House, Susanna was relieved to feel that the temperatures were a bit cooler. She placed her order for iced tea and baked chicken and marveled at the efficiency of the Harvey House waitresses in their crisp uniforms of black and white.

It wasn't long before the table was filled with plates of steaming food and iced drinks. Gary dug right in to his heaping pile of potatoes and gravy. Mother gave a sniff. She sampled the tea and seemed to find it acceptable. And why not? As Susanna understood it, the coffee and tea were made from water that had been tanked in from Kansas City. Every Harvey House along the line made their coffee and tea this way so that no matter where a traveler happened upon the line, they would have the same quality and delicious taste.

Susanna felt the tension in her neck begin to ease as she thought of the possibility of a bath and a long sleep. She had been so busy the last two weeks, helping her family get ready for this move, and it seemed she hadn't had a moment to herself. The last year had been hard. Losing Mark to influenza was ever at the forefront of her thoughts. They had been the best of friends since grade school. Now he was gone, and while Susanna felt that she'd dealt with the first impositions of that loss, she was uncertain about her next stage of life. Mark had insisted she remarry, and she had promised him she would, even knowing she never could. The hole left in her heart wasn't likely to be filled by another man, and if it wasn't to be filled, then why bother to marry at all? Still, she felt a sense of guilt, knowing she had given him her word.

"This beef is delicious," her father declared. "This man Harvey knows what he's doing when it comes to food. I wonder if he's ever thought about expanding to other train lines. It seems foolish to stay with just the Santa Fe."

Many of her father's ventures had started with less, and Susanna moved the conversation to something else. "Do you recall when the first reservations at the hotel are slated to begin?"

Her father looked up and shook his head. "I can't say that I do. Harrison wrote it all in the paperwork. I shall have to sit down with the books and papers and study them."

"Well, I believe you said the first reservations were to begin Monday. That gives us just two days to make certain everything is in order." Susanna cut into her chicken. It looked perfect.

"Two days to get that place into shape for a grand opening hardly seems enough time," her mother said, lifting her chin defiantly. "I don't see how we can be expected to manage. We'll need to hire workers."

"Mother, we are the workers."

The older woman began tearing up again and dabbed her eyes with her linen napkin.

Susanna shook her head. "But we will be working together. Tomorrow is Saturday, and we will be able to divide up the work and see what is left to be done. It appears everything is in order. We shall have to make the beds and perhaps scout out some fresh flowers. I like the little arrangements they have here in the Harvey House. Perhaps we can ask where they've acquired them."

Mother turned to her husband. "This is so unfair. Herbert, I cannot live in a hotel. I'm sorry. I simply cannot."

"What do you suggest I do, my dear?" Father said with a sigh.

She straightened. "Buy me a house. At the very least, rent me one. I shall be completely at peace if you just manage that."

Susanna's father looked at his wife and

then back to his plate. "I'll do what I can, dear."

⁓

Herbert Ragsdale knew there was very little he could do to please his wife. She had already threatened to leave him for the comfort of friends. The entire situation was a mistake, and he'd made certain she knew that. Harrison was merely trying to impose his will on them, as he and Father had always done where Herbert was concerned. Surely this was all just a grand joke on Harrison's part to teach Herbert yet another lesson that he somehow believed had been missed.

Pushing a slice of the Harvey House's famous pie around his plate, Herbert found it difficult to look his family in the eye. Because what if it wasn't a grand scheme? What if he'd truly lost everything? What if Harrison wasn't just pretending that Herbert was broke?

Herbert had watched the bank officials post foreclosure signs on his property. He'd seen the auction people come and start categorizing his beloved furnishings. The bank manager himself had collected all of the jewelry he and Gladys owned. If this was just a scheme to shame his younger brother, Harrison had gone to complete extremes.

A sense of dread washed over Herbert.

Was it possible it was all real? Could Harrison really allow Herbert to lose all that he'd worked so hard to maintain? He put down his fork and noted that his wife was watching him apprehensively. Even Susanna and Gary had a look in their eyes that he couldn't quite identify. Was it betrayal? Did they feel he'd failed them? Surely not. How could they? He might have trusted the wrong person, but he had done nothing wrong. One of these days he would make the right investment and win them a fortune.

He forced a smile, but they only looked away.

Would they always believe he'd failed them? Curse Harrison for putting that idea in their minds, if so. This was all his brother's game. That was all it was. And the sooner Harrison showed up in San Marcial, the sooner Herbert would set him straight.

A week later, after a quiet but successful hotel opening, Susanna was determined to find her parents proper accommodations.

The townsfolk seemed enthusiastic about their new hotel, and so far there had been half a dozen guests with the promise of more. Susanna had even managed to get into something of a routine. Each morning she went to the rooms that had been vacated by guests. She opened the window to air out the room, then stripped the covers and hung them over the foot rail of the iron bed in order to air those as well. She then put the sheets and pillowcases into a pile for laundry. She dusted and swept and then moved on to the next room in order to let things settle before finally returning to make the beds with clean linen and close things back up. It seemed a good order in which to handle matters.

But even with this sense of accomplishment and organization, Susanna couldn't ignore that her mother had caused something of a personal riot in the family. Mother hated the hotel and simply would not live there a moment longer. She'd already gone to the train station four times to check the schedule for trains back to Topeka.

There were certain things her mother would complain about for a time and then let go, but Susanna knew the idea of a proper home wasn't one of them. Mother was impossible to please. She complained or cried from morning to night. Susanna had done her best to reason with her, but Mother wouldn't hear it. She just kept on with the demand that someone needed to find her another place to live.

"I wasn't born to this kind of life," Mother

would reiterate. "I cannot bear it. My constitution is such that I will surely die."

Day after day she remained in her room, crying or raging. From time to time she came out long enough to make everyone miserable. Susanna found herself reaching a breaking point, even though she knew this was Uncle Harrison's punishment for her parents.

She had brought a good amount of money with her, although she hadn't yet had time to go to the bank. Between her mother's fits and her father's incompetency, Susanna found it necessary to do most of the chores to see the hotel properly run. Once Father was able to check in a guest and direct them to their room, he took over the front desk, but that didn't help with the laundry and cleaning responsibilities, which her mother should have had to do. Mother, however, refused, leaving Susanna to work alone. She rarely addressed Susanna directly unless it was to nag and whine about their living accommodations or lack of luxury.

"This is completely uncalled for," Mother announced as Susanna ironed sheets one day. "We are above this kind of thing. You must contact Harrison and demand what is rightfully yours," she said when Father entered the room.

"Maybe you should contact him and tell

him yourself," Father replied, plopping onto the small sofa.

Mother began to cry again, and Susanna knew a great argument was soon to follow. Mother would tell Father he was a fool to allow his brother to do such an abominable thing to him. That a competent man wouldn't let himself be pushed around.

Susanna focused on the ironing as her mother began her tirade. Father wasn't truly a bad person. He was just unwise. He was fooled by his own sense of importance and supposed wisdom. Just as her mother had illusions of being an important member of high society, her father firmly believed himself to be a financial master. This setback was just a minor inconvenience, and as soon as his brother was able to straighten things out in Topeka, all would be forgotten.

She sighed. Her parents had a strange inability to face reality. But, of course, others had aided in their delusion. Even Uncle Harrison admitted that much. That was, in fact, why he felt he must take a hard stand now. Otherwise, Gary would turn out to be no different.

Poor Gary. Susanna had tried to speak to him, but this situation had changed him. He was angry and disrespectful. He blamed Father for ruining his life and future plans.

He had been bound for college in the fall, without direction or purpose. His grades were abominable, and had it not been for the promise of hefty donations by their father, Gary wouldn't have even qualified for attendance. Now, with the money gone and no donations forthcoming, Gary's invitation had been rescinded, and college was no longer an option.

Susanna really couldn't blame her brother for his anger. She was beginning to have plenty of her own. If she'd been smart, she would have remained in Topeka with her in-laws.

2

When Mother's campaign of whining and crying only escalated the next day, Susanna decided enough was enough. Uncle Harrison might not want her parents living elsewhere, but frankly, if they didn't move off the premises, Susanna knew there would be trouble.

She took it upon herself to start scouting for a house. Anything would do, she told herself. She could use her own money. They didn't need to know about it. She spoke to several store owners before happening upon one who happened not only to know of a small house for sale but also owned it. Carson Medford appeared to be in his sixties, yet there was a twinkle in his eye and a spring in his step that suggested he was far from old. He left his store in the care of his hired clerk and escorted Susanna to the house's location.

"I used to live there with my wife, but after she died, it seemed ridiculous to have all the room over the store sitting empty and me living in a house that I could just as easily sell."

They approached a charming adobe house. It was rectangular in appearance with a couple of deep-set windows on the front.

"It's only a few blocks to the hotel. This would work out very nicely," Susanna declared.

"I haven't even advertised it for sale. Things move pretty fast around here, and there's always a headquarter official looking for a house. I don't know why, but as I prayed about it, I didn't feel compelled to put it up for sale yet. But when you asked, it just felt right."

"So you're a man of God." She smiled. "I, too, put my trust in the Lord. I began praying for a house when I realized how miserable my mother would be staying at the hotel."

"We're all pretty inspired by the new hotel. Your uncle spared no expense, and it has urged the rest of us to spruce things up. We've got over a thousand people living in town now, so we might as well make it as nice as we can. Here we are." He unlocked the front door. "It has two bedrooms. It's not a big house, as I said, but it is solid. The walls are a foot thick, and the house stays cool in the heat of the summer and warm when the cold weather comes."

"Does cold weather ever come to the desert?" she asked.

"Absolutely. We had us a blizzard not two winters back. It comes heavier in the higher elevations, of course, but we've had our share of cold and even snow." He led her into a room on the left. "Here's the kitchen. You can see that it has an icebox. The train brings in ice regular, so it's not a problem to have ice delivered. We're pretty modern here."

"I would say so." She smiled and continued her inspection.

"The smaller of the two bedrooms is off the right of the living room, and the larger is on the left." He opened the door to the smaller bedroom, and Susanna stepped in. She could see it working well for Gary. "There's an outhouse in the back and a couple of cauldrons for laundry near the outside pump."

"Sounds quite convenient." Of course, her mother wouldn't think so.

After seeing all there was to see, she knew it was time to hear the price and negotiate the details. Could she manage it for herself? This would be her first big venture without her father-in-law, husband, or Uncle Harrison to guide her. She glanced heavenward and whispered a prayer.

"And what is the price you are asking for this house?" She decided it was best to get right to the point.

Mr. Medford looked at her rather sheepishly. "Well, the fact is . . . I had a higher price in mind, but the Lord gave me another number to ask."

For whatever reason, his words put Susanna at ease. "Very well, and what is that price?"

"Three hundred dollars."

She thought of the money she had back in the hotel safe. She had brought exactly four hundred dollars with her from Topeka. There was more than enough to pay cash and have money left over until she could arrange with the bank for more.

"And the furniture stays with it?" She glanced around at the sparse but adequate pieces.

"It does. Two beds, one in each room, kitchen table with four chairs, and the sofa in the living room. And like I said, the laundry cauldrons stay."

"I'll take it. It seems the Lord is looking out for the both of us today."

Mr. Medford nodded. "I've never known Him to do otherwise."

She smiled at the old man and extended her hand. "Neither have I."

"You will just have to wear it wrinkled," Mother declared to Gary as he fussed over his Sunday shirt. "I don't know how to iron it. I've never had to do such things for myself."

"I could stay home. You're the one who always protests wrinkles. We are supposed to look our best all the time in case we come across someone who will promote our destiny."

"Well, they certainly won't come from this horrid place. Decent people wouldn't be caught dead here."

Susanna had just arrived from the hotel and looked at her mother. "How did the house suit you last night?" She had borrowed linens from the hotel to make the beds and give it a homier appeal before showing it to her mother and father. For now she'd told them they could rent the house. She had no desire for them to know she had bought it outright. If they knew she had money, there would be no end to her misery.

"It certainly isn't what we are used to," her mother replied, "but it is better than that hotel. I simply could not show my face in church with the explanation that I was living behind the work desk of a hotel. The shame would have been too great."

Susanna knew she'd only made the situation worse in some ways. Her mother had complained and cried and gotten her way once again. Susanna wasn't teaching her anything but that such actions continued to work. But it had given Susanna great peace of mind. With her parents and Gary staying at the house, she had taken the hotel manager's rooms. As far as she was concerned, she'd gotten the best of the arrangement.

"The Methodist church services start in ten minutes," Mother announced. "We need to go now, or we'll be rushed in getting there. I hate that we must walk everywhere. Herbert, you simply must arrange for us to have a carriage."

"Mother, there is nothing far enough away to merit a carriage. We can walk to all of the stores, the church, and the Harvey House." Susanna shook her head. "Even the railroad depot is close. And we certainly cannot afford to purchase a carriage and horses. Nor do you have any place to keep them, so we would have the added expense of a livery."

"Oh, you are always so uncaring, Susanna. My nerves simply will not take walking everywhere. Especially when it's hot."

"I'm sorry, Mother, but you will have to get used to walking in the heat. Besides, you'll have plenty of work at the hotel to do, so being out and about won't be a problem. I won't be here forever, and you'll need to take over my duties."

Her mother looked stunned. "I can't. I won't. I wasn't raised to do such things." She looked at her husband. "I haven't the constitution for it."

"Don't go on so, Gladys. We'll get it all figured out. Maybe Gary can take over Susanna's chores when she leaves us."

"I'm no washerwoman," Gary declared. "Cooking and cleaning are women's work. I'm going to check into a job at the Santa Fe."

"What about helping me with the hotel?" Father asked.

"The hotel is your punishment, not mine," Gary replied.

The look of surprise on Father's face left Susanna certain a fight was about to erupt.

She shook her head and reached for her brother's arm. "We're going to be late for church."

They headed out of the house, and Susanna remarked at how much cooler it had been inside.

"The adobe keeps the house so nice and cool. Won't that be a blessing, Mother?"

"Electricity would be a blessing. I honestly don't know why things are so primitive. The railroad has electricity, and you would think the town could afford it."

"Uncle Harrison said it's coming. That's why he had the hotel wired for it. It was no doubt a great expense, but he plans for there to be fans in every room."

"He can afford it," Mother countered. "Which is why it's a grief that he won't help us for a short time while your father finds something new in which to invest. It's hardly his fault that the other venture came to an end."

Susanna could not understand what thoughts must be inside her mother's head. Did she not comprehend that the choices Father made had robbed them of their financial security? Did she not understand that her husband's pride had put them in this position? Her mother wasn't generally naïve about money, but when it came to her husband, it seemed he could do no wrong and any complication was someone else's fault.

A group of brown-skinned children ran past them. They were laughing and bantering back and forth in Spanish. Susanna smiled. How wonderful to be so carefree.

"Savages," her father murmured.

"Savages, father?" Susanna stared at him, shocked. "They're children. And from the look of it, they're headed to church."

"I suppose they could have been brought to the Lord," he murmured. "I'm still not

convinced that such wild people can understand what it is to be tamed and settled."

"Well, perhaps it would be wise to keep
such thoughts to yourself, Father. After all,
it's nearly 1900. I would say your thoughts
are a bit archaic and out of place."

"You know what your brother said, Herbert. Some of the Indians are even working
for the railroad," Mother announced. "Not to
mention"—she lowered her voice to a whisper—"the Mexicans."

Susanna rolled her gaze toward heaven.
How in the world were her parents ever to
live and succeed in San Marcial, where the
better part of the people around them were
either Indians or Mexicans? They held such
prejudices and didn't see anything wrong in
openly admitting their thoughts. She could
only imagine the fights Gary would get into.
He'd never lived around people of color. Topeka had small groups of such folks, but they
stayed to certain parts of town, as was expected of them. Susanna seriously doubted
Gary had ever spoken to someone with skin
of a different color than his own. This would
bring new experiences for them all.

They arrived at the Methodist church,
and to Susanna's delight, Carson Medford
was there, welcoming folks into the building.

"Ah, Mrs. Jenkins," he said, beaming a

smile. "I'm so glad you could make it. Are these your folks?" he asked, nodding toward her parents.

"They are. Mr. Medford, this is my father, Herbert Ragsdale, my mother, Gladys, and brother, Gary. Family, this is Mr. Medford. He's the one who . . . who . . . had the house for us."

"It's a solid house, to be sure," Susanna's father declared. "I'm grateful that it was available so quickly."

"The Lord always has these things worked out. Welcome to the Methodist church. I think you'll enjoy worshipping with us," Mr. Medford declared. "We can raise the roof with our singing."

"How interesting," Mother said, forcing a smile.

"Let me guide you to a seat." Mr. Medford led the way, taking them to an empty row second from the front.

Mother nodded with a look of smug satisfaction as she gazed around at the other congregants. At their church in Topeka, the more important the family, the closer they sat to the front. This spot would very much meet with her mother's approval.

The organist began to play, and the entire room filled with music as the congregation rose. Susanna got to her feet and accepted a hymnal from Mr. Medford before he headed back to his duty at the door.

"Page thirteen. 'Blessed Be Thy Name,'" he whispered.

Owen Turner slipped into the back pew just as the singing concluded. He hadn't meant to oversleep, but lately he'd been so tired from putting in extra hours. As a supervising boilermaker and repairman for the Santa Fe shops, Owen was always needed for one job or another, and nothing took its toll on him like the hot summer months of San Marcial.

The offering plate was passed, and he contributed as he did every week. His friends LeRoy and Lia sat on the opposite side of the church with their two boys. Seven-year-old Emilio gave him a wave, causing nine-year-old John to do the same. The boys giggled, which drew their parents' attention. LeRoy looked across to where Owen sat and gave a nod before thumping both of his boys on the back of the head. LeRoy's pretty wife, Rosalia—Lia to her friends—gave him a smile and continued to sing.

Owen tried to focus on the music, but the fact was, it had been hard to drag himself out of bed that morning. He'd gone to bed plenty early, but his neighbors hadn't, and all their thumping and hollering left him unable to sleep. Now they were soundly snoring, and he was trying to stay awake in church services.

Prayers were offered, and then Pastor Lewis took the pulpit. A huge smile split his face. "What a wonderful day to be in the house of the Lord!"

"Amen," many of the people responded.

"I was just telling Agnes this morning what a blessing it was to know you'd all be here and that together we would share the Word of God. Doesn't that just light your candles?"

Owen had to chuckle along with the others. The old Texan always had a way with words. Except when reading Scripture. For that, he was quite formal.

The congregation stood for the reading of God's Word, and Pastor Lewis blessed the passage coming and going.

"Let us read from Luke fourteen." Everyone rose in unison except for a few folks at the very front. Owen figured they were new to the procedure as they struggled to their feet.

"Father, we ask for wisdom and understanding as we consider Your Word. Amen."

"Amen," the congregation murmured.

Pastor Lewis read the Scripture passage,

then ended in his usual manner. "Thus saith the Word of God."

Everyone knew this was their cue to sit. Everyone but the new people. Owen could see now that they were strangers to the church. He was particularly intrigued by the shapely young woman standing beside an older matron.

"Folks, this is a good passage about thinkin' of ourselves less and honorin' others more. God doesn't want you puttin' on airs and runnin' around looking for ways to make yourself seem important. When you got a weddin' to go to, who's important? The bride and groom, right? Don't much matter if you're there or not, unless you're one of those two folks. Sure, you were invited, and you might even be kin, but the most important people are the ones who are gettin' hitched.

"Now, don't get me wrong, a weddin' is a good time for everyone. A great celebration, and probably all the ladies in the church cooked up their best dishes. That's always my personal favorite part." He paused with a grin, and the people chuckled. "But anyhow, the Lord wants to teach us humility and understandin'. If we don't practice it, we might call attention and embarrassment on ourselves. See, here Jesus is talkin' about not sittin' down at the best seats and then having to be asked to leave them for sittin' at the far table. Just start out with the far table. The food will be just as good there as at the head table." He chuckled. "Maybe better."

The people laughed or smiled as the pastor continued.

"Don't always be thinkin' of yourself as so important. Throughout the Bible we're told to think of other folks as better than ourselves. If we do this, we'll treat them with respect and honor them with our conversation and actions. It doesn't take a whole lot to show someone they're important to us."

He continued preaching about seeking humility. Owen understood this better than most. He'd spent a good part of his life avoiding the attention of folks around him. Unlike his younger brother, who craved attention. Unfortunately, his brother's desires had often backfired on him, somehow managing to leave Owen wounded in the crossfire. Daniel just seemed to have a knack for being at the wrong place at the right time.

Owen pushed the thought aside. He'd come to worship the Lord, not to think ill of his brother. That kind of thinking could come at most any other time and often did.

"I can't think of a single time," the pastor declared, "when takin' the lower place of importance served a man poorly. If he was already considered no account and unimportant, his decision to act as such left him without disgrace. And if he truly was important . . . well, it gave the host a chance to esteem the fella and bring him honor and a little attention. Better to let someone else sing your praises than find yourself tryin' to get folks to see how important you think you are. Especially if you aren't that important." He grinned out at the congregation. "But you know, each of you are important to the Lord, and because of that you're important to me. I want you each to know what a blessing you've been to me.

"Now, I see we have some new folks with us today, and while I don't know exactly who they are or how they will affect my life or yours, I'm asking you all to make them feel welcome after the service. And with that, I think Ralph has another song for us to sing."

The song leader nodded to the organist, and the music started up once again. Owen smiled. Pastor Lewis always made his day better.

When the services were concluded, Owen slipped over to speak with LeRoy and Lia. The boys were immediately all over him.

"Uncle Owen, you gonna take us fishing today?"

"Not today, boys," their father answered.

"Remember, we're heading to Poppy's ranch to celebrate his birthday."

"You're welcome to join us, Owen. My father loves you," Lia declared. "We're taking the train both ways, so it won't take long at all."

"No. I didn't sleep well last night and believe I'll take a nap."

LeRoy laughed. "Take one for me too."

Owen promised he would, then made his way outside. He glanced around, hoping to find the new folks so he could give them a proper greeting as the pastor had asked them to do. He spotted the older man and woman along with a young man he presumed was their son. They were talking to Pastor Lewis and his wife. Owen rounded the corner of the church and made his way toward a gathering of folks, where he found the young woman who'd caught his attention.

"Owen, I'm glad you're here," one of the ladies called. "Come meet Mrs. Jenkins."

Missus, eh? Well, somehow that figured. Owen gave a wave to acknowledge he'd heard the request and made his way over. Mrs. Jenkins glanced up, smiling, and for a moment Owen felt his breath catch. She stepped away from the others and extended her hand. He reached to take hold in greeting.

Just then the squeals of children at play built to a crescendo as a herd of children came barreling at them. Two little girls were leading the way with a jump rope between them. One headed right and one left, resulting in Owen and Mrs. Jenkins being caught in the middle.

Owen grabbed hold of Mrs. Jenkins just as the rope snagged him behind the knees. The girls seemed immediately to know what they'd done wrong and ran back toward each other, further entangling the two adults. As Owen and Mrs. Jenkins began to fall, he rotated to take her weight atop him so he wouldn't crush her. With a *whoosh*, they landed on the ground, bound face-to-face by the rope.

Owen couldn't help but smile at Mrs. Jenkins's surprised expression. "Welcome to San Marcial," he declared, laughing.

To his surprise, she started laughing as well. The folks around them laughed as Owen sorted out the rope and got to his feet. He reached down to help Mrs. Jenkins, who was by now laughing so hard that she could hardly sit up. Her humor at the situation only made him like her all the more. It was a pity she was married.

He took her hand, but instead of pulling her to her feet, Owen was nearly forced to his knees. It was like trying to gather water. Her mirth made her completely useless. The people around her laughed all the more and offered a hand, but it seemed almost impossible to get Mrs. Jenkins to her feet even though she was but a slip of a gal.

Finally, however, they had her upright. She dabbed at her cheeks and shook her head as she met Owen's gaze. "Well, I suppose I've made quite the impression."

By now the older man and woman, as well as the younger man, had come to see what the ruckus was. The older woman looked quite put out. "Susanna, conduct yourself."

"I am, Mother. I am but doing a poor job of it."

"Nonsense," an older woman from the church declared. "This is the best time any of us have had in ages. It does a soul so much good to laugh."

"Being laughed at is hardly the impression a widow needs to be making," the stranger said, shaking her head.

"We're not laughing at her, ma'am," Owen said, realizing that he still held fast to Mrs. Jenkins's arm.

"Of course they aren't," Mrs. Jenkins declared. She looked at Owen. "Thank you for the rescue. I'm Susanna Jenkins."

"Owen Turner."

The pastor joined them. "I see you've met the Widow Jenkins, Owen. Leave it to you to get wrapped up with one of the purdiest gals to grace our spread."

The comments about Mrs. Jenkins's widowhood were not lost on Owen. He looked at her, unable to keep the surprise from his expression as he let go of her arm. "I'm so sorry."

Mrs. Jenkins nodded. "Thank you." She sobered and began to dust off her dress.

People began talking of other things, and Owen felt he'd somehow overstepped his bounds.

"These are my parents, Mr. Turner," Mrs. Jenkins said, "Mr. and Mrs. Ragsdale. And my brother, Gary."

Her introduction furthered his embarrassment. "Pleasure to meet you all. I'm Owen Turner. I work for the Santa Fe, as most of us do."

"I'd like to talk to you about it," Gary said. "I don't know anybody here or anything about the railroad, but I'm thinking about getting a job with them."

"Well, maybe you'd all like to be my guests for lunch." Owen wanted to kick himself. Why had he just done that? "At the Harvey House," he hurried to add.

"We were headed there," the older man

declared. "It would be very neighborly of you to have us as your guests."

Owen nodded. "Then it's settled. Come on. I always have a table waiting for me on Sunday."

3

Lunch with Owen passed quickly, and before she knew it, Susanna was walking by his side as they made their way back to the hotel. Mother and Father had left the restaurant early because Mother had declared the heat was making her ill, but both seemed to like Owen well enough, as they insisted he would be invited to dinner one evening soon.

Gary remained to discuss his sudden fascination with the Santa Fe Railway, making it perfectly acceptable for Owen and Susanna to be together without causing a stir. Still, Susanna couldn't help but wonder what others might be thinking after their pandemonium in the churchyard that morning.

"It sounds like a real adventure working with the railroad. Do you think I could try my hand at it?" Gary asked Owen.

"I'm sure with all the different jobs available that you could find something you'd enjoy or at least be good at."

"Could I work with you?"

Owen looked from the younger man to Susanna and back again. "Well, it's entirely possible, but I can't say for certain. I do have say in hiring for my department, however."

"Then that's what I want. I think it would help a lot to know the person I was working with. I mean, you seem like a nice enough fellow."

"I'm a hard taskmaster," Owen countered. "You should know that about me. I believe in hard work. I put in a full day's work and then some. I expect those working with me to do the same."

"That makes sense to me," Gary replied. He sounded so naïve.

"Working in the shops is like nothing you've ever known," Owen continued. "It's usually one-hundred-twenty degrees, if not more, in there during the summer. It melts the fat right off your body and bakes your brain. It won't be easy. You'll have to get your mind around that fast, or you'll never last. You really ought to think about it for a few days, Gary. You only just arrived, and frankly, running a hotel would be a whole lot easier."

"Maybe so, but I don't like the idea of working for my father," Gary said. "Now, if you'll both excuse me, I'm going to explore. This town seems pretty interesting to me."

Susanna shook her head as Gary went whistling down the street. "You may regret that," she murmured. "My brother is new to a life that includes working."

"I had a feeling your folks came from money." Owen grimaced. "I hope that wasn't too forward of me."

"Not at all." Susanna looked at him. "I much prefer being straightforward about things. So in that vein, I offer a warning about Gary. He's never worked a day in his life. He's used to people doing things for him, and responsibility isn't something he's had to face. If you hire him, you'll have your work cut out for you."

"Is he of good character?"

She paused and considered that for a moment. "I've never known him to steal or cheat. He has lied on occasion, but usually about things so immaterial as to make you question why he'd bother to lie. He's lazy, but that may not be entirely his fault. He's been taught to be so. I think he'll have to be taught to find value in work and to see that some things in life need a more serious evaluation."

"You are very honest."

"Why be otherwise? You'll find out soon enough for yourself. By being honest, at least you'll know you can trust me."

"And that's important to you?" he asked, smiling.

She paused and turned to him. "I'm not entirely sure why, but yes. It is important to me. My parents are rather odd and my brother entirely spoiled, but from me, I want you to know honesty and appreciation." She smiled. "I could have landed on the bottom of the pile this morning, but you made certain I didn't. I'm very appreciative of that."

He chuckled. "It was a rather quick decision on my part, but I'm glad I could accommodate you."

They continued toward the hotel, and Owen picked up the conversation again. "Why have you all come to San Marcial?"

"Reformation." She shrugged. "At least for Mother and Father. My goodness, I'm surprised to be admitting as much."

"Why?"

"It's all so personal and troublesome. I've never been the type to share such intimate details with strangers." She looked at him, surprised at the level of comfort she felt. "Suffice it to say my father hasn't been one who made good choices in life, and his brother is trying to teach him to do better.

Uncle Harrison built this hotel and asked Father to run it for him after a financial setback caused my folks to lose most of their money." She further surprised herself and Owen by reaching out to take his arm. "I'd appreciate it if you said nothing about that aspect. My parents are prideful—much too prideful—but I wouldn't shame them on purpose. They are mortified to be in this position."

"I assure you I'll keep your secret."

She smiled and let go of his arm. "Thank you." She glanced at the hotel's double doors. "Well, this is it. My home for the time being."

"Do you intend to stick around?" he asked.

Susanna shrugged. "I'm really not sure. I came to help, but otherwise . . . I just don't know."

Owen Turner met her gaze. "Well, I for one hope you stay awhile."

The next morning Susanna was pleased to find her father at the hotel on time and ready to work. He stood behind the front desk looking over a sheet of paper.

"What's this?" Susanna asked.

"We had two telegrams on Friday asking for rooms tonight. We may be very nearly full by nightfall." He frowned and glanced up at

Susanna. "I'm not sure it's right to have you living here at the hotel to manage things at night. Some resident might try to take advantage of you."

Susanna looked around the small lobby. "Well, I don't know how else to make it work, since you and Mother refuse to live here. Someone must be here at all times for the guests. Hotels require full-time management, as you are coming to see. The first week of business was enough to prove that, but with you refusing to live here, you don't get the full picture."

"I didn't refuse. That was all her doing. I rather liked the quaint little rooms." Her father pushed back his shoulders. "The place has given me all sorts of ideas for improvements to make more money. Money for myself."

"You should probably focus on what Uncle Harrison wants you to do and not give so much time and energy to other plans."

"Well, there are always ways to better yourself, if you're looking for it. I might even get into real estate here. I heard some men talking at church yesterday about how this town has grown and is continuing to do so. If I could get my hands on some land and build a house, I could turn around and sell it for twice what I paid. The Santa Fe intends to expand their shops and offices, and that will mean more people who need houses."

"Yes, I'm sure that's true. But, Father, you have a job to do, and Uncle Harrison expects you to be faithful to it. You can hardly run his hotel *and* build houses. Besides, what do you know about building houses?"

"Well, I'd hire it out. There's bound to be builders in the area." He smiled and then held up the new hotel ledger. "This is for the guests to sign. I couldn't find one for the people last week. Now we'll be official. I just need to locate a pen for them to use."

Susanna nodded, but apprehension filled her stomach. Why couldn't her father be content just to take what was given him and rest in that for a time? All her life she had watched him scheme and dream, always certain that the next chance for riches was just around the corner.

Grandfather Ragsdale had been a man of fortune and good luck. Whatever he touched turned to gold and silver, bless his heart, and Susanna's father was convinced he had the same ability. But he didn't. He wasn't even as gifted as Uncle Harrison in reasoning out a good deal over a more dangerous risk.

How she wished her father could step outside of himself for a moment and understand what he had done to his family and what he

55

was continuing to do. They had had a good life in Topeka. Potwin was a neighborhood of beautiful homes and wealthy people. It was the only place Mother wanted to live, and while they hadn't been able to buy something truly grand in the heart of the district, Father had found them a home on the edge. It had been a lovely two-story with a large porch and beautifully groomed grounds.

And around the corner and down a block had been Mark's childhood home. It wasn't attached to the Potwin addresses but was still a very nice house with an equally lovely porch. Susanna had spent many an hour on that porch, plotting and planning with Mark. She had never cared about the address of his house or the social standing of his family. His father was a tradesman—a shoemaker—and Mark had a desire to own a store in which he could sell his father's shoes. That dream had come true, and before they knew it, the shoes were being requested all over the country. Word-of-mouth sales had turned the little store into a very successful endeavor.

But now it was gone. Susanna and her father-in-law had lost their heart for it after Mark passed. Together they sold the store to another, who took the workmen her father-in-law had trained and continued to sell Jenkins handmade shoes. The money she'd made from the sale, along with Mark's life insurance, was enough to keep her comfortably for the rest of her life. As long as she was smart with the money. She couldn't make risky choices like her father had and expect it to last, so she had sought her father-in-law and uncle's counsel and was content to live on a budget. With an occasional splurge, such as buying the little adobe house.

Uncle Harrison had admonished her to say nothing to her family about her money. He'd told her this last disastrous decision made by her father was the final straw that broke the camel's back. Uncle Harrison was determined that her father learn a lesson once and for all.

"Susanna, if he doesn't change and start listening to wise counsel, he'll be left with nothing. I can't even be honest with him about the money left to him from our father's estate."

She could see the truth of her father needing to change but hated how it had shamed the family and caused her mother such sorrow. Of course, most everything caused her mother some form of grief. Still, losing her social status was almost more than Gladys Ragsdale could bear. It was good they had left Topeka, because her mother had declared she would never leave her bedroom again—unless they carried her out feetfirst to her grave.

"Are all the beds made?" Susanna's father asked, disrupting her thoughts as he returned with a pen in hand.

"Yes. Everything has been dusted, the beds arranged, and towels and soap made available for the guests to use in the bathroom."

"I don't imagine they're too happy about having to use an outhouse. How primitive."

"Yes, but efficient. The only alternative is to provide chamber pots, and I certainly don't intend to clean them," Susanna replied.

Her father shuddered. "Nor I, and I suppose the fact that they have a room to bathe in assuages their disappointment."

"Let's hope so."

By noon, the first of their reservations had arrived. He had driven a produce wagon down from Socorro, just south of Albuquerque, bringing with him a large supply of food, as well as a box full of puppies. Susanna had fussed over the sweet pups, wishing she could take one for herself, but she held back, not knowing what her future might hold. She reminded herself that she was here to help her parents get established in their new life. Nothing more. She had no idea if she would stay on once they were better able to manage for themselves, or if she would head back to Topeka. The truth was, she had no idea what she wanted out of life anymore.

She left the hotel shortly after her father got their guest checked in and took the laundry to the little house, where she knew she'd find her mother either sleeping or reading. Susanna was determined to help her mother realize her duties of cleaning and cooking but knew it wouldn't be easy. Keeping house was the job of maids, as far as Mother was concerned. And doing sheets and towels for a hotel was something she would just as soon send off to the Mexican laundry. Unfortunately, Father said there wasn't money for such things, and the task fell once again to Susanna.

"Mother?" she called as she entered the cool house. How wonderful that the temperatures were so much nicer inside. That had to please her mother.

"I'm in the bedroom," her mother called in a weak voice. "I have a terrible headache."

Susanna left the bundle of laundry at the door. "Well, we need to figure out what to fix for supper. I thought maybe you could go with me to the grocer's store."

"Heavens no. Not with my headache. I told your father we needed to hire a cook and housekeeper, but he has given little thought to it."

Susanna walked over to her mother, who sat propped up in the bed. "You must face the truth of our life, Mother. You and Father cannot afford servants. You've lost your fortune and need to be responsible for yourselves. Cooking and cleaning won't be that hard for just the three of you. Although if Gary gets a job with the railroad, his clothes will be most difficult to keep clean."

Her mother fixed her with an annoyed glare. "I wasn't born to clean and cook."

"You might not have been born for it, but you are now in that position. Hiring someone to help would simply cost too much. You must face facts. The money is gone. The house in Potwin is gone. Your finery and social standing are gone. I don't say this to hurt you but rather to help you face the truth. That life is gone."

"Then my life is gone," her mother countered. "I'm too delicate and will surely die. Either the heat or the work or this godforsaken land will kill me."

Susanna hated hearing her mother talk in such a manner. "You haven't even tried to fend for yourself, Mother. Come to the grocer's with me, and we'll find some simple things to fix for supper. I even brought a cookbook. I'm sure I can help you learn to make a few things."

"I don't want to learn. I wasn't born to live like this." Mother leaned back into the pillows, drawing her arm over her eyes.

Her patience running thin, Susanna shrugged. "Then I guess you will go on wasting money at the Harvey House until you come to the end of the salary Uncle is paying Father. It's quite ridiculous to spend money there when a few groceries in the house would make a much better solution."

"I cannot cook. Would you further shame me?" Mother declared, suddenly sitting up. "The women in my family didn't have to cook for themselves."

"The times have changed." Susanna gave her mother a sympathetic pat on the arm. "I'm trying to help you."

"Then hire me someone to cook and clean. That's the only help I can abide right now."

Susanna thought about it and nodded. She put the laundry to soak, then left the house. How in the world would her parents ever survive? Should she hire someone on? It was made clear to her on Sunday that many of the Mexican women would love to earn extra money with part-time work. Perhaps, at least temporarily, it would resolve the issue and make matters better. Maybe once Mother had that pressure taken off her shoulders, she would be willing to reevaluate the situation.

Most likely it would just make matters worse. Susanna felt confident that once a maid was hired, it would be impossible to get rid of her. Mother would cling to anything that gave her the security of her old life. So what was the answer? Susanna could hardly do it all.

She sighed and headed for the store. There would still need to be food in the house. She could provide that much for the time being. She would also need laundry soap. There was very little left at the house. Doing up the sheets and towels every day took plenty of soap, and Susanna wasn't about to skimp on cleanliness. She'd have to ask Uncle Harrison what exactly he'd had in mind when he built the hotel without a laundry of its own, but for now, the responsibility was hers. Like everything else.

"This is officially the Rio Grande Division of the Santa Fe Railway," Owen explained to Gary. "But most folks call it the Horny Toad Line, due to all the toads you find smashed to smithereens on the rails."

"Boy, it sure is hot in here, just like you said," Gary interrupted.

Owen overlooked his lack of attention for the moment. "It is, and this is morning. It will get ten times worse by late afternoon."

"I heard all the Mexicans take a break in the afternoon. They call it *see*-something."

"*Siesta*. They quit during the hottest hours, then come back to work after the sun begins to set. But we're not Mexicans, and on the Santa Fe, we keep working straight through. I like to arrange easier work to be done in the afternoon, if possible."

"Owen, is this the new man?" a tall, beefy man asked as he approached with a determined gait.

"Yes, Mr. Payne. Gary, this is Timothy Payne, the supervisor for this part of the shops. Mr. Payne, this is Gary Ragsdale. He's just moved here, and his folks are running the Grand Hotel."

Mr. Payne nodded. "I watched it go up. Should provide some much-needed rooms. Gary, Owen tells me that you've never worked before. Railroad work isn't easy, and there won't be much in the way of second chances, since first mistakes often get you killed."

Gary's face paled despite the heat. "I understand. Owen told me the same thing. I know I'm not really cut out for this work right now, but I hope to prove myself."

"I hope you do as well." The older man looked at Owen and motioned across the room. "We'll need that boiler remade by Friday instead of Monday. Can we get it done?"

"You bet we can," Owen assured him. "It's been going well. Hopefully the next fireman will be better acquainted with problem gauges."

"Yeah, you can hope." Mr. Payne left them then, calling out to someone across the open shop. "Davis!"

"Are you sure you want to give this a go, Gary?" Owen asked. "It really is going to be the hardest thing you've ever tried."

Gary nodded, but Owen could see the boy wasn't convinced. Owen took him to one of the workstations where several men were working.

"These are some of the men you'll be working with temporarily. We call them boomers. They like to move around the country and work various jobs, never really settling down to one shop or location."

"That sounds adventurous," Gary declared, extending a hand to the man nearest him.

Owen made the introductions. "That's Hercules Monroe. We call him Herc. This is Gary Ragsdale, fellas. He'll be joining us."

Monroe nodded and shook Gary's hand. "This is William Foxtail. He's part Apache, but we just call him Bill."

"A real-life Indian, eh?" Gary grinned.

Bill nodded and leaned closer. "Stay on my good side. My grandfather taught me to scalp when I was just a boy."

Gary's eyes widened, and he took a step back as the boomers laughed.

Owen chuckled. "There won't be any scalping on my watch."

A third man stepped up and put his hand in Gary's. "Name's Martin Thomas Clarmont. Folks call me Empty—play on my initials."

"Empty." Gary nodded. "I'm glad to meet you fellas. I'm pretty excited to see what you do here and learn all about it."

"Well, the first thing I notice about you is your lack of muscle. We swing hammers in here and bend iron," Empty said. "I'm guessin' you've never done that."

"No, I haven't. But I'm willing to learn. This will be my very first job."

Empty looked to Owen, who gave a nod. "We all have to start somewhere."

4

The first of August dawned with a cloudless sky that promised no relief from the sun as the day wore on. Susanna got up at first light and began preparations for the day. There would be four guests checking out to catch the morning train, and she had no way of knowing if her father would be at the hotel in time to see to them.

Even more important, at least in Susanna's mother's opinion, was an invitation to a midmorning gathering of the Methodist Women's Society. The invitation had come on Sunday, when Mrs. Payne stopped Mother on her way out of the church.

Susanna had seen her mother's apprehension melt away as Mrs. Payne explained she wanted to have Mother and Susanna to luncheon to introduce them to a few of the ladies from church and make them feel properly welcomed. This appealed to Mother, who felt it was a good way to assert her position amongst the community members. Susanna, however, wasn't at all sure what position she would insist on having.

As soon as Father arrived, Susanna turned the front desk over to him and made her way to the little adobe house, where her mother was already flitting about, trying to figure out what she would wear.

"Where's the laundry you always bring?" her mother asked.

"I thought I'd wait and do it tomorrow, since we have the gathering today. There were only four rooms rented, and I can clean those up this afternoon."

As if she hadn't even heard, Mother looked at Susanna, who had donned a gray and lavender print day dress. The lightweight material was perfect for the heat of the day, but Susanna knew her mother would consider it much too casual. Even if it was designed by Worth.

"You can't wear that," Mother said.

"But I'm going to, and that's all we'll say about it. I've barely come out of mourning and must use what I have at hand. In the future I will arrange for other clothes, but for now this must do."

Mother turned back to her own wardrobe. "I don't want to be remiss in my dressing. This might very well be a small town in the middle of nowhere, but these women still read *Godey's*, I'm sure. Not only that, but I'm told important railroad officials come here often. It could be that some of these women are no different than I am—temporarily required to live their life in rural repose for the sake of their husband's duties. We cannot neglect our appearance."

"I'm a shoe salesman's widow." Susanna smiled. "Honestly, Mother, no one will care."

Her mother gave a huff. "If you won't dress appropriately, then I must." She pulled on a snug-fitting mauve jacket and adjusted her lace jabot. "Now for the perfect piece of jewelry."

Mother was in her element as she prepared for the gathering, but Susanna did her best to temper matters. Especially when Mother pulled out a sapphire and ruby pin. Not only did it not match the mauve, but it was too extravagant.

"Mother, it's much too informal a gathering to wear an expensive piece of jewelry. Maybe just use Grandmother's cameo?"

"Bah, they need to know I'm from good breeding and that we have money."

"But you don't have money any longer,

and frankly, I'm surprised you got away with keeping your jewelry." Susanna shook her head. "You'd probably do well to keep it hidden."

"The bank didn't know about my entire collection, nor shall they." Mother put the piece aside. "But I suppose you are right. It is too early in the day for such things. Still, I want to make a good impression. Perhaps my pearl brooch."

"Perhaps you could just be kind and attentive. Show some friendship. Remember, these ladies have husbands who work for a living, and now your husband also works. We are no better than they are and need to accept our place."

"Susanna, honestly, you do go on and on about the silliest notions. We are merely experiencing a brief situation. Your father was lied to and then robbed. That's hardly his fault, and we will be fine in just a few months. He's assured me. I don't like the circumstances we find ourselves in, but it's only temporary. Your father is even thinking we might relocate to San Francisco. Apparently, he has a lead on an investment there." She fastened on the cameo.

Susanna hoped her mother didn't see her eyes roll heavenward. Why could her parents not understand or accept that this situation was far more permanent? Uncle Harrison had told them so. He'd made it clear that had he not given them the hotel to run, they would have been left on the streets in Topeka. Mother thought him just being unkind, while Father felt confident there was a quick and easy path to solvency and success. But there wasn't, and Susanna was hard-pressed to get them to understand the truth of the situation.

They arrived at Mrs. Payne's little two-story house at precisely eleven o'clock, as instructed. Susanna both dreaded and looked forward to the outing. She wanted to get to know the women from the church and gain a sense of belonging. But she knew her mother would make a scene at some point, and she dreaded the very thought. How could she possibly explain?

Mrs. Payne ushered them into the front room. "I want you two to have these chairs so you'll be able to see everyone. The ladies are quite excited to welcome you to San Marcial, so we thought we might have a pounding."

"A pounding?" Mother asked.

"Yes." Mrs. Payne pointed to the corner. "We've all brought gifts of food and other things you need to set up decent housekeeping. You won't have to shop for some time."

"How wonderful," Susanna replied. "Mother and I were just discussing getting our cupboards in order." From the look of the overflowing table, they wouldn't have to shop for quite a while, except to buy perishables.

"I was discussing hiring a maid," Mother said, ignoring Susanna. "I hope perhaps someone here might recommend a young woman who can clean, do laundry, and cook."

"I'm sure we can," Mrs. Payne replied. She seemed momentarily confused by this interruption in her plans but quickly recovered. "I'll bring refreshments."

"Let me help, Sylvia," one of the other ladies volunteered, jumping to her feet.

It was only a matter of minutes before the dining table was covered with a variety of foods, as well as coffee, tea, and iced lemonade.

Everyone was encouraged to help themselves. Mother seemed put out not to be waited on, so Susanna, hoping to avoid a scene, offered to bring her a plate. This satisfied her mother momentarily but left her alone to tell the women around her whatever she chose to say. The very thought terrified Susanna. Her mother would think nothing of exaggerating and outright lying to make herself appear important.

Susanna brought her a plate with several tasty-looking treats. There were delicate little sandwiches, as well as sweet treats that were sure to please, along with some of the most enticing fruit Susanna had ever seen. Susanna also brought her mother a cup of tea. Mother always declared that nothing was quite so soothing as a good cup of tea. Hopefully, this one would qualify.

"We, of course, come from old money back east," her mother was saying. "The family lineage is positively abundant with nobility and wealthy financial geniuses like my husband."

Susanna wanted to turn and walk away. "Mother, here is a cup of tea. I know you'll enjoy it."

Mother nodded at the offering and noted the charming china. "This is lovely."

Mrs. Payne smiled. "It was my mother's china, passed down to me."

Mother sampled the tea and smiled. "Very good. I think there is nothing quite like an excellent tea. We get ours from a wonderful shop in Kansas City that specializes in fine teas."

The women seemed impressed and offered pleasing comments that left Susanna free to exhale and head back to the refreshment table to get her own plate.

Mrs. Payne joined her, refilling a platter of cucumber sandwiches and beaming a smile. "I'm so glad you could come today. We are all so pleased to have a new family in town."

"Thank you. This was such a sweet surprise. I'm sure once Mother adapts to her new life here, she'll be ever so grateful for your kindness."

Mrs. Payne nodded. "It must have been hard to leave such a life as she had in Topeka." She bit her lip, then shook her head. "I'm sorry if I spoke out of turn. I heard there was a great difficulty."

"There was, but hopefully it will be dealt with and straightened out." Susanna tried not to give away too much. She didn't want to shame her mother, but at the same time she wasn't one to lie or shy away from the truth.

"And you are a widow?"

"Yes. It's been a year since my husband died of influenza."

"Were you married long?" Mrs. Payne asked, her expression sympathetic.

"It felt longer than the three years we enjoyed because we were childhood friends as well."

"A true love match, then?"

"Definitely."

"You are such pretty girl. I think all of us are rooting for you and Owen to get together. How like the Good Lord to throw two people into each other's path in such an unexpected way."

Susanna looked up from her plate. "I'm

not sure I understand." She finished gathering her treats and started back to her chair. Mrs. Payne followed.

"Well, several of us have been hoping to find a wife for Owen. He's such a good man. When you two were entangled with the children and their jump rope, it seemed a perfect introduction. Imagine telling your children years from now that you met when you got all tied up at church."

Several of the other women chuckled, but Susanna's mother expressed her displeasure. "Hooligans. Children should be better supervised. My daughter is a widow, after all. She's still in a state of mourning. It's only been a year."

"A year is plenty long enough for one so young," one of the ladies protested. "I think we do our young people a disservice by strapping them with traditions and rules that have nothing to do with them."

"Well, Queen Victoria doesn't think that way, and neither do I," Mother replied. "She's maintained her mourning for nearly forty years."

"Yes, and she was much older than Susanna when she became a widow," Mrs. Payne pointed out. "Also, she had plenty of children to keep her company. Your daughter is quite young and has no children. She needs to be about life and happiness. Owen Turner is a good Christian man, and I think he'd be perfect for her."

The other ladies quickly agreed, and Susanna felt her face warm. She'd had no idea these ladies were already putting her and Owen together. It wasn't that she didn't like the man in question, but she honestly had not had time to consider any such possibilities. Her parents were still too precariously placed to leave them to their own resources.

"Let me introduce everyone, in case you don't remember from church," Sylvia Payne declared. She went around the room, letting each woman explain who they were and how they might fit in Susanna's and her mother's lives.

When the last woman was introduced and explained that she was married to one of the railroad's head office workers, Susanna could see that her mother was more than a little bored. As far as she was concerned, none of these women had any place in her life. Susanna, on the other hand, was quite charmed. There were several older ladies who had even encouraged her to join their quilting club.

"I've never quilted," Susanna admitted, "but I would love to learn."

Her mother looked away from her when she made this statement. At least she had chosen to remain silent and not made known her thoughts on sewing.

A young woman joined the group late. Mrs. Payne brought her to Susanna and her mother. "This is Rosalia Branson. Everyone calls her Lia. Lia, this is Susanna Jenkins and her mother, Mrs. Ragsdale."

"I saw you at church. I'm pleased to meet you now." Lia smiled, and there was something about her expression that Susanna immediately liked.

"Lia, Mrs. Ragsdale wants to hire someone to work for her. I know you were talking about taking on a job. Perhaps you would like to discuss what Mrs. Ragsdale has in mind?"

"Oh, yes please. I can cook and clean and mend and do laundry. I'm only looking for a few hours each day while my boys are in school, however."

"That sounds very suitable to what would work for us," Susanna's mother declared. "I'll let Susanna arrange it all. You may give her your references." Mother all but waved Lia away from her.

Susanna stared at her mother for a moment, then turned to Lia. "We can discuss it after this. I don't want to spoil the party atmosphere with talk of work."

Lia nodded. "I nearly forgot. I brought a pound of coffee. I left it by the door." She hurried away, then returned with a bag in her hand. "I know it's not much, but LeRoy says coffee is a staple of life that you can never have too much of."

Susanna laughed. "Sounds like great wisdom. My father drinks his weight in the stuff. Thank you for your thoughtfulness." She took the bag and held it while Lia helped herself to the table of food.

"Here, I can put it on the table for you with the rest," Sylvia Payne said, coming to take the coffee from Susanna. "I'll have my husband bring everything over to the Medford house after supper." She laughed. "I guess it's the Ragsdale house now, but we all knew it as the Medford house for the longest time."

"It's a lovely little house, and it stays so nice and cool."

Sylvia nodded. "I often tell Mr. Payne that if we're going to remain here for many years, we should get an adobe house. The heat can be so unbearable, as I'm sure you are realizing."

"Yes."

Susanna cast a glance at her mother, who seemed to be fading as woman after woman tried to make it a point to converse. If only they knew what a snob her mother truly was, they'd never make the effort. It was probably good they didn't know. How she wished her mother could realize the value of just being honest about her situation. Susanna wasn't sure, however, that her mother was capable of comprehending the truth. Neither of her parents seemed to live in reality. Uncle Harrison had made it clear that until they could accept their lot, they would go on believing themselves wealthy and capable of great waste and risk. She was supposed to be the voice of reason helping them see the truth. Unfortunately, she'd done nothing but perpetuate the problem by buying them a house and now arranging a maid.

But the latter was for herself as much as anyone. She couldn't continue with the additional workload. She sighed.

"You sound tired," Lia said, coming to stand beside her. "Is the heat starting to get to you?"

"The heat has been difficult, I'll admit." Susanna smiled. "I don't really mind it, though. I've never cared for the cold and much prefer this desert heat and dryness."

Lia nodded. "You'll have to be careful about your skin. You're so very white. It's a beautiful color, but you will no doubt burn, and the dryness will make it rough."

"I do burn and freckle." Susanna liked Lia. She was outgoing and full of life. "I plan to be very careful with parasols and large-brimmed hats." She smiled and changed the subject. "I hear that you have children."

"Yes, two boys. Emilio and John. They are my joy." Lia's entire face lit up as she talked about them. "Their father's too. I'm sure you'll get to know LeRoy. He works in the department next to Owen's."

Susanna couldn't help wondering what she meant by that comment. It seemed everyone had already decided that she and Owen would be a couple.

"I think your mother is taking ill," Sylvia said, pulling on Susanna's sleeve. "The heat, poor thing."

Susanna handed her plate to Sylvia. "I'd best get her home."

"I'm not sure how you can manage it. She's all but fainted dead away. I don't have a cart, but there is a wheelbarrow. I could get my gardener to take her home in it."

Susanna almost choked on her reply. "If she cannot walk, we will consider that."

Sylvia nodded and hurried from the room. Susanna made her way to her mother, who was being fanned by three women.

"She just seemed to take bad," said one older woman. Susanna couldn't remember her name. Matilda . . . Mary . . .

"Thank you for giving her such good

care." Susanna leaned down to whisper in her mother's ear, careful that no one else could hear her. "They're going to take you home in a wheelbarrow if you're unable to walk."

Susanna straightened as her mother's eyes popped open. "Oh my. I'm feeling a bit better." She waved the women away. "I'm sure I can manage for myself, but I should go home to lie down."

"Don't overdo it, Mrs. Ragsdale. You are among friends," Agnes Lewis, the pastor's wife announced. "We'll take good care of you."

Gladys Ragsdale got to her feet. Susanna was certain no one would ever be allowed to take her home in a wheelbarrow. Not if her mother still had breath in her body. Susanna kept a look of sober concern fixed on her face when what she wanted more than anything was to burst out laughing at the very thought.

What a day.

Owen looked at the work Gary was doing and shook his head. "You aren't pounding in the right places. See how Herc and Empty are doing it? They heat the iron, then Empty puts the block hammer in a specific place. It's all about getting the proper shape. You can't just put it any old place. Then Herc comes with the sledge and makes hard hits to form the metal. It's a precise operation."

"It just looks like you're hitting it over and over without any real change," Gary said.

"It's a subtle change, but it's lining up properly with what we need it to be," Owen declared. "Sometimes it's not immediately evident what's being accomplished. Kind of like when God is working on our hearts."

Gary frowned and shook his head. "I don't know about that, but it seems to me there has to be an easier way to get this metal shaped like you want it."

"There are machines that can bend metal and shape it, but this requires precision, and doing it by hand is the only real way to have it turn out the way I need it. Now, please, stop trying to cut corners."

"What do you mean by that?"

"You're trying to come up with a better way—an easier way—but sometimes good things take effort and time. Just trust that we've been doing this long enough to know what's needed." Owen gave him a smile of encouragement. "Now, pick up your sledge, and let's try again."

The afternoon seemed to drag by. Gary was constantly heading to the water bucket for drinks of water, and then, of course, he needed the privy. He was sweating no more or less than the others, but he was clearly more uncomfortable. Owen had assumed this would be the case, since Gary had never worked a job—particularly one in the desert heat with railroad ovens. It was a harsh initiation, but he had asked for it, and Owen had warned him.

By the time the whistle was blown to end the workday, Owen could see that Gary was more than happy to follow the boomers off for cold beer and female company.

Owen, however, delayed him and sent the boomers on. They would have plenty of time to be a bad influence on the young man.

"You did good for your first day, Gary. I suggest you take a swim in the river. That's what I like to do. I'm headed there now, if you want to join me."

"I don't have a suit."

Owen laughed. "None of us do. You can either swim in your undergarments or without them. Some even go in fully dressed as a way to wash their clothes at the same time. There aren't any women around, so it's perfectly acceptable however you choose. Come on. I'll show you where we go."

He left the shops and led Gary down a narrow path behind the roundhouse and along the railroad fence. There was an opening in the fence just big enough for the men to file through one at a time, and on the other side was the river. They moved past the shop and rail yard grounds to where the iron railroad bridge offered a little shade. Here, there were already a dozen men shedding their clothes and seeking the water for refreshment.

"It's a great way to end a day," Owen said as he started taking off his overalls. He glanced at Gary, whose simple white shirt and gray trousers were now covered in sweat, soot, and oil. "We've got to get you some better work clothes. After our swim, come back with me to the company houses. We'll ask around and see what we can find that someone can spare."

"I know these are ruined. I've got holes where the sparks caught my cuffs on fire."

"Yeah, they'll do that, but don't worry. We'll get you set up in decent style. I wanted you to see what the job entailed before you went all out."

"I can't say I enjoyed it, but it wasn't as bad as it could have been." Gary smiled. "And if I'd known about cooling down with a swim, I might have had a better disposition."

Owen slapped him on the back. "Well, how about this? Last one in the water buys supper at the Harvey House!"

He pulled off his cotton shirt and tossed it aside before dropping to the sandy soil to get rid of his shoes. Gary laughed and did the same, just as Owen had hoped. He wanted more than anything for Gary to have a sense of camaraderie with the men and with him. Mr. Payne would say it wasn't good to fraternize with your subordinates, but Owen had seen good things accomplished by being a friend as well as a boss. It was a balancing act, to be sure, but just as respect had to be earned, so did friendship. Trust wasn't something Owen gave easily, but he hoped to be able to put faith in this young man.

5

Despite the swim he claimed to have taken after work, Gary showed up to the table for supper that evening dirtier than Susanna had ever seen him. Mother was appalled and demanded he go change his clothes, and Susanna suggested he take a bar of soap they'd received from the pounding and use it liberally.

"You're always picking on me," he declared.

"Well, I certainly cannot eat dinner with you smelling this way," Mother declared, sticking her nose in the air. "The smell of oil or whatever it is has already given me a headache. Susanna, I'm going to my room. Bring me a tray."

Susanna nodded. What else could she do? Father was just coming through the door, and

Gary was marching around the room, ranting about having already washed off in the river. She looked at the casserole she'd heated for supper. It was compliments of Mrs. Lewis, the pastor's wife. She had explained it was Mexican in origin, with a very mild amount of spices, since she didn't know what the family might be able to stomach.

"What smells so good?" Father asked.

"This is something Mrs. Lewis called enchilada casserole," Susanna explained. "It has corn tortillas and beef and cheese and spices. She tells me it's quite good. I haven't yet tried it." She placed the glass dish on the table. "I also sliced some ham and fried it, and cut up some fresh vegetables. It's very simple fare but all that I could manage in between helping Mother rearrange the bedroom."

Father glanced toward his bedroom. "I didn't get to talk to you after you came back to clean the hotel rooms. How was the party?"

"It was lovely." Susanna went back to the tiny kitchen to retrieve the platter of store-bought bread and butter.

"And did your mother at least enjoy being the center of attention?" Father asked, once again casting a quick glance toward the bedroom door. No doubt he feared his wife overhearing his snide comment.

"She did for a time." Susanna brought the tray of vegetables and placed it on the wooden trestle table. "She didn't understand the concept of them bringing gifts of food and laundry soap."

"What was that all about?" Her father took his chair and reached for a pitcher of iced tea.

"It's called a pounding. Everyone brought a pound or two of something to help set up our kitchen. They even brought cleaning supplies. It was quite a kindness, as it saves us having to spend a great deal to stock up on staples in order to cook properly. Or clean, for that matter. One of the ladies gave us five pounds of soap she'd made."

"Interesting." He poured tea for himself and then looked at Susanna. "Tea?"

"Yes, please." She took a chair at the table and wondered how much longer Gary would be.

"And your mother . . . she accepted these things graciously?"

"I don't think she fully comprehended what was going on," Susanna admitted. "However, the heat started getting to her, and she became rather faint. We needed to leave early to get her home, and Mrs. Payne suggested her gardener could bring Mother in a wheelbarrow."

Her father nearly spilled the tea. "She what?"

Susanna smiled. "You heard me right. There was no carriage or wagon to bring her home in, so Mrs. Payne suggested the only thing she could. It perked Mother right up, and she walked back without difficulty."

The edge of her father's lips curled. "I'm sure she did."

"Mr. Payne brought the food goods and soap just a little while ago. It really was the greatest kindness."

Her father nodded. "I suppose a small town like this has its strange practices."

Susanna heard her brother coming from the opposite side of the house. He had changed his clothes but hadn't dressed for dinner as he might have in Topeka. He wore a button-down shirt without a starched collar and had simply tucked it into a pair of tan trousers. He wasn't even wearing shoes.

This garnered a look of reproof from Father, who was dressed in a full suit with vest and tie. "We are hardly barbarians, to come to the table in such a state," he declared.

"I figured you'd rather have me here than wait for me to properly dress," Gary replied. "Besides, what's the purpose in dressing for dinner here? We aren't going to be entertaining the governor."

A small lizard of some sort skittered across the tile floor, causing Gary to startle and do a little dance.

"That's why we wear shoes," Susanna interjected. "It could have been a snake."

Gary scowled. "We didn't have these problems in Topeka."

Father's face reddened, and Susanna feared there might be a fight between them. Ever since Father had lost his money, Gary had lost his respectful attitude.

Susanna offered to fill her father's plate and then Gary's with the enchilada creation. The two men sampled it hesitantly, but upon tasting the dish, decided it was acceptable and dug in. Susanna loved the spices and flavors that came from the casserole. She would have to find out how it was made. She had learned a lot about cooking during her marriage to Mark. He had liked simple fare, but from time to time she had experimented using one of the cookbooks she'd been given as a wedding present. Mark had heartily approved of her adventurous nature, even if there were one or two dishes he received with less enthusiasm than others.

"This is really good. I like it a lot," Gary said, passing his plate for more. "I tried something called a tamale at work today. It was a lot of ground corn on the outside and meat inside. They were really hot with spices that made my eyes water. The fellas laughed at the way I could hardly eat it. Owen said I'd get used to the spices in time."

"How was your workday?" Susanna filled his plate and handed it back.

"It's hard work. Hot too. So hot. I don't know how a man bears it, but I did." He puffed out his chest in pride. "Owen took me to the river afterwards. A lot of the men go swimming there, while some go for cold beer and to shoot pool. I might try that tomorrow."

"You're too young to be drinking until all hours," Father said. "I won't have a drunkard as a son."

"I don't intend to be a drunkard. But I do intend to make friends. If we have to live in this horrible town and work for a living, I intend to make the best of it."

"Good for you, Gary. Friends are important. I'm sure Owen will be a good one to have."

"Aw, he's my boss. I can't really be friends with him." Gary reached out to stab a slice of tomato. Next he took several cucumber slices, some ham, and finally a slice of bread. "But the boomers are there, and they're good to me. I can go with them to play pool. I guess there's poker too, but that's done in back-rooms. It might be illegal, but I don't know for sure, 'cause it seems all the men know about it and do it. I guess a lot of money changes hands."

"Poker, eh?" Father murmured.

"Well, don't get yourself in trouble." Susanna began to prepare a plate for her mother. She knew Mother wouldn't appreciate the enchilada casserole but put a tiny bit on the plate anyway. She then added ham and some of the fresh vegetables and placed some bread and butter on the side. "Do you suppose Mother would like iced tea or hot?" she asked, knowing the answer but hoping to draw her father into considering that his wife had once again taken to her bed.

"I guess hot tea, but the day has been so wretchedly warm that she might prefer the iced. Maybe start with it." He shook his head. "The hotel is rather warm. I don't know how Harrison thinks people are going to want to stay there."

"It cools down in the evening, Father. I find it rather comfortable at night." Susanna poured her mother iced tea, then stood to fetch another tray. She arranged the food for her mother, then remembered to grab silver and a linen napkin at the last moment. "I'll be right back."

She went to the bedroom door and gave a light knock. Her mother's voice was barely audible. She was trying to prove how weak she was to whoever was coming to see her.

"Oh, it's you, Susanna. I'm afraid I'm just so weak from the heat."

"I thought you might be, so I brought you iced tea with sugar. It should perk you right up, although I know you prefer hot tea." Susanna arranged the tray on the bed so that it was near her mother, who had changed from her clothes into a dressing gown and now lay atop the bed with a book.

"I don't suppose we have any cake, do we?"

"No. I haven't had time to bake." Susanna offered nothing more. If Mother wanted cake, she could figure out for herself how to get it. "I'll be with the boys if you need anything."

She didn't give her mother time to protest but returned to the table to find her father and brother arguing.

"I don't want to help you at the hotel," Gary said firmly. "I like what I'm doing."

"You like being a dirty laborer? I didn't raise you to take on such work. You were meant for greater things. I want you to go to college this fall."

"And how will you pay for that? We have no money because you lost it all." Up until now, Gary had said very little about their change of status. It seemed a hard day's work had brought out the frustration in him. "I lost all of my friends because of your inability to manage your accounts. You were the laughingstock of Topeka and no doubt elsewhere. I was glad to leave so that I could be spared further embarrassment."

Father slammed down his fork. "How dare you speak that way to me? We had a minor setback. Nothing more. You cannot gain great capital without taking risks of equal greatness. It is hardly my fault that the man involved in the investment was a crook, nor that your uncle wouldn't stand by me."

"If you'd taken Uncle Harrison's counsel in the first place, you wouldn't have made such a mess of it," Gary countered. "You think you're so wise, but you aren't." He got up from the table, shaking his head. "And so we must live like this."

He stormed off to his room, leaving Susanna and her father to stare at one another.

Susanna wondered if there was anything she could say to help the matter, but she decided her father wouldn't hear it, even if she offered praise. He knew in his heart of hearts that this mess was his fault. He had to know. Even with all the denial and blaming of the conman who'd sold him out, he had to see that he had rejected advice from others more qualified to judge. He had to accept that he was responsible. Didn't he?

"Your brother will never know how these things work," Father groused. "He's too impatient to learn. If he could only see the way industry and finance requires a man to make choices that others might see as far too dangerous in order to bless that man with riches and security. Perhaps one day when we are resettled and recovered from this, I will be able to teach Gary how to judge the situations for himself."

She frowned and tried to keep her focus on her food. What could she possibly say? It was as if her father lived in a world of his own making.

After supper, Susanna cleaned up, knowing no one else would. She put away the food and clean dishes, then went to her mother to say good-bye before heading over to the hotel.

"Everything is put away, Mother. I'm hoping to speak to Lia tonight to see how soon she can start working for you."

"Oh, I do hope it is soon. I simply cannot abide a dirty house, and of course there is no one to fix breakfast. Your father had to bring breakfast from one of the local cafés this morning. It was greasy and cold by the time it reached me." Mother gave a little sniff.

"You can always eat cold ham and make toast. We have sliced bread."

"I wouldn't know how to make toast," her mother protested.

"Well, perhaps it would be a good idea to learn." Susanna kissed her mother's forehead, then headed for the door. "I'll see you sometime tomorrow."

Father was looking over a letter that had come in the mail when Susanna bid him good night.

"I'm heading out," she said.

He glanced up, but there was no offer to see her safely back to the hotel or even to thank her for taking care of everything. Her parents really were the most self-focused people she'd ever known.

"Your uncle Harrison is coming to see how things are going. He wants to make sure we have everything we need. I'm going to speak to him about these arrangements. It really is a deplorable town, and it's criminal for your mother and I to have to live this way." He looked down at the letter. "He really is quite unkind to imagine this will work."

Susanna shook her head and headed for the door. There was no sense in even offering a reply.

The day had cooled to a pleasantly warm evening. Susanna wanted to contact Lia and arrange whatever she could for her services. Again, her conscience was pricked at the knowledge that she was only furthering her mother's spoiled behavior. Still, it was Susanna who would suffer if she didn't arrange for a maid and cook. It would fall to her own shoulders and double her workload. She sighed. Helping at the hotel was far more work than she wanted as it was. She had hoped her mother might see the need to offer a hand, but of course that was the furthest thing from her mind.

A few blocks down Main Street, Susanna noted the crossroad she wanted and turned left. Lia had said their house was at the end of the road. Susanna admired the small adobe house. Two boys were racing circles around two men in the front yard.

One of the men was Owen Turner. When he spied her, he smiled and gave a wave.

"How nice to see you again," he said, coming to greet her. "Come meet the gang."

The two boys came running and clamped themselves onto Owen's legs. "Now you have to carry us," one of the boys declared.

Owen made great stomping strides as the boys squealed in delight. "On my right leg is Emilio, and on my left is John. That exhausted man behind me is their father, LeRoy Branson. LeRoy and boys, this is Mrs. Jenkins."

"How nice to meet you all," Susanna said, laughing. What a difference this company made. They instantly cheered her. "I've come to see Lia. Mother wants to hire her to do some cooking and cleaning."

LeRoy came to greet her. "Nice to meet you, Mrs. Jenkins."

"Oh, please, everyone calls me Susanna." She shook LeRoy's hand. It was a firm, calloused handshake that reminded her of his job. "You work with Owen at the railroad, right?"

"I don't work alongside him, but I am at the shops. We're the two who keep the Santa Fe actually running."

Owen laughed. "Sometimes it definitely feels that way." The boys peeled off his legs and went running.

"Come on inside," LeRoy said, heading for the house. "Lia is there."

Owen and Susanna walked toward the house in unison step. He offered her a smile. "How's the hotel business?"

"So far, so good. I have pleasant accommodations to myself, so that is very nice."

"And the guests have been polite? No one getting out of hand with you?" Owen looked at her as if to assure himself of the truth.

"No. Things have been quite pleasant. But we're just getting started."

Inside the little house, Susanna marveled at the homey feel. There were beautiful multi-colored curtains at the windows and tile on the floor that was equally colorful.

"Your house is so charming," Susanna said when Lia came to greet her. "I love these tiles."

"Thank you. They are special to me. My uncle made them."

"He is a very talented man. An artist."

"*Sí*, he is," Lia agreed. "Would you like something to drink?"

Susanna shook her head. "I just came from supper with my family. I thought I'd best try to arrange for your help before I let another day pass."

"Come and sit, and we'll talk about what you need."

"I don't suppose you need us, so we'll just go back outside and enjoy the evening," LeRoy said. He bent and gave Lia a quick kiss.

Susanna waited until the men had gone before explaining what she had in mind. "I want to tell you about our situation," she began. She had already decided to be completely honest with Lia. Susanna explained her mother's elevated opinion of herself and her father's delusional ideas about finance. She tried her best to be kind and even show

respect—after all, they were her parents—
but she knew Lia would learn the truth soon
enough. "My brother is spoiled and has no
idea how to conduct himself. I fear for him
and am more than grateful that Owen has
taken an interest in him. However, Gary is
naïve and is certain to get himself into trouble."

"It's easy enough to do around here. Not
all the men are good," Lia admitted. "There
are some very rough characters in San Marcial."

"And no doubt they will see my brother
coming from a long way off and take advantage of him."

"Then we must pray for him."

Susanna was embarrassed to admit she
hadn't considered that. Her religious train-
ing was mostly superficial, although she
and Mark had prayed and read the Bible together. "I suppose I've been so caught up in
the changes that I hadn't thought about the
need for prayer. But you're right."

"I will pray for him faithfully, just as I do
my boys."

"Thank you, Lia. I am grateful."

"We will be good friends, you and me. I
already know it."

Susanna hadn't had a good friend since
Mark had passed away. She had closed herself

off from everyone. Perhaps a good friend was exactly what she needed. She smiled.

"I can do a few hours now while the boys are out of school," Lia began. "My sister María can watch them. They love to play with their cousins. Once they are all back at school, I can work most of the day if needed."

"I think a few hours in the morning and a few in the afternoon would work well for now. Mother will need help cleaning and with laundry. She will also need help with cooking."

"I can do this," Lia replied. "I can come over first thing and help with baking and laundry. On days without laundry, I can clean first thing. In the afternoons I can make supper and help with whatever else there is. On laundry days, this would be a good time to take in the clothes and iron them."

"Speaking of laundry, once the boys are in school, I will need help with the hotel laundry. We can do it at my folks' house because of the outdoor cauldrons Mr. Medford left. It's so hard on me to strip all the beds and then go wash all the bedding. It's not usually that dirty, but it still requires the time and effort. I wish Uncle Harrison had thought to put in a washing station at the hotel, but I have a little wagon for transport, so we'll make the best of it."

"I'd be happy to help with that."

"Wonderful. Once it's clean, I can bring it back to the hotel and spend my evenings ironing it."

They talked about the arrangements after school started and settled on a price. Susanna thought the payment was more than acceptable. It was far less than she might have paid in Topeka. Uncle might protest, but this was something she was doing for herself, and he would have to live with it. Her only other choice would be to leave San Marcial.

"Well, I should get back to the hotel." Susanna got to her feet. "I see the sun has set, and there's not much light left. No sense in me getting lost."

"I'm sure Owen will be happy to walk back with you," Lia said as they made their way outside, where the boys were still running circles around Owen and LeRoy. "Won't you, Owen?"

Owen came toward them. "Won't I what?"

"Won't you be willing to walk back with Susanna? It's getting rather late, and who knows what rowdy souls she might encounter."

"Of course I'll walk you back. I was waiting around with just that in mind."

Susanna smiled. "That's very kind of you."

"It's perfectly selfish," Owen admitted. "I get to keep company with a pretty girl."

LeRoy laughed. "I'd say Owen gets the better end of the deal. Susanna will just have to suffer through."

Susanna didn't say a word about how much she liked the arrangement. She bid Lia good-bye, then headed back toward the hotel with Owen at her side.

"I appreciate the escort. I'm still not that familiar with everything."

"It'll take time, even in a small town. Maybe Sunday you would like to take a walk with me after church. Better yet, a ride. Do you ride horses?"

"I do. Quite well, in fact." She grinned. "It was a definite pleasure of mine growing up."

"Well, then we will definitely ride. I'll borrow a couple of horses, and we can take a picnic lunch after church and go off down the river. I know a lovely place. When we get back, we can ride around San Marcial, and you can get to know where everything is. I'll even point out the places you should never go."

She laughed. "Sounds intriguing."

"It's meant to. I have to entice you somehow."

"You had me enticed with the horseback riding," she declared, unable to admit that anything that involved Owen would have drawn her utmost attention.

"Then it's a date."

6

After church that Sunday, Susanna dressed with special care in a brown split skirt and a brown-and-yellow calico blouse. The sleeves of the blouse were long and the neck high. She hoped it would keep her skin from the harsh burn of the sun.

She looked at her carefully pinned up hair and decided to pull it all down and go with a simple braid. The honey-brown mass spilled down her back in waves. Taking up her brush, Susanna stroked it into order and then braided it into a single plait.

Last, she took up a straw hat with a wide, full brim that would offer plenty of shade. She glanced in the small mirror hanging over her dressing table. It had been a long time since she'd really studied her image in a mirror. Since Mark's death, she hadn't cared what she looked like. Now it seemed like it might matter.

She turned to the left and then the right, catching only a bit of her image in the small mirror. She pinned on the hat and looked again. She smiled at her silliness and chided herself for acting like a schoolgirl with a crush. Owen was quite charming, but it was too early to pretend to have feelings for him. Or was it?

Owen was waiting for her when she finally exited the hotel. He had two horses saddled and a blanket roll and pack on the back of one of the horses. "I have lunch for us compliments of the Harvey House. I hope you aren't tired of their fare just yet."

"No, of course not."

"This is Daisy," he said, leading her to the sorrel mare. "She's a little spirited when she hasn't been ridden, so you'll need to keep a tight rein on her. I could have gotten you a sidesaddle, but with her I think you'll be glad to ride astride."

"This is fine. Thanks for the warning." Susanna rubbed the mare's face. "I'm sure we'll be good friends, won't we, Daisy?"

Owen helped her mount, then jumped up on the tall bay next to Daisy. "This is Mannie. He's my horse of choice when heading out for leisurely rides. He's got a good temper with a hint of daring. I once jumped a high fence with him, and it was as if he were doing nothing more important than crossing a ditch. He's quite the ride."

"Is he yours?"

"He will be. I've been paying him off in installments. Lia's father owns him and Daisy. He rents horses to the livery here in town."

"How nice." She got a feel for the saddle, finding it just a trifle big. It would suffice, however.

"Well, follow me," Owen said, reining his horse away from the depot and Harvey House and toward the long, meandering river.

Susanna noticed the long mesa across the river. "Does that have a name?" She pointed.

"Mesa del Contadero is the official name, but most folks just call it Black Mesa. We can climb it sometime if you're up for an adventure."

"Sounds like fun, although I think I'd have to buy a different pair of boots." She glanced at her riding boots. They were far too nice and the soles too slick for getting traction on a climb.

"The shoemaker's widow has no proper boots," he said, laughing.

"It would seem you know all about me."

"I asked Lia a lot of questions." His smile only widened. "I hope you don't mind."

"Not at all. So long as I get to do the same."

He chuckled. *"Con mi permiso,* which is Spanish for *with my permission.* Lia taught that to me first thing. She said it was a good thing to know."

"I'll keep that in mind."

They rode side by side in silence until San Marcial was well behind them. Susanna didn't know when she'd last felt so carefree and happy. There was just a hint of breeze that made the sun not quite so unbearable, and she was glad to be rid of her family—at least for a little while. Their unhappiness and complaining threatened to put a stranglehold on her most days.

"Tell me about yourself," Owen said, breaking the silence.

"I thought Lia already told you everything."

He shook his head. "She's only told me what you've let her know. I want to know it all. I want to know about your husband and your life in Topeka."

Susanna was taken aback. "You want to know about Mark?"

"Of course. He was important to you, and I want to know about the things that were important to you."

Susanna smiled and gave a little shrug.

"What can I say? We were lifelong friends. I'd known him since grade school. We were in the same class, and it was like we were always meant to be friends."

"What was he like?"

"Sensible but fun-loving. Kind and gentle, but assertive and self-confident. But it was his father who made the shoes, as Lia mentioned. Jenkins Shoes. You might have heard of them."

"No, I don't think so, but please go on." He gave her a smile that caused her heart to skip a beat.

"Well, his father made these shoes that became quite sought after, and Mark knew when he was still a boy that he wanted to sell his father's shoes."

"He didn't want to make them?"

"No. He never felt that was his talent. He was good, however, at everything involved in running a store and marketing the shoes. He worked day and night with his father to learn all that he could about the shoes and how they were made, but he never felt making them was his gift. And it wasn't. Being in charge of the stores and working to distribute the shoes was definitely what he was good at. By the time he died, he had managed to get five different stores in five major cities in just a couple of years. The shoes were quite popular."

"When did you marry?"

"When I was twenty. That was four years ago."

"Why did you wait so long if you'd been in love since childhood?"

"Mark didn't want to marry until he could afford to furnish me with a home that was free and clear of debt. He figured we'd marry when I was twenty-five. That would have been next year." She shook her head and smiled. "But he was that good at marketing the shoes. He managed to build a lovely store and a large work warehouse for his father and the men he trained, pay it all off within the first two years, and buy a small house for us."

"It sounds like he was quite the man."

Susanna felt a bittersweet pang of love. "He was. He was a good man."

"And how did he die?"

She gazed out across the Rio Grande. "Influenza. We all had it. It was just a bad cold for me, but Mark took very ill with it, and the doctor said he developed pneumonia. He knew he was going to die. I don't know how." She couldn't help but remember those last few hours. "He coughed so hard I thought he'd turn himself inside out." She shook her head. "He coughed and coughed, and no matter how much medicine the doctor gave him, it didn't seem to help. We had water boiling with herbs and made poultices for his chest with menthol. The doctor even had us brew very strong coffee and get him to drink it. That helped a bit, but not very much. His fever began to climb, and try as we might, we could not get it back down. Then the coughing stopped. He had no more strength for it. His mother and I never left his side as we bathed him in herb water and did whatever we could to see him through.

"Then, around eight o'clock in the evening, he opened his eyes and spoke. He was wheezing but otherwise could be clearly understood. He told us he wasn't going to make it. His mother went for his father, and while she was gone, Mark gripped my hand and told me that he loved me and always had, but that he didn't want me to spend my life in mourning. His folks were back by then, and he made them promise they wouldn't grieve him forever. He wanted them to enjoy their lives and for me to remarry as soon as I felt I could. I didn't even want to consider it, but he made me promise. He said he couldn't die in peace knowing that I might spend the rest of my life lost in sorrow."

"So you promised."

"I did." She swallowed a lump in her throat. "By ten that evening, he was gone. We'd been married just three short years, but we'd had a lifetime of love."

"I'm so sorry."

She shook her head and met his eyes. "Don't be. I'm not. Death is hard to face, but to have known life without him would have been harder. I'm grateful for the time we had. I am determined to regret nothing."

"That's a hard one."

"I suppose it is."

She let the horse have her head, which was a mistake. The sorrel picked up her pace and began to trot. A moment later, she was into a gallop.

Susanna held her seat and worked to bring the mare back under control. "Whoa, Daisy," she called, pulling back gently on the reins. The horse seemed determined to run, but Susanna continued to impose control.

Finally, the mare slowed and reared up in protest. Susanna kept her seat, leaning into the horse like one born to a saddle. The horse gave two more jumps in protest but finally calmed.

Owen caught up with her. "You are quite a horsewoman. I'm impressed with the way you ride."

"She's a great mount but obviously doesn't get out on a regular basis. We probably should have run her first thing and gotten the orneriness out of her."

"She seems to have settled down now.

And this is a great place for our picnic. There are trees along the river just over there."

Susanna looked to the north. "It's a very pretty place."

Owen dismounted and helped her down from Daisy. They walked the horses the rest of the way. Owen handed her both sets of reins, then pulled the blanket from the back of his horse and spread it on the ground. Next, he took off the saddlebags and put them on the blanket, then took off the saddles before taking back the reins.

"I'll water them and tie them off while you search through those saddlebags and see what we have for lunch," he said. "Keep an eye out for snakes. They love an escape from the heat just like we do, and you can often find them in the brush around the trees and river."

Susanna nodded and glanced around, a little unnerved. She sank onto the blanket, keeping a close eye out for anything that moved. Since their arrival, she'd heard horrible stories about giant spiders and scorpions and poisonous lizards, as well as snakes. It was enough to make her rethink a life in San Marcial. For the moment, however, everything seemed tranquil and without danger.

Susanna smiled at her own nervousness. She reached into the first of the pouches. Best just to get lunch out and ready. Doing something mundane and normal would put her fears to the back of her mind.

Owen had purchased ham and cheese sandwiches for their main course. Besides these, there were two large apples. In one of the other bags was a mason jar of lemonade. Surprisingly, it was still cold. There were no glasses, so she presumed they would share the jar. In the last pouch were two of the large quarter-cut pieces of Harvey House cherry pie wrapped in waxed paper. The pieces were a little squished but otherwise no worse for the wear.

"Well, I'm not at all sure how you intended for us to eat, but I have found plenty of food," Susanna announced as Owen returned from overseeing the horses.

He laughed. "Fingers. We'll probably make a mess, but I don't figure there will be anyone to see, and we can wash up in the river."

"Rather scandalous that we're out here all alone," she replied. With another man she might have felt completely out of sorts, but Owen made her feel strangely safe.

He looked stricken. "I never thought about safeguarding your reputation. I apologize. I suppose we should have asked Lia and LeRoy and the boys to join us."

"I suppose, but I don't mind. I've always

lived my life in a way that I hoped was respectful and above reproach. If folks want to think ill of us, they will no matter who might accompany us."

Owen lowered himself to the blanket and nodded. "I couldn't agree more. Shall I offer grace?"

"Please."

Susanna bowed her head, and Owen said a brief but heartfelt prayer.

Once he concluded, he grabbed one of the sandwiches and began to unwrap it. "I hope you don't mind the simplicity."

"Not at all." She picked up the other sandwich. "I cherish it. I'm not one to stand on formalities. That would be my mother."

He smiled. "Tell me about your folks. I've never met people who seemed more unhappy or uncomfortable. I've heard all sorts of stories about them." He shook his head. "I probably shouldn't have said that. I don't mean to sound like folks are gossiping about them."

"I'm sure they are, and probably most of the stories are true." She frowned. "My father was born to a rich man. My grandfather could touch a coin and triple its value without even trying. My uncle Harrison is the same way. He has a natural understanding of investments and how and when to take a risk.

My father unfortunately thinks this gift is also his."

"But it's not?" Owen asked.

"No. It never has been. You can't convince him, however. Uncle Harrison and Grandfather Ragsdale were well aware of my father's flaws, however. They were cautious and careful to safeguard his inheritance, but Father never understood that, nor did he ever figure out how to invest wisely. Grandfather died some years ago, and Father was given a lump sum to work with, but unbeknownst to him, an additional portion of his inheritance was given to Uncle Harrison for management. Uncle Harrison was able to double that amount, but my family knows nothing about it—at least I don't think they do. Through the years, Uncle Harrison has had to go behind my father's back and clean up messes he's made, and this inheritance has had to be used. Thankfully, Uncle Harrison is gifted in earning it back." She frowned, remembering how her uncle had shared all of this just a few weeks back. Susanna had been so embarrassed for her father.

"He never told Father how much of a mess he'd made of things until recently, when Father lost everything and Uncle Harrison let him fall despite there being inheritance still available. He told me he had to do this, or when he died and Father realized the full amount was his, he'd no doubt squander it and be left a pauper."

"I'm sure your folks couldn't have been happy at that turn of events."

"No. They thought it a joke at first. A poorly executed one, but nonetheless a joke. Uncle Harrison told them that my father had refused to be taught, and so they had to face the consequences."

"That would have been hard to endure."

"It was terrible. My mother has always believed herself to be of the highest society. She came from a political family who had more power than money, so she was always seen in the right circles, but everyone knew she was of little worth financially. When she married Father, she was finally able to attach herself to money. But even so, she's never been accepted among the truly elite. Those in power with longtime wealth realize exactly what she and my father are and how they operate. People have always known and laughed at them behind their backs. I never knew this until I had my coming-out ball. I remember overhearing girls I thought were my friends talking about how ridiculous it all was. I heard them say that we were of no account—that Father was a fool and my mother a braggart who had nothing to brag about.

"I remember asking Mark about it, and of course he knew. He explained some of it to me, but he didn't tell me all. It wasn't until Uncle Harrison explained before we came here that I finally knew how bad it truly was."

"And what did he tell you?" Owen asked, still not having taken a single bite of his sandwich.

Susanna motioned to him. "Eat. It's not important. You have probably already guessed. My uncle paid my father's debts and moved him down here. Uncle built the hotel, having heard that San Marcial was a booming community slated to grow even bigger because of the Santa Fe Railway. It was just going to be an investment, but after what happened, Uncle Harrison saw it as a teaching opportunity. My father is to run the hotel and make a good show of the business and a tidy profit for my uncle. Uncle Harrison will judge his work and decide his future."

She began to nibble on her sandwich and found that she was quite hungry. It wasn't long before she'd devoured the entire thing. Owen too seemed hungry. He ate the sandwich and apple and was quickly working on the pie when Susanna got up the nerve to ask him about his life.

"So, turnabout is only fair. Tell me about your childhood. Where did you grow up?"

"Albuquerque, and elsewhere before that. My father was a train engineer."

"Ah. So that's how you came to work for the Santa Fe?"

"Yes. Trains were always a part of our life. I often snuck on board when I was young, especially after my mother died. I was just twelve when she passed away from an infection." He drew a deep breath. "I had a younger brother too. Your brother Gary reminds me of him."

"Had? Is he gone?"

"Yes."

It was all he offered, and Susanna didn't pry.

Owen continued, "My father passed on a couple of years back. He loved being an engineer and died doing what he loved when his train derailed near Winslow."

"I'm sorry to hear that. So your family is all gone?"

"Yeah. I'm the only one left." He finished off the pie and leaned back on his elbows. "I tried my hand at a variety of railroad jobs, but working with the boilers was what I found most intriguing. I even trained in Topeka, which makes me smile when I think of how you were there. The world really isn't so very big after all."

"No, I suppose not." Susanna studied

him a moment, wondering if she might ever have seen him. But truth be told, she had only had eyes for Mark back then.

It was pleasant under the shade of the twisted cottonwood, but after a time, Susanna couldn't help but notice the growing heat.

Owen seemed to read her thoughts. "I think we should head back. Today's a scorcher without any clouds to ease the temperature." He got to his feet. "I'll get the horses saddled."

"I'll pack up our things here," Susanna offered.

He reached down to help her to her feet. She stood and was quite content to let Owen hold her and gaze into her eyes. It was a lovely moment.

"I have to tell you that this has been the best day I've had in some time," he said.

Susanna could see the sincerity in his eyes. "It's been the best for me as well. Thank you for suggesting it."

He dropped his hold on her. "Thank you for coming along."

7

The next week Uncle Harrison arrived. He inspected the hotel with Susanna's father following in close step. Susanna manned the front desk while the two men made their way around the hotel, which at the moment was empty.

Susanna had already stripped the rooms where people had stayed the night before and remade made the beds with fresh linens. Her mother had encouraged her not to change the linens every day—after all, who was to know, unless the sheets were mud-smeared or stained? But Susanna didn't like the idea of letting different people sleep on the same sheets. She wanted their guests to know the room was completely clean—bedding and all.

"Well, the rooms aren't as big as I thought they'd be, but the furnishings are good, and if need be, you could fit another bed into most of the rooms," Uncle Harrison declared as he and Father made their way down the stairs.

Uncle Harrison was a large man who appeared rather imposing to most. He was six foot two and broad shouldered with a thick waist. Susanna had once seen a photograph of Queen Victoria's son, who was to be king one day. Uncle Harrison was the spitting image of that man and just as intimidating as if he were a king.

"Susanna, how are you, my dear?" he asked. She had been in the back and not quite dressed when he arrived, so she hadn't yet greeted him.

"I'm doing well, Uncle Harrison." She embraced him as he kissed her cheek. "And how about you? How was the train ride?"

"Completely without error. I came in my own car, and it was luxury at its best. I cannot complain. And how about you? Is life treating you well?"

"It is. I'm quite content." She beamed a smile.

"Now, where are your mother and brother?"

Susanna could tell her father hadn't broken the news of their living elsewhere. She looked to her father, who was quick to look away.

"Mother is no doubt at home in the little adobe house I arranged for them," Susanna said. "Gary, however, is working for the railroad. He wanted to try his hand at manual labor."

Her uncle's scowl was deep. "You aren't living here at the hotel, Herbert?"

Susanna's father shrugged. "Gladys couldn't abide it here. She was a nervous wreck. Susanna found us a little house only a few blocks away, and she manages much better there."

"That wasn't our arrangement. Someone must be on the premises at all times."

"There is someone," Father hurried to explain. "I come every dawn and stay until evening, except for mealtimes. Susanna is here all evening and night."

"She lives here alone? That is hardly appropriate. You and your wife were to live here, not your daughter."

"Yes, well, perhaps you can take that up with Gladys over lunch."

Uncle Harrison merely rolled his eyes and then fixed his gaze on Susanna. "What about that brother of yours? Can he stay here with you? I don't want you living here alone. This town has a reputation of being a bustling place with a lot of strangers. You need to be protected."

"I'm sure Gary might consider it. We can ask him," Susanna assured him. She couldn't imagine why Gary would care.

"Let me see the books," her uncle demanded. "May we use the living quarters, Susanna?"

"Of course." She led the way and opened the door to her rooms.

They were exactly as Uncle Harrison had them built. Susanna hadn't added any personal items to make them her own. She wasn't sure how long she'd stay or if her family would find it necessary for whatever reason to take back the rooms. In fact, her entire world still felt as if it were turned upside down, and no place felt like home.

Her uncle and father took a seat at the small table while Susanna fetched them coffee. Father had the books open and was showing her uncle the records and then comparing those numbers with the bank deposits. Susanna herself had double-checked his entries and knew they were right, so she had no concerns that her father might have failed in this area.

"Good," Uncle Harrison declared. "I'm glad to see we've had a few walk-ins from the train. Some will want the convenience of the Harvey House, and that is perfectly fine. I believe that, while we are competition for them, they have their purpose and place as well. Some people will prefer to be away from the tracks." He looked back and forth across the ledger as if searching for something. "Where's the accounting of expenses in the day-to-day running of the place? Laundry, for example."

"Susanna does the laundry."

"That's not what I told you to do, Herbert. There's a good Mexican laundry in town. They'll pick up whatever you have to be done and deliver it the next day."

"But just look at the money we've saved." Susanna's father looked proud.

"And have you given that money to Susanna?"

Her father's look changed to indignant. "Of course not. I need that money for our living expenses."

"You aren't entitled to that money. I set a salary, and I set expenses."

"I have a friend who is happy to continue helping with laundry at the house," Susanna offered. "Perhaps I can simply pay her."

"Do you have receipts for laundry items you've been forced to purchase?" her uncle asked.

"I'm sorry, I never thought about it," Susanna said with a shrug.

"Herbert, from now on you will pay this

friend of Susanna's to do the laundry. Susanna has enough on her plate in cleaning the rooms and wash areas. How ridiculous that you and Gladys can't even do that much."

"I've had a representative from the railroad ask me about signing an arrangement for them to use our empty rooms for visiting workers," Susanna's father said, quickly changing the subject.

Uncle Harrison frowned. "Laborers?"

"I believe they were speaking of clerical headquarter workers, Uncle." Susanna brought the cream and sugar, along with spoons. "They have offices here, as you know."

"Well, clerical officials would be acceptable, but not laborers. We can't have them staining the sheets and tearing up the furniture with their rowdy ways. I've not yet seen laborers who didn't imbibe alcohol, and once drunk, they present quite the problem." Uncle Harrison frowned all the more. "Which is another reason you shouldn't be left alone here at the hotel, Susanna." He looked at his brother. "You and your wife should live here."

"But we can't. Gladys would be ill all the time."

"Your wife feigns illness every time her mood changes. The two of you must open your eyes to the truth, Herbert."

Susanna saw a glint of anger in her father's eyes. "None of this would be happening if not for you. You could easily make this go away."

Uncle Harrison had his coffee cup midway to his lips and stopped. "You honestly blame me, don't you?"

Susanna hated to see the brothers fight. She hated fighting of any kind, but what could she do or say to change the situation? Her father was being unreasonable, and his older brother had done nothing but attempt to help him see his erring ways.

"If you had released funds to me, I wouldn't have lost my home," Father insisted.

Her uncle put his cup on the table. "You lost your home because you took a gamble we all warned you not to take. We told you that the investment wasn't sound. We warned you we had explored it and found it to be less than reliable. I begged you to hear reason, and you know this full well."

"You were never one to take big chances," Susanna's father countered. "How was I to know this wasn't just one of those times when you were being overly conservative?"

"Herbert, all of your adult life you have been unwilling to listen to counsel from others who know more than you." He fixed Susanna's father with a sad look. "Our father knew a day just like this would come. He hoped you would learn early in life that money management required so much more than risk-taking, but you've been unwilling to learn anything from me. I'm afraid that even giving you this opportunity was a mistake."

"I think the summer heat is making us testy," Susanna interjected. "We should walk over to the house. It's much cooler there. The adobe keeps the temperatures much nicer, Uncle. You probably should have built the hotel of adobe." She smiled, hoping he would be willing to end the confrontation. "Besides, it will soon be time for lunch."

"Yes, well, I suppose we can do that," her uncle said. He still studied his younger brother with undisguised disappointment.

"I'll let Gladys know you're coming," her father said, getting to his feet. "I'll send the Garcia boy over to watch the desk, Susanna."

She looked at Uncle Harrison, who was scowling. She hadn't had a chance to explain to her uncle about Father bringing in a boy to watch over things during mealtimes. She wondered how he would take the news.

Father was gone before she could offer any protest or encouragement. That was best for now, she figured. Uncle Harrison was beyond angry.

"I'm sorry for interfering," Susanna said

after her father had gone. "I'm afraid I've made a mess of things."

"Tell me about this house they're living in."

"I bought it. Mother immediately started in upon our arrival and was so unreasonable I could hardly bear it. She was ready to climb aboard a train bound for who knows where, and of course Father would have followed. I thought maybe if I found them a better situation, they would both relax and see the blessings they had to work with. Instead, it has only made matters worse. Mother refuses to do anything for herself, and so it fell to me. Frankly, I don't have time to keep up with the cleaning and laundry here and take care of the family at the same time. I hired a lady from church to help with cooking and cleaning at the house."

"So they are back to being waited on hand and foot."

"If not by this woman, it would be by me. I'm afraid I can't long bear my mother's sobbing and complaints."

"Susanna, you must be strong. I asked you to come here to be my eyes and ears, not to make matters worse." Her uncle, although understanding, was firm in his tone. "Your mother has to learn to take care of things for herself. She needs to take over this hotel and know what it is to work. Your father needs the same thing. Perhaps you should go back to Topeka."

She thought of Owen and shook her head. "I don't think that's the answer."

"Perhaps not, but without you here, they can hardly expect you to do everything."

"Well, at least father has been coming to work regularly every morning. And at dawn. He wants to be here to check people out as they leave and make certain they pay their bill. He appears to be trying to do what you asked of him."

"No, because he isn't living here and taking full responsibility. He was to live here and be the hotel's full-time manager. Your mother was to clean and maintain the laundry for each room. They were to endure this punishment to teach them to appreciate what they had. They have no more understanding of why they're here than when I first imposed this punishment on them."

"I doubt they ever will. They're set in their ways, Uncle Harrison. The lessons should have come when Father was young."

"Believe me, there were lessons aplenty. Your grandfather was more than patient."

"Hello, I am here," announced a voice from the lobby.

"That will be Manuel. He'll watch the

front desk in case someone comes to check in. It's doubtful, since we won't have a train in until later today, but I told Father he shouldn't just lock the front door and expect that there would be no one."

"Of course not. It's a business," the older man said, rolling his gaze heavenward. "Oh, it vexes me." He shook his head. "Who is this boy, Manuel? Is he reliable?"

"Yes, of course. He's a sort of adopted son to our pastor and his wife. Manuel's family died during an epidemic when he was quite young. The pastor and his wife took him in, and he's been with them ever since. He's quite reliable. Why don't you let me introduce you?"

Susanna went to greet Manuel. "Manuel, this is my uncle, Harrison Ragsdale. He owns this hotel."

Her uncle looked at the young man and gave a nod.

Manuel was wearing an older but neat suit with a white shirt and starched collar. He smiled and greeted the older man. "I'm glad to meet you."

Uncle Harrison nodded again but said nothing.

"Someone will be back by one o'clock," Susanna promised.

With her uncle beside her, Susanna led

the way to the little house. She prayed her father and mother would both realize the importance of this visit and take it seriously. She prayed her mother would stop with her pretenses and avoidances and face the truth of what was expected of her. Most of all, Susanna prayed for peace between her parents and uncle.

Uncle Harrison was impressed with the coolness of the house and immediately expressed as much. He handed Susanna his hat. "It's remarkable that the adobe accounts for this. I must order a study of this, for I plan to build additional hotels in the south. It would be to my benefit to consider this manner of construction."

Susanna drew Lia out of the kitchen. "Uncle Harrison, this is Lia Branson. She helps out a few hours each day and has made our luncheon."

"I am happy to meet you," Lia declared with a smile. "I will have your lunch ready soon."

Mother and Father came out of their bedroom. Mother looked more than a little miffed at the interruption to her day.

"Harrison," she said, nodding. "I see you have come."

"Gladys." He gave a nodding bow. "You are looking fit."

"I am hardly that. I've been wasting away. This climate is not good for me at all."

He chuckled. "Well, for someone on death's door, you look remarkably well."

She frowned and shook her head. "I can see you are without reason."

"I have plenty of reason, my dear lady." Uncle Harrison looked around the small living area and then to the door Susanna's folks had just come through. "I presume that is a bedroom."

Susanna nodded. "And on the opposite side is another small room where Gary stays."

"But we will soon change that and get him to stay at the hotel with you. Honestly, Herbert, you lack all sense in letting your widowed daughter live there alone. What were you thinking? As I made clear, the hotel was where you and Gladys were to live."

"I cannot abide that place. I simply cannot. It's much too hot, and I will faint if I have to stay there even an hour," Susanna's mother said, shaking her index finger at her brother-in-law. "You are heartless, and I wonder what your wife would say if you imposed the same on her."

"My wife understands her station and has never put on the airs that you do, madam."

"Oh!" Mother huffed.

"As I was telling Herbert at the hotel, the

entire idea of you coming here was to learn how to work for your living. To see the value in going at an investment from the inside out. Learning to appreciate what you have, rather than constantly trying to get what you don't."

Mother took out her fan and began to wave it rapidly. Susanna feared she might decide to faint for dramatic effect and jumped in.

"I'm sure Gary won't mind coming to the hotel, Uncle. There's room enough for both of us to stay there quite comfortably."

"Hardly," Mother said, pausing the fan. "There was only one main room with two tiny bedrooms. Jail cells are bigger than what you sentenced us with."

"And your husband could just as easily end up in one, if he doesn't learn to manage his money better," Uncle Harrison responded. "Do you realize the conman who robbed you is being hunted by the government? He is responsible for criminal acts against the government. What if he chooses to implicate your husband as a partner in his acts?"

"He wouldn't dare. Herbert has never done anything criminal."

Susanna saw her father's face pale. This meeting was getting worse by the minute. Thankfully, Lia was setting the table with food.

"Oh, look. It would appear lunch is served." Susanna touched her mother's shoulder. "We should be seated."

It was such a different life than what they had known. In times gone by, a bell would have chimed or a servant would have announced the meal. They would have come to the table, where servants would have helped them into their chairs and then served them from a sideboard. Now the food was placed on the table, and it was more or less a free-for-all.

Pushing her mother toward the table, Susanna helped her into a chair and then quickly took the seat to Mother's left. Father and Uncle Harrison joined them, but the looks on their faces suggested great reluctance.

"Would you like me to say grace?" Susanna offered. She realized she was doing anything and everything to keep some feeling of normalcy, but it was the normalcy from her own world. Father and Mother didn't pray over meals.

Father nodded, and she bowed her head. "Lord, for what we are about to receive, we thank You. Bless this food to our bodies and bless the hands who have prepared it. Amen."

"Amen," Uncle Harrison replied. Mother and Father remained silent.

Susanna picked up her plate. "Uncle, Lia has made pork tamales for us. They are her family's recipe. She always fixes us something from her heritage so that we can experience food from the Mexican culture, but without the strong spices. Would you care to try them?"

"I would. It sounds rather intriguing." He gave her a smile.

"The rest of our fare is recognizable enough. Salad and chicken in cream sauce. Tonight we'll have more of the same with a dessert added. We try to be frugal with our food budget."

"It is appalling to have to eat the same things day after day," Mother muttered. "I have a boiled egg and toast every morning for breakfast."

"On Sunday we have ham or bacon as well, and some mornings oatmeal is served, so Mother does have options," Susanna said.

"It's a terrible way to live," the older woman snapped.

"Better than starving," Uncle Harrison said as Susanna handed him a full plate of food. He smiled down at the fare. "Looks positively delicious."

They ate in silence for a few moments, with Mother and Father actually sampling the tamales. Susanna thought them delicious and could tell by the way her father ate that he too enjoyed them. Only her mother picked at them as if they would bite her.

Lia headed for the door a few minutes later with the promise to return later in the day. Susanna was more than grateful for her friend's help and started to comment on the meal, but her uncle spoke up before she could say anything.

"What do you pay her to work here?"

"That is hardly any of your concern, Harrison," Mother said. "Go ahead and go, Lia. We'll see you later."

Lia did as instructed, but Susanna could see the matter was far from over. Her uncle had that steeled look of determination in his eyes.

"Who is paying for her?" he asked again.

"I am," Susanna said without hesitation.

"Of course, you aren't. Herbert is," her mother corrected.

Harrison looked to his brother. "Which is it?"

Father looked momentarily embarrassed. "I suppose Susanna is. I haven't given the woman any money."

Mother looked surprised and glanced from her husband to Susanna and back.

"And for this house?" Uncle Harrison pressed.

Father picked at his tamale. "Again, Susanna. She offered to find the place and did so. She's not asked me for money, and I offered none."

Susanna's uncle turned to her. "So you are using your own money to pay for your parents to have undeserved luxuries."

"This is hardly luxury," Mother proclaimed loudly. "And why shouldn't a daughter help her parents in their time of need?" She pushed back from the table. "Honestly, you are a cruel man, Harrison. You shame us at every turn. I'm certain Herbert intends to pay Susanna for her kindness. God knows she's the only one to offer us kindness."

"I kept you from being put out on the street and moved you here to allow you to escape the shame and humiliation you were certain to face in Topeka. Don't you consider that a kindness?" Uncle Harrison replied. "Both of you are spoiled children expecting the rest of the world to see to your needs, but it's time you grew up. I forbid Susanna to spend another dime on either of you."

"You can hardly forbid my daughter to do anything," Mother countered. "She is a grown woman, and if she chooses to help her family, then it is because we raised her to see the value of supporting family in their time of need." She got to her feet. "I feel faint. Your aggressive nature is more than I can stand. I must lie down." She exited the room without another word, slamming the bedroom door for emphasis.

Susanna looked to her uncle, who shook his head and went back to eating. Father ducked his head and kept his gaze on his plate as if to make himself invisible.

It was a sad moment in Susanna's life. Her parents were like willful children who refused to be corrected. What in the world would happen to them if they didn't change? Even she didn't have enough money to keep them indefinitely.

~~~

"Gary, I've shown you three different times how to do this. You aren't paying attention," Owen said, taking the sledge from him.

"I'm trying. I guess I just don't understand."

"Or you aren't listening." Owen had reached the end of his patience. It was over one hundred degrees in the shop, and everyone was on edge.

Mr. Payne came over, clearly angry. "Owen, I looked over that boiler you remade. It's substandard and needs to be redone. Who did you have working on it? The man obviously doesn't know what he's doing."

Gary paled despite the heat. He threw Owen a pleading look. For a moment, Owen's anger mounted. Gary actually expected Owen to smooth things over—just like his brother used to do. But try as he might, Owen couldn't bring himself to admit it was Gary. He liked Gary, and even though the kid was difficult to train, Owen didn't want to see him get fired.

"It was my fault," Owen said, doing what he vowed he'd never do again—taking the blame for someone else's poor work. "I'll see it's fixed."

Payne nodded and looked at the metal piece they'd been working on all morning. "When are you going to have this done?"

"Not sure now, but hopefully by tomorrow—end of the day."

"See to it. We have a schedule to keep. Every 1400 hours we have to remake these boilers and do so in a manner that will keep them going another 1400. I can't have substandard work."

Mr. Payne walked off, and Gary breathed a heavy sigh.

"Thanks for covering for me. I thought I'd done a good job."

Owen hadn't had a chance to inspect the piece, so it really was his fault in a way. "I should have looked at it. I won't take the blame next time, Gary. If you can't do the work, you'll have to go. There are plenty of other jobs on the railroad. Maybe this one doesn't suit you."

Gary shook his head. "No. I'll figure it out. I want to work with you. I'm sure I can do better."

Owen nodded. "You'll have to."

Gary was no sooner home that evening than his mother was harping at him to clean up. He was filthy and knew he smelled bad, but he wasn't in the mood to be bossed around. Nothing had gone right at work, and even though Owen was patient, it was all such a mess, and Gary wished he could just slip away unnoticed. Nevertheless, Uncle Harrison was coming to dinner, and Gary was expected to be there and to dress properly.

He washed as best he could, even taking a bar of soap to the shirt he'd been in all day. He didn't know why, but it seemed a smart thing to do. He left it soaking in the washtub and for the first time wondered who would be responsible for cleaning it. All his life, other folks had taken care of such things, and he'd never once considered who might be cleaning up after him.

Dinner was a somber event. His folks were

in bad moods, and Susanna seemed anxious about something. Uncle Harrison looked Gary over at the beginning of the meal but said nothing. Now that they were ready for dessert, he eyed Gary again as if considering his worth.

"I'm proud of you, Gary. Your sister tells me you've been working in the Santa Fe shops, learning metalwork."

"Yes, sir. I'm working with the head boilermaker, Owen Turner."

"How do you like it?"

"I'm not sure. I'm not very good at it."

"Of course you aren't," Mother said, reaching out to pat his arm. "I didn't give birth to a laborer. It's appalling that you've taken on this job."

"Not at all," Harrison declared. "I'm impressed. Besides Susanna, you are the only one to show real initiative."

"That isn't fair," Mother protested. "My poor husband has done your bidding at the hotel, and you act as if it were nothing."

"It certainly isn't the hard work your son is doing." Uncle Harrison gave Gary a smile. "Good job."

"Thank you, sir." Gary wasn't sure what else he could say. It was clear the tension was growing.

His mother began to sniff. When she did

this, a full storm of tears was certain to follow. Father noted it as well. He looked at Gary in warning, but it was too late.

Mother burst into great wailing sobs. "You have ruined our life, Harrison. Just look at what you've done to my son. He is a gentleman, and yet you've turned him into the lowest of the low." She got to her feet, crying into her handkerchief.

Gary looked at Susanna, who merely shrugged. They'd seen this many a time, usually over something far more trivial. There was nothing to be done. No comfort to be offered. This was their mother's moment to prove to Uncle Harrison that his treatment had gone beyond reason to very real and heartfelt pain.

She staggered across the floor as if blinded by her tears and reached the bedroom door with a dramatic wave of her arms. "I don't know if I shall be alive in the morning. This sorrow is surely too great to bear."

She opened the door to the bedroom and disappeared inside. The four left behind sat in silence, looking at one another as if wondering if they should do something more.

"I'll take her some dessert later," Susanna offered.

"I'm going back to the hotel," Father declared, getting to his feet. He glanced at the food on his plate. "I'll take this with me."

Gary continued eating. The food was very good, and the new work left him feeling half-starved most of the time. Owen had warned him he'd drop weight even as he built muscle. Herc said the same thing. He told Gary he'd be muscle-bound by Christmas. He tried to imagine what he'd look like. He'd need new clothes. Of course, before then, he'd probably have to spend some of his money on better work clothes. Owen had gotten him a few things from some of his friends and from a collection of clothes the railroad workers kept for new men. Still, they didn't fit well, and Gary would be better off with his own. Thankfully, he didn't have to pay room and board like the others did.

He finished his dinner and excused himself while Susanna and Uncle Harrison continued talking. He had told Herc and Empty that he'd meet them later for an evening of pool. Tomorrow was Saturday, and they'd only be working half a day, so the idea of stepping out for some entertainment appealed to him. He'd have to swing by the hotel and see if Father could advance him a little money since payday wasn't until Monday.

In his bedroom, Gary took off his good suit and pulled on a blue cotton shirt and older gray trousers. He pulled on his everyday coat, then grabbed his straw hat. He opened his bedroom door just enough that he could hear his sister and Uncle Harrison as they conversed.

"You must never let them know about your money, Susanna. Your father will demand you give it to him for his investments, and your mother will expect you to spend it on her until every penny is gone. You're a wealthy woman, but you must safeguard your future."

"I'm trying to be wise, Uncle. But I could hardly stand the whining and scenes Mother made. You saw how she was tonight regarding Gary. I'm afraid I'm just not tough enough to listen to such things for long."

"Well, now that you've bought this house, I suppose there's nothing to be done for it. Get Gary to stay at the hotel with you so you won't be in danger. That's all I can recommend, since your folks won't move in there like I want them to do."

Gary used that moment to appear. "Did I hear my name mentioned?"

Susanna startled but smiled. "Yes. Uncle would like you to move in with me at the hotel. He doesn't think it's safe for me to live there alone."

"I can do that," Gary said, having already determined it would be a nice reprieve from staying with his folks. "I'm headed out to meet some friends right now, though."

"You can wait until tomorrow to move," Uncle Harrison declared. "I'll be at the hotel tonight, so I can be available for your sister. Thank you for your consideration, however. You're turning into a remarkable young man. I'm sure your father is proud."

Gary shook his head. "I don't care if he is proud. I didn't do it for him. He's ruined my life, and I just want to find a way to be nothing like him."

8

I like it better living here than with Mother and Father," Gary admitted a week later.

"I can't say that I blame you." Susanna had made toast and boiled eggs for breakfast. "Are you hungry?"

Gary nodded. "I'm always hungry these days. Owen says it's because of the way my body is trying to adjust to the hard work."

"How's that going for you?"

He slipped into a chair at the table. "I'm not good at it, Susanna. I'm not good at much of anything."

"In time you will be. You just have to put your mind to it."

"Herc and the boys tease me because I've never had to work. Herc said he had to cut down trees for firewood when he was just a boy of six and lived up in Minnesota. I played with toy soldiers in the nursery when I was six."

"I'm sure everyone has their story, just as you do. Don't give up, Gary." She placed three boiled eggs and two pieces of toast in front of him. "I'll get you some coffee."

"I won't give up, but . . . well, Owen may give up on me. I just don't seem to understand the things he wants me to do. I'm trying, though. I really am."

"Did you tell him that?" She brought the coffeepot and placed it on a hot pad near Gary. She quickly retrieved her own breakfast plate and joined him at the table. "I'm sure if you're honest with Owen, he'll be patient with you. Besides, today is Saturday—so just a half day. You won't have to work quite so hard."

Susanna offered a short prayer, and they dug in. Gary noted the time and began to eat a little faster. Susanna wondered what Owen thought of her brother. It wasn't like he'd ever worked before. Surely Owen would remember that. Still, should she say something to him when they were next alone?

Gary was soon off to work, and moments later Susanna's father appeared, ready for his workday. He was late but seemed in a surprisingly good mood. Susanna took the opportunity to ask a favor.

"Father, later today some of the women

are getting together to quilt. They've invited me to join them so I can learn. I don't know how long it will last, but I assume I won't make dinner with the family. I wondered if you would consider returning to the hotel after dinner this evening and keeping the front desk for me."

"Of course. I'd be happy to. I think the time away from your mother will help her to calm down."

"Is she out of sorts even now that Uncle Harrison has returned to Kansas City?"

"She's worse than ever." Father shook his head and sighed heavily. "I think she hoped to change Harrison's mind when he was here, but you know from what transpired that this was never even remotely possible."

"Uncle Harrison only wants you and Mother to change your ways."

"It isn't his right to run my life," her father replied, turning the guest log to check the names. "Just because he's been more successful—had better breaks—doesn't mean he's smarter than me."

Susanna could hear the misery in her father's voice. How did one face their failures without acknowledging their inadequacies?

"We all make mistakes, Father." She tried her best to tread carefully. "Even you."

"I admit that I made a mistake. I should

have done things differently, but it's too late to change things now, so why dwell on it? Harrison would have me wallow in it and cover myself in sorrows. How am I to move forward if I can't seek another means of financial gain? How can I redeem myself?"

"Uncle is giving you a chance to redeem yourself by managing this hotel. He believes you and Mother should work to make it a success and prove yourselves."

"To whom? Him? I already know I'm fully capable of great things. I've had a life of great gains and losses. I've lived with great successes. Losses too, of course, but I've always bounced back."

Susanna shook her head. "The only way you came back from those losses was because Uncle Harrison paid your debts." She winced a bit, realizing her words would hurt.

"But it's my money he used! He thinks I don't know that."

"Don't know what, Father?"

"About the separate inheritance. Our father didn't trust me, so he left my money in Harrison's care."

Susanna hadn't realized her father knew about this and wasn't about to admit she knew. "Why do you think he did that?" She hoped reflection on the matter might help him face the truth.

"He enjoyed controlling me. Harrison too. They think me incapable of managing my own affairs, but it isn't true."

"But it is. You lost everything because you refused to be counseled on this last investment."

"That's not true. I listened to their counsel. I simply didn't accept that they were right."

"And you were wrong. Wrong in such a way that you lost your home, Father. Your home of over twenty-five years."

"Only because Harrison wouldn't cover the bank note. It was petty and childish of him. He loves seeing me humbled."

"Why would he love that? Why would he purposefully seek to humble you when he's the one who begged you not to invest in this last venture? Perhaps you don't remember, but I was there when he told you how dangerous it was."

"He's always been an alarmist."

"He's always managed to come out on top with his investments."

Her father looked at her, and his expression saddened. "So he's convinced you as well."

"Convinced me of what? The situation speaks for itself. The losses are indisputable. Uncle Harrison has had no call to convince me of anything."

Her father shook his head. "He's convinced my own children that I'm unable to manage my own affairs. It wouldn't surprise me at all if he were arranging to have me put away in a madhouse, and then what will happen to your poor mother?"

Susanna clung to her patience. "No one is trying to have you put away, Father. Uncle Harrison only wants you to come to your senses and learn to invest wisely before all of your money is gone."

"I'm sure that's what he told you," he said, shaking his head, "but just look around you. He's brought us here so that no one will realize what he's doing. He will have his way unless I'm able to get together a sizable amount of money and find a reasonable investment. I'm sure I can earn back our home and clear my name. If only I can lay my hands on several hundred dollars."

Susanna's heart nearly broke for him. She gave him a hug and headed back into her living quarters. It felt like a hopeless cause.

That afternoon, Susanna put aside her concerns about her parents and focused instead on learning to make her first quilt block.

"This is a very simple block. A nine-patch," Mrs. McGuire explained. "It's an easy one for you to learn first. We'll teach you a number of squares. They'll all be different, and once you have enough, we'll help you put them together for a sampler quilt. That way you'll have something to look at when you decide you want to make, say, a quilt of all nine-patch."

Susanna paid close attention as the women advised her on threading her needle, on taking the smallest of stitches, and on keeping a clean quarter-inch seam. By the time they took a break for a little supper, Susanna felt fairly confident of her ability to make a straight stitch line. When the end of the evening neared, she had made not one, but two nine-patch blocks.

"I'm amazed by how pretty they are," Susanna declared as she finished ironing the squares.

"There are all sorts of tricks you can use with different fabrics," Mrs. Lewis told her, stepping up to take the iron as Susanna finished. "I think you'll find yourself quite good at this. You seem to take to it well."

"I can't imagine making my own big quilt, but I'm so excited to learn." Susanna was already imagining the quilt laid out on her bed. She had so enjoyed this evening with the ladies from church.

Lia came to admire her pieces. "Are you glad you came?"

"Oh, yes!" Susanna held up her two squares. "I'm so happy."

The ladies laughed. "I've never seen anyone quite so excited about a nine-patch square," Mrs. McGuire admitted.

As the ladies gathered their things and the quilting party broke up, Susanna set her squares aside and helped Lia clean up.

"Where are your boys tonight?" Susanna asked. She couldn't help but wonder if Owen might be with them.

"Owen and LeRoy took them fishing. I'm hoping if they caught a mess, they'll have them all cleaned before bringing them into the house. I don't mind cooking them—fish fries up fast—but cleaning them will take much too long."

"I'll stay and help—but you'll have to teach me how." Susanna laughed. "Sometimes I feel like I've never learned anything useful. Growing up, I was taught piano and embroidering, but nothing practical."

"Well, piano can be very useful for church, and embroidering is just fancy sewing. If you can do that, you can learn to make clothes. Just look at what you accomplished tonight."

The sound of the boys returning caused both women to stop what they were doing and head for the kitchen. Lia was there first as the men entered with the fish. They had thoughtfully cleaned each one.

"These are ready for the skillet," LeRoy declared. "And I think we're all hoping for a bite tonight."

"I'll put them on right now," Lia said, taking up the large cast-iron skillet. She put lard in the pan and added wood to the stove. "I kept the stove warm all night, so it will heat right up." She looked over her shoulder at Susanna. "Want to stay and have some fish?"

"Please do," Owen said from behind LeRoy. "I'll walk you home afterwards."

"Well, with a reward like that, how can I say no?"

They all laughed, and Susanna joined in.

Emilio took her hand. "You can sit by me, Miss Susanna."

John was not to be outdone. "No, she can sit with me."

"I have two sides," Susanna told them. "I will sit in between you both. How's that?"

The boys grinned. "Then we can both have you."

"What about me?" Owen asked.

"Oh, you don't need to sit with her," John explained. "You and Papa can sit side by side. You're friends, and we're friends with Miss Susanna."

"Aren't I Miss Susanna's friend?"

Susanna looked at Owen and noted his raised brow, as if questioning her on the matter. She smiled and gave a shrug. Owen only grinned.

"Right now, Miss Susanna is going to help me fry fish. So you boys go sit down and let us work. We'll have this fixed up *muy rápido*—very fast."

Susanna watched as Lia used several spices to enhance the flavor of the fish but mainly kept it simple with salt and pepper. There weren't that many filets to fry, so the cooking went quickly.

"Susanna, do you see that crock over there?"

She glanced the direction Lia pointed. "Yes, of course."

"It has tortillas. Would you bring it and that jar of salsa beside it? LeRoy likes to eat his fish like that. You might like it as well. It's not too spicy."

Susanna laughed. "I've already learned that when a Mexican says it's not too spicy, I'd better be ready for fire. Your idea of not being too spicy is different from mine."

"Then I will bring some cold milk for you to drink. It helps to cut the burn." Lia flipped the last of the fish onto a plate. "You'll see."

They sat down to the late snack, and Susanna couldn't remember when she'd had such a pleasant time. The fish was delicious, and putting it in the tortillas with salsa was a perfect way to eat it. She was grateful for the milk, because as she'd suspected, the salsa was a bit spicier than she was used to. Owen laughed at her as she fanned her tongue, and Emilio and John mimicked her several times before the meal was complete.

"I know two little boys who need to get washed up and put to bed," Lia declared as soon as the children finished their food.

Susanna could see they were starting to droop. Sitting still to eat had brought out all the exhaustion in them.

"I'll wash your dishes." Susanna got up and began gathering the plates. "And you can wash your boys."

"I'll dry," Owen offered, then added with a grin, "The dishes, not the boys."

"That lets me off the hook altogether," LeRoy said, sounding quite pleased with himself.

"Oh no." Lia shook her head. "I'll wash and you can dry boys."

He laughed and got to his feet, grabbing first John and then Emilio. "Let's just throw them in the river and then put them to bed."

"No, Papa," they squealed, suddenly finding energy again to resist.

LeRoy laughed and carted them off to

another room while Susanna grabbed the last of the dishes and headed to the kitchen.

Owen already had the hot water from the stove's reservoir ready and was filling the dishpan with soft soap.

"I thought I was going to wash and you dry," Susanna said.

"You are. I just was getting things ready for you." He stepped aside and grabbed a dish towel. "I don't know about you, but I'm beat and ready to hit the hay."

"Yes, it has been an exhausting day, and I'm sure my father is more than ready to return home from the hotel. He was good enough to stay there and work this evening so I could come here. I think Mother has been particularly taxing since my uncle's visit, and Father was happy to distance himself."

"Was it that bad?"

Susanna washed and rinsed the first plate, then handed it to Owen. "It was, but you don't want to hear about that. Tell me how things are going with Gary."

Owen frowned, and Susanna couldn't help herself.

"That bad?"

"You don't want to hear about it."

"But I do. I've seen a real change in him. One that I didn't expect at all."

Owen nodded. "He just doesn't seem

to understand instructions. They're simple enough, but something about it eludes him. He makes mistakes—the same ones over and over. I can't seem to get through to him."

"He had trouble in school that way too." Susanna shook her head. "It's like something is missing in his ability to reason. I feel sorry for him because he honestly seems to want this to work out this time. I've never seen him more dedicated."

"I'll keep doing what I can to help him, but if he can't do the work, I'll have to turn him over to someone else."

They had the dishes done in short order and found that LeRoy and Lia were still busy with the boys. Owen told them he and Susanna were leaving and would see them later, then took Susanna's arm.

"I'll see you home."

"Thank you," she said, reaching for her two quilt squares. "These are what I made tonight. I'm so pleased with them."

"And to think, from these two will come a mighty quilt." He grinned. "I look forward to seeing the finished product."

"Well, it will take a while, I'm sure."

They walked down Main Street, mindful of some of the celebrating going on. The saloons were alive with music and revelry.

"The boys are letting out their aggressions,"

Owen said, shaking his head. "It never fails that Saturday brings out the wild in everyone—railroaders, miners, and cowboys."

"Even you?" she asked with a teasing tone in her voice.

"The wild in me is long gone. I'm pretty quiet and boring. I hope that doesn't disappoint you."

"Not at all." Susanna turned to see his face in the fading light. "I'll take quiet and boring."

Her attention was diverted as a man came flying out of a saloon and into the street. He landed on his backside and rolled end over end. Another man stood in the doorway of the drinking establishment. He was a big man with a dirty apron covering equally dirty clothes. He tossed a hat toward the man on the street.

"And stay out until you can keep your opinions to yourself." The barkeep glanced toward Owen and Susanna before heading back inside.

When the man on the ground finally managed to get to his feet, Susanna was stunned to see it was her brother.

"Gary! What in the world is going on?"

He shook the dirt off his clothes and picked up his straw hat. "Nothing. We were just having some fun."

"It doesn't look like fun."

"It wasn't anything. See, I'm not even drunk."

"Well, thank God for that. I'd hate to have to deal with you if so."

Gary frowned and looked at Owen. "Why are you with him?"

Susanna bristled. "Not that it's any of your business, especially given the circumstances, but Owen is walking me back to the hotel after my quilting party."

"Humph!" Gary turned away. "You could walk home without him."

"And encounter rowdies like you without someone to protect her?" Owen asked.

"I'm not a rowdy, and no one's going to bother her. The fellas know she's my sister."

"And that's supposed to keep her safe?" Owen refused to let it drop.

"Well . . . I don't know." Gary looked away and shook his head. "I just don't like my sister cozying up to my boss."

Susanna stopped mid-step and turned to her brother. "Gary, you may not be drunk, but you are running off at the mouth. I'm a widow. I'm in charge of myself now. You're a good brother, and you've told me over and over how much you like Owen. I don't know what has you in a mood now, but maybe some sleep would be best before you open your mouth again and cause irreparable harm to yourself."

Gary looked at her for a moment, his eyes narrowing and then closing for a moment. Finally, he opened his eyes wide. "Sorry. Maybe I drank more than I thought."

Susanna nodded. "Hopefully it won't happen again." She smiled and pointed to the hotel. "But no harm. We're back, and you can sleep it off."

Gary nodded and left them before anything more could be said.

Susanna turned to Owen. "I don't know what got into him. He's never been that way with me."

"You were always with one man in the past," Owen said gently. "He grew up seeing that and expecting you and Mark to be together. This is something new for him."

She smiled. "Something new for me as well."

9

Gary, I think it's time we try to find you a different job," Owen told the younger man. "You aren't cut out for boilermaker work, and boilers are much too important to just skim by doing a so-so job. None of the railroad work can take that kind of attitude, but there are other jobs you might find more interesting."

Gary frowned. "You're just getting rid of me because I don't want you keeping company with my sister."

"And why is that?" Owen asked him. "Have I done anything wrong? Have I treated her with anything less than the utmost respect?"

Gary shook his head. "I just don't want her getting hurt. That's all."

He was embarrassed to be caught in the

middle of his sister's affairs, but he'd given this a lot of thought. If she got tied up with Owen, then the money she had would be tied up too, and she'd stop helping the family. It hadn't really worried him before, but lately Gary thought about it more and more. He hadn't realized she was rich until Uncle Harrison's comment. Susanna might be their only hope for getting back to normal. Why should he work if she had the money to send him to school?

"I don't have any intentions of hurting your sister, Gary."

"Well, then, don't fire me. She'll be really mad if you let me go. She's going see it as a real problem. We're really close. That's why I'm living at the hotel."

Owen looked at him for a moment, then shook his head. "I'm not firing you. I'm just trying to figure out a job you'd be good at. There are a lot of different things to do around here, as you well know. Boilermaker isn't the only position. You might even like something on the rail itself or on the train. Maybe you could learn to be a brakeman. It's dangerous, but you might enjoy it."

"And get myself killed? I've heard terrible stories about getting crushed between cars. No, thanks."

"Well, it was just an idea. There are a lot

of other things you might consider. There are even office jobs. You might find that more to your liking than working so hard out here."

Gary shook his head. "Reading is hard for me. I just want to stay here in the shops. I know I can get good at this."

"But we don't have time for you to gradually improve. I need a good man right now." Owen paused, looking rueful. "I can't keep covering for you."

"If you like my sister, you will. Otherwise, I'll tell her that you ruined it for me—that you've been against me from the beginning."

Owen frowned. "You know that would be a lie."

Gary did, and for the first time, the idea pricked his conscience. Before in life, whenever he needed to press someone into helping him, it wasn't a difficult matter. He'd find some way to make them see things his way. It was basically how he got through school. But Owen was different. Owen had been kind to him—a real friend.

"I'm sorry. I just don't want to lose this. I guess if you have an idea for another job, I'll try it," Gary said, shoving his hands into his pockets. "I'm not trying to be difficult."

"You aren't a bad kid," Owen said. "I want this to work out for you. We just need to find something you're good at."

Gary shook his head. "I've never been good at anything."

Owen frowned. "You will be. Maybe I need to figure out a different way of teaching you."

By the look on Owen's face, Gary knew he'd won. Somehow, he was just going to have to show Owen that he could manage this job. He didn't want to end up with someone else telling him what to do. At least this way, Owen was interested in Susanna, and that gave Gary a tiny bit of leverage. After all, Owen wouldn't want to ruin his chances with Susanna by causing trouble for her brother.

"Come on." Owen motioned to Gary. "We need to punch out the rivets on the boiler that came in this morning. I'll show you what we need to do."

"You won't be sorry, Owen. I'll do well. You'll see."

"You gonna join us at the pool hall?" Empty asked Gary after the whistle blew at the end of the workday.

"I might, but I'd rather play poker. I made a nice sum the other day," Gary replied. "Say, you guys ought to come over to the hotel first. I bet we can get my sister to serve up something to eat. She's been cooking for me at the hotel, and she's pretty good. I happen to know she has an applesauce cake just waiting for my attention."

"Applesauce cake sounds mighty good, but I'd rather have a steak," Bill Foxtail declared.

Gary shrugged. "We'd probably have to bring her the steaks, but that's simple enough. We'll swing by the butcher's and get some steaks. It'll be harder for her to say no that way."

He grinned. Maybe this way she'd get to know his friends a little better and stop focusing on Owen.

The men made their way to the butcher and ordered three steaks. As an afterthought, Gary ordered another smaller steak for his sister. No sense in showing up without something for her as well.

Gary's mind was still on the things he'd said to Owen earlier. He didn't know why he'd acted that way. He felt so confused lately. He hadn't known about Susanna having money, and it was starting to bother him that she'd allowed the family to end up in San Marcial when she could have kept them in Topeka. Of course, Uncle Harrison was to blame as well, but the two of them seemed unfeeling about the family's future. Especially where Gary was concerned. He was on the threshold of manhood and finding his place in society. He'd never appreciated that before now, but when he thought of how much it might have benefitted him to find a wealthy girl to marry, well . . . it made him angry to think he'd been denied that.

They reached the hotel and found Susanna just coming downstairs. Gary frowned when she smiled at him. She really did care about him. He knew that much. She had always been there for him.

"To what do I owe this visit?" she asked, looking at the three men standing behind her brother.

"Hey, Susanna." Gary forced a smile and motioned to his friends and the paper-wrapped meat. "We came to ask you a favor."

Susanna gave him a hesitant look. "What do you have in mind?"

"We were hoping you might cook for us. We bought some steak. Enough for you too. And maybe you'd let us have some applesauce cake too."

Susanna glanced at the clock. "I suppose I can cook the steaks. I don't have much else to go with them, though. If you want to run and get an onion and some potatoes, I can fix that up as well."

"I'll go get 'em," Herc said, turning for

the door. "Ain't nothin' I like more than fried onions."

Empty and Bill exchanged a look and nodded. "Sounds good," Empty said.

"I told you she's a great sister. She'll make someone a good wife too." Gary looked at Susanna, thinking of the three men he'd brought home with him. A frown crossed his face, however, rather than a smile. None of these three were good enough for her.

Gary pushed the thought aside. It wasn't like Susanna was quick to make decisions. Maybe she'd see that his friends were a lot of fun and just want to spend time with them. But that really wasn't appropriate for a young widow, was it? He bit his lip. Why was he acting like this? Susanna was her own person, and he'd never tried to interfere in her life. But before there had always been Mark. Mark had been there since Gary first had memories. Mark was a good man, and he'd always been kind to Gary.

"Well, since your friend has gone for the potatoes and onions, why don't you guys get cleaned up?" Susanna suggested.

Gary stared at her as if really seeing her for the first time. She was a good woman, and here he was trying to cause trouble for her. He should never have brought the guys to her for supper. Now if they did like her, he'd have to find a way to dissuade them from pursuing her.

"Come on, guys, let's go get cleaned up." He looked at Susanna. "We won't get things dirty here. We'll go down to the river."

"I would appreciate that. When your friend gets back, I'll tell him where you've gone. By the time you've managed to clean up, I should have things ready." Gary nodded and motioned his friends outside just as his father came in the front door.

"Father," Gary said with a nod. Empty and Bill gave Father quick nods as well as they shuffled out the door.

"What are you doing here?" his father asked.

"The fellas and me came to ask Susanna to fix us some steaks."

"Steak? Who has money for steak?"

Gary laughed and dug into his pocket "I do. I made a nice bit playing cards last night. Here's the money I borrowed." His father looked at the wad of money in Gary's hand as he peeled off several bills and handed them over. "I'm good at cards."

"I used to be pretty good at them myself." His father looked at the money in his son's hand. "Why don't you help me out now? I need to get four hundred dollars together. There's an investment in a silver mine south of here that

I'd like to get in on. If you'd spot me the money now, I'll see to it that you get it back doubled."

Gary shoved his money back in his pocket. "No. I'll go with a sure thing."

"That's hardly fair, Gary. I've done everything for you."

Gary shook his head. "You've done nothing but ruin my life. I would be at the university instead of working as a laborer if you hadn't been so foolish. You don't even care. You've never cared about me—or Susanna, for that matter. You only care about your next scheme."

Father looked shocked, but it didn't stop Gary. He had no idea where Susanna had gone. He supposed she was setting things up to cook in their little kitchen.

"You know that isn't true, Gary. I only ever cared about making money because of my family. You know I've done all I can to keep our family living the life we were meant to live. It's your uncle's fault that we've failed and ended up here."

"No, it was your fault. I know that and so does everyone else. You're the only one who seems incapable of accepting the truth."

"How dare you talk to me that way? Everything you have is due to my generosity. You wouldn't even be here if not for my willingness to keep you living at home."

"So put me out. Uncle Harrison wants me here at the hotel to protect Susanna. Yet another thing you failed to consider." Gary wasn't sure where all of this rage was coming from. He was angry at Father for their change of fortune. He was angry that he'd been shamed along with the family name. Things should have been different—would have been different—had Father only been reasonable.

"I have the onion and potatoes," Herc said, coming through the open front door.

Gary went to his friend and took the vegetables. "I'll get Susanna fixing them. You go on with the others to the river and get cleaned up."

Herc glanced at Gary's father and then back to Gary. He seemed to understand the unspoken tension. "Sure. See you there." He turned and exited without another word while Gary headed for the private living quarters.

Susanna stood ready and waiting. She smiled at the size of the potatoes and onion. "He must be really hungry."

"We all are. I'm going to go get cleaned up with them. Father's out there," Gary said, nodding toward the hotel lobby.

"He'll be heading home for his own dinner soon. I'll let him know not to expect us," Susanna said, smiling at Gary.

Gary nodded. He thought about saying something more to his sister about his friends. He didn't know if they would act out of line with her or not. He hoped they'd be polite. Now that everything was set in motion, he couldn't for the life of him understand why he'd thought putting his sister in this position was a good idea. He supposed he wanted to keep her from getting too close to Owen, but the boomers were no better. In fact, they were a whole lot worse. Owen had told him how boomers moved from job to job. They were more interested in seeing the country than working a job. Gary had even thought such a life might appeal to him, but the more he thought about the life he could have had, the less interested he was in the life that his friends could offer. And he certainly didn't want that life for Susanna.

But what now? The family money was gone, and he'd tried to throw himself headlong into working, even though he wasn't any good at it. Susanna had money—Uncle Harrison had said as much. Maybe Gary should talk to her about sending him to college. Maybe he could still have the life he'd intended.

But then what? For all his intentions to go to college, it had never been about learning or bettering his mind. It was something rich sons did, whether they had a propensity toward learning or not.

Gary made his way toward the front door and found his father still standing there as if ready to pounce on him.

"Look, Gary, I know you've been angry at me. I know you blame me for this," Father said, waving his arm. "But I can fix everything if I can lay my hands on some money. You can help me. You get paid every week. You said you were good at cards. It shouldn't be that hard to turn your pay into the money I need. This silver mine is a sure thing."

Gary shook his head. "Then play cards for yourself, or use the hotel money."

"But you have the money now and could help me." His father looked at him expectantly. "Just imagine if we were able to get this investment. It might mean heading back to Topeka in a matter of weeks. Isn't that what you want? Surely you don't want to keep having to work in that horrible shop. You were raised to be a gentleman, Gary."

"Yes, I was, but you ruined that. You ruin everything, and now you want to try to fix it by making more bad investments. I won't be the one to help you. I'm going to help myself. Maybe Susanna will spend more of her husband's money to help you, but I won't give you a dime."

Herbert bristled at his son's attitude but then shrugged it off. As soon as Harrison tired of this game, Herbert knew all would be well. In the meantime, he was quite capable of playing cards and making a little money. He remembered blackjack being rather amusing in his younger days. Poker required more focus, but surely it couldn't be that difficult.

The problem would be getting the startup money—the ante for the games. He studied the check-in desk, and his gaze drifted toward the door to the living quarters. Gary's words about his sister echoed in his ears.

Where there was a need, there was always a way.

Susanna was busy peeling potatoes when her father came into the back room. She could tell there was something on his mind.

"What's happened now? I thought I heard you and Gary arguing." She diced the potato and reached for another. The lard was just starting to pop in the cast-iron skillet.

"How much money do you have?"

She looked at her father, then back down at the food. She wasn't sure what he meant by the question. "I have a few dollars in my purse."

"No, I mean how much money do you have in the bank? In investments?"

She refused to look up from the potato. She had dreaded this moment, knowing it would come but hoping it might go on being overlooked. After all, it had been a year since Mark died, and Father had never once asked her how his death left her situated.

"Are you well off?" her father asked. "I mean, you had no trouble buying the house here. I thought at first it was simply a rental, but then I overheard someone say you had bought it. I never really gave it thought, however, even then."

"You like the house, don't you?" she asked, hoping to change the subject. "I told Uncle Harrison he needed to consider building future hotels out of adobe. I'm amazed at how much cooler they are."

"How rich are you?"

Susanna put the last of the potatoes in the skillet and then began to cut up the onion. "I don't feel I need to answer that question, Father. My husband arranged for me, and that's all I will say."

She heard her father take a seat at the table. She glanced up to see him shaking his head. Whatever was on his mind, she didn't think the matter was going to go away. Even so, she said nothing. She diced the onion, added it to the potatoes, and focused on frying them together. She found herself whispering a prayer, hoping God would make her father forget about everything and refocus on something else. Perhaps a group of guests would show up? Maybe Gary and his friends would return quickly.

"I never thought you would betray me," he said.

She held her tongue. She wasn't sure what had brought this conversation about, but she was going to do her best to avoid it.

"You should probably go on home for supper, Father. Mother will wonder where everyone is. You can let her know that Gary wanted me to cook for him and his friends. It's just a one-time thing, however. I'm sure we'll be there for supper tomorrow." She barely drew a breath. "I wonder what Lia has made for dinner."

"I'm sure it won't be steak. We cannot afford steak."

"Lia makes amazing meals for you. You've never lacked. Honestly, I think her cooking is some of the best I've ever had. I've been having her teach me to cook in the Mexican style."

"We eat chicken and pork—poor man's

food," her father said accusingly. "How much money do you have?"

She turned and faced him. This wasn't going to go away. "I have enough. That's all I will say on the matter. I am no longer your worry. I am a widow with funds of my own. My husband saw to my needs, and that is all anyone needs to know."

"You must have a considerable sum, or you wouldn't be so unwilling to discuss it."

"I don't want to discuss it, Father, because it is not necessary to discuss."

"You probably have enough that you could have kept us from losing the house . . . and everything else." He looked at her with a betrayed expression. "How could you?"

"Father, you are making assumptions you have no right to make. I only came to San Marcial because Uncle Harrison begged me to do so to help you and Mother get established. He didn't bid me to come here to pay your way. The help I've offered has been purely from selfish motives, I'm sorry to say."

"You can deliver us from this hell." Her father gazed at her as if she were the answer to all of his questions. "You owe this to us."

"I owe this to you? And how do you figure that?" She turned back to the food just in time to keep it from burning. She worked quickly, pulling the potatoes and onions from the skillet and replacing them with one of the steaks.

"You're our daughter. We provided for you for all those years, and now you can provide for us. I demand that you give me charge over your bank account and investments."

Susanna turned to see that he was serious. She'd never seen him quite so firm in his demands. "No. My money is not yours, nor will it be."

"I won't tolerate this. I need that money. I need it now."

His tone was unlike anything Susanna had ever heard. "Father, I don't wish for this to come between us, but I will leave San Marcial for good rather than be harassed by you."

"You know nothing about how to invest."

"And neither do you." She hadn't meant to say it out loud, but the words spilled out before she could stop them.

"We're back!" Gary called from the lobby.

Susanna gave her father a pointed look. "I'm willing to forget this ever happened. We needn't argue in front of Gary and his friends."

"I won't forget this. I won't forget your betrayal. We will talk more about this after supper."

Susanna shook her head and refocused on the food. Now what was she going to do? Her father was usually a kind, soft-spoken man, but the craving for money and his desire to invest in one thing after another had turned him into someone she didn't know. How had he figured out that she had money? Uncle Harrison certainly wouldn't have told him. Maybe he'd just added up the fact that she'd purchased the house and hired Lia without seeking reimbursement. She supposed she should have been more careful.

She put one of the steaks on a plate and then popped another into the skillet. This wasn't going to be resolved easily. Once Father told Mother that she had money, there would be no end to the nagging and whining.

A train whistle sounded. That would be the evening train preparing to leave. Susanna fought the urgency to make a run for it. She wasn't going to be able to stay once her mother learned the truth. There wouldn't be any peace of mind. She sighed and began to pray in earnest.

Dear God, help me, please.

10

Susanna knew that sooner or later she would have to deal with her mother. She had just hoped it would be some time in the future rather than ten minutes after her father left.

"Susanna Ragsdale!" her mother bellowed from the lobby of the hotel just as Susanna sat down to eat with her brother and his friends.

"I guess I won't be joining you," she said, smiling as she got to her feet. "Gary, please clean up after yourself and your friends. I have a feeling I'm going to be busy for a while."

She made her way to the front desk, where her mother was anxiously pacing back and forth. With one look, Susanna knew her father had told his wife everything and then some. Susanna reached for the sign that would explain to their one and only guest for the evening that she was on supper break. The sign declared she would return at six-thirty. A glance at the clock showed that gave her a half hour to calm her mother.

"Why don't I walk you back to the house, Mother?" Susanna headed for the front door of the hotel.

"We can talk right here. Right now."

Susanna stood at the open hotel door. "Not unless you wish everyone to know your business, including Gary's friends, who are eating with him in the back room."

Mother glanced toward the open door behind the hotel's front desk. "Very well." She gave a huff and exited the hotel, glancing over her shoulder to make certain Susanna followed. "I can hardly believe what your father has told me. I'm so ashamed and hurt by you that if this is true, I can scarcely think of how we can go on."

Susanna easily caught up with her mother's strides. "I'm sure you'd rather wait to address this until we are back in the privacy of the house."

"The house you bought because you're rich," her mother declared.

"The house I bought because you made such a scene about living at the hotel," Susanna countered. "The hotel Uncle Harrison generously provided for you and father and Gary. I shouldn't even have to be here. I am a widow, and my in-laws are in To- peka, where I was happily living and may yet return."

That shut her mother up for a moment. Susanna picked up her pace in order to reach the house before her mother unleashed yet another tirade of words. Once they were in- side, however, Susanna braced herself for the assault.

"Your father tells me that you're rich. That you have more than enough money to have kept us from losing our home and prop- erties. That you could have delivered us from the hands of the bank, and instead chose not to lift a finger to help."

Susanna said nothing. Instead, she walked to the table, which Lia had set with salad, dinner rolls, and some sort of meatloaf. Su- sanna picked up a plate and helped herself. If she couldn't eat her steak with the boys, she would at least eat here.

While Susanna filled her plate, Mother raged about Susanna's selfish nature and how impossible she'd always been as a child. She started in on how Mark had changed her, made her less congenial, more self-absorbed and selfish.

"I've never been more humiliated and embarrassed. More hurt. You have betrayed me and your father, and I demand you make this wrong . . . right."

Susanna had the fork halfway to her mouth. "And what would make it right, Mother?"

"Now you're being reasonable." Mother took the seat opposite Susanna at the table. "You must turn your money over to your father for management."

"So that he can lose it as he has his own?"

Mother's face turned red. "How dare you be so cruel? He did not lose his money. A ruthless conman stole it. He robbed your father. It is hardly the fault of the victim."

"A victim who was warned by no fewer than a dozen people to avoid the man and his schemes." Susanna popped a piece of meatloaf in her mouth and smiled. Lia had such a way with seasonings and spices. Susanna would have to learn what Lia had done to this meat.

"Your father has a right to make his own choices."

"And he did," Susanna said, reaching for the pitcher of iced tea. "Now he must live with the consequences. I'm sorry for you both, but that is hardly my fault."

"No, but it is within your power to fix. You could have given us the money to save our place in society." Mother wagged her finger as she often did when making her point. "I will not tolerate any more of this godforsaken place. You will make all the arrangements, Susanna. You will give your father the money he needs to reinvest in our future. You will help us get to California, for surely Topeka is lost to us now."

Susanna took a long sample of the iced tea. She placed the glass on the table and met her mother's gaze. "No. I will not."

Her mother began to huff and puff as if she were about to hyperventilate. She took up her fan and waved it wildly. "You will not defy me in this. I deserve better."

"Mother, I am sorry for your circumstances. I am sorry that Father was taken in by that deplorable man. I'm even sorrier that he wouldn't listen to his brother and others he supposedly respected, because had he listened, none of this would have happened." Susanna took another long sip from the iced tea, hoping—praying, really—that her mother would calm down and see the truth of the situation. "I cannot and will not give you money left to me by my husband for my future. It is invested, and I cannot take it out, even if I wanted to. My father-in-law is handling it for me."

"Your father could manage it better. He should be the one managing your affairs."

Susanna shook her head. "Mother, you

and Father have got to see the truth. I love you both very much, but this is not going to be easily resolved. Father has to see that he is not good with investments. He doesn't have the same skills as Uncle Harrison. He needs to understand that truth. You do too. You are not a grand society dame, and even those who tolerated you because of your association to the Ragsdale fortune have never treated you with respect. You are better off without them."

"This is deplorable. Your uncle has convinced you of something that simply isn't true. You must help us now. You are our daughter, and you owe it to us."

Susanna looked at her mother's hopeful expression and shook her head. It was all just too sad. Her parents could not bring themselves to see the truth. What if they were never able to see it? What would happen to them?

Her appetite was gone, and Susanna got to her feet. "I am not giving you and father any more money. I've paid for this house and for Lia's salary. That's all. Father earns a salary for his work with the hotel, and you two must make your life on that salary. I'm sorry."

She headed for the door, but her mother was there before her. Never had Susanna seen her move so quickly.

"You have to help us. You *have* to. You will be no daughter to me at all unless you make this right. I have been shamed and humiliated and will be mortified should anyone else learn of my condition. I demand it of you. If you love me even a little, you will help us. If you are unwilling to help . . . I will never speak to you again. You will be dead to me."

Susanna felt tears come to her eyes. She had never expected this from her mother. In all her years of melodramatics, Mother had never issued such a threat.

"Then I am dead," she whispered and walked out the door.

Owen arrived at the hotel anxious to see Susanna and invite her to another picnic on Sunday. He'd been thinking of it all day and figured he might as well go ahead and ask her. When he came into the lobby, however, there was a man standing by the desk and no sign of anyone else.

"They aren't here. The sign says they'll return at six-thirty. This is an appalling business practice. I can scarcely believe they manage a hotel this way," the stranger said.

Owen shrugged. "There must have been some sort of problem that took them from the hotel. Usually they have a young man stand in for them during the supper hour."

"It's completely unacceptable," the man countered. "I paid good money for my room, and I demand proper attention."

Just then Susanna came through the front door. Owen couldn't be certain, but it looked as though she'd been crying. She came to the front desk and moved aside the sign that said she'd return at six-thirty.

"May I help you?" she asked.

"I should hope so. Where have you been? I've had need, and you've been elsewhere."

She pointed to the sign. "It says I'll return at half-past six, and here it is only a quarter after. I'm early." She smiled at him. "So how may I help you?"

"You can start by discounting my room for your lack of attention to the needs of your guests."

"I'm sorry. I'm unable to refund or discount the rooms. What other thing might I help you with?"

"Nothing. Nothing at all. I'll take my things and go. I will, however, be reporting this to each and every person I can. I will tell them the Grand Hotel is not worth their time or effort. Unless, of course, you want to reconsider and discount my room."

Susanna shook her head. "I'm sorry. I am unable to do that."

The man stormed off, muttering to himself all the way up the stairs.

Susanna watched him go, then turned to Owen. "Well, this day just gets better and better."

"Are you all right?"

"I've had an argument with my parents." She looked down at the hotel registry. "And now with Mr. Corders."

"I think he's just looking for a free room. Some people are like that. They go around complaining until they get free stuff."

Susanna nodded. "I suppose so."

Mr. Corders came barreling back down the stairs, suitcase in hand. "It's most unfortunate that you care so little for your guests. The hotel will be an abominable failure at this rate."

He left without bothering to stop at the desk, and Owen watched as Susanna stared after him. She looked as if she might burst into tears at any moment. He couldn't help but wonder what she'd argued about with her family.

"What can I do for you, Owen?" she asked.

"Maybe it's what I can do for you. Why

don't you put the sign back up and come walk with me? You look really upset."

"I am." She shook her head and reached for the sign. "But it says I'll return at six-thirty, and I'm not sure once I leave that I'll come back."

Owen smiled. "I'll see to it that you do . . . eventually."

Susanna put the sign on the desk and came around to join Owen. "All right, Mr. Turner. Take me for a walk."

Owen laughed and took her arm. He escorted her onto the street and looked down the dirt road first one way and then the other. "I have an idea. Have you been to La Plaza Vieja—Old Town?"

She shook her head. "That area farther up the hill? I've heard of it but not been there."

"Good. We'll take a walk there. It's up away from the river on the rise. It's where many of the Mexicans settled. They knew about the river's tendency to flood."

"And the railroad company did not?"

"The railroad needed to be near the water. The railroad company's counting on the embankment they've put in to keep them safe. The land has seen a flood or two, but so far it hasn't been all that bad, and they're hoping to keep it that way."

They walked past the post office and then

the school. Owen pointed out the new swings. "The children have already been trying those out. Some of the railroad workers put them in. There's going to be a couple of teeter-totters too."

"I'm sure they'll enjoy them."

"The men?" He chuckled. "I'm betting they'll try them out before turning them over to the kids."

She smiled at this as they continued past the Methodist church.

Owen let go of her arm. "So what has you so upset?"

"My father and mother found out that I have money."

"Money?" He shook his head. "Their money?"

"No. My own." She met his gaze and shrugged. "My husband left it to me. Life insurance money and money from the sale of his stores."

"Oh, I understand." He hadn't thought of her as a rich woman, but it was starting to sound like perhaps that was the problem. If such a thing could be deemed a problem.

"Somehow they learned about it, and now they expect me to turn it over to them. My father has some investment he wishes to make, certain that it will make him rich very quickly, and my mother expects me to immediately arrange for us to move to California, where a much better lifestyle awaits her."

"California? Why California? I would think she'd want to return to her home."

"No, she was shamed there and has no desire to have to explain or reveal the truth. California has become the focus of their interest."

"What will you do?"

"Nothing."

They had reached the top of the rise where the old Protestant church stood. Just beyond was the adobe Catholic church with its bell tower. To the right of the church was a grocery store. Several old women stood outside with their baskets, talking in Spanish.

"I wish I could speak Spanish. It sounds like such a beautiful language," Susanna said, watching the women.

"I speak enough to get me into trouble, but I'm learning more. Lia and LeRoy speak it, and I've learned by practicing with them and their boys. I'm sure Lia would teach you too." Owen pointed to the small grocery store. "They bring in a lot of supplies from Mexico. Some of the ingredients the old folks love and can't get in American stores."

They continued walking, with Owen sharing bits and pieces of information he could remember. "The old women here do what they can to make the area beautiful. They plant gardens, and though there's plenty of tamarisk, they work to cut it out."

"Why? It seems like anything green around here would be good."

"There's a high salt content in the leaves, and it causes the soil to be unfriendly for other plants." He led her toward an old schoolhouse and then around the bend in the road to where the black iron gates of the cemetery stood open. "Of course, no community would be complete without a place to bury the dead."

They walked past the gates, and some of the first graves came into view.

"These are dated during the Civil War," Susanna declared.

"Yes. The Battle of Valverde in February of 1862." Owen touched the top of a cross-shaped marker. "It was a big battle, with over twelve hundred casualties. Most of the fighting took place north of Black Mesa and east of the river, and some of the soldiers were buried in mass graves by the river."

"Who won?"

"I think the Confederates did. I don't know much about the actual fight. It seems like a long time ago, doesn't it?"

She nodded. "It does—a lifetime and more." She gazed at the peaceful resting places of the cemetery. "Thank you for bringing me here. My spirit is already calmer, and that was something I didn't think possible."

They started walking again, making a wide circle back toward New Town, and Susanna continued to speak.

"I'm sorry I'm poor company. I just don't know what to do about my family. Even Gary was in a mood."

"That's probably my fault. I talked to him about trying a different job. He's just not able to understand what I need from him, and he's making a mess of things and always expecting me to cover for him . . . something I vowed I'd never do again."

"Again? You sound like there's a story behind that."

He nodded. "There is. Maybe for another time. Right now, I want to help you with your problems."

She smiled. "There's nothing to be done. My mother informed me I'm dead to her if I don't help them. My father wants to invest and needs my money to do so. I promised my uncle I wouldn't interfere anymore in his plan for them to bear their own consequences. So maybe my only choice is to go. Leave San Marcial."

"No!" Owen hadn't mean to react so quickly, but he whirled her toward him and held fast to her arms. "Please don't."

Her eyes widened. "Don't?"

"Don't go. I don't want you to go."

Susanna shook her head. "I don't want to go, but I might have to in order for them to learn their lesson. I'm not good at being nagged or whined at."

"I understand that, but I . . . well, I'd hate for you to leave. We've just started to get to know one another." Owen realized how tight his grip on her arms was and let go. "I'm sorry. I just want to say that . . . I've come to care for you. I want us to be friends. Good friends." He couldn't bring himself to offer her more.

She studied him for a moment, seeming to understand. "I want that too. I've come to enjoy our talks."

He nodded and started walking again. "I'm sure we can figure this out, Susanna. We just need to give it some thought."

11

Gary brought his friends to the hotel again nearly a week later. Susanna was glad he hadn't asked her to cook for them but was less than pleased to have the men just hanging around, keeping her from being able to work on her quilt squares, since they had taken up the table with their card game. Empty was teaching Gary some new game that was sure to net him a hefty profit.

"I think you should head home, Gary," Susanna said. "It's nearly suppertime, and Mother and Father will be expecting you."

"Aren't you coming too?" her brother asked.

"You know the situation."

"We can always get something to eat at the cantina. Charlie has the best Mexican food," Empty said. "Why don't we all head over there? The games will start after nine." He gathered up the cards and stuffed them in his pocket as if it were already decided.

"I guess I'd prefer that to listening to my parents tell me how bad things are," Gary admitted.

Bill whispered something to Herc, but Susanna focused on her brother. "I'm sure they'd like to at least see you, Gary. They must miss you."

"They probably miss you too," her brother replied. "But I don't see you rushing over to comfort them."

She smarted at his comment but tried to show little reaction. Instead, she picked up a cleaning rag and began to wipe down things in the kitchen. "All I know is that you are still on their good side, and we should try to keep some sort of communication open between us." She looked at the others. They already knew the worst of it. Gary wasn't silent on the matter at all.

"I don't think it matters unless we're willing to give them money, and then they're more than happy to talk to us."

"I still think you should make an appearance at supper. They'll want to know how you're doing at your job."

"No, they won't. They're ashamed of me working a job."

Susanna glanced at his friends, who were now examining Herc's new knife and trying to ignore her conversation with Gary. For a moment she wondered if any of them had family. Maybe they could relate to what Gary was going through.

"I haven't talked to either Mother or Father about my job," Gary said, shaking his head. "And I don't want to either. They'll just ask for money." He got to his feet. "I don't blame you for telling Father no. I told him the same. I've been making a nice pot of money saving my wages and playing cards on the weekend."

"That's hardly a better way to invest than what our father has chosen. You know there are men who will take advantage of you." It was her concern about this that truly pushed her to separate him from the boomers. If Gary went home for supper, maybe he would forget about gaming.

"Gary's good with cards," Empty chimed in. "I've never seen anyone quite so natural at it. He's even better at blackjack than poker." The boomer gave her a smile, as if that might make everything all right.

Susanna sighed and put her cleaning rag aside. "It's still gambling and involves great risk. You don't want to spend an entire week working hard for the Santa Fe only to have someone steal it away from you in a card game."

"But that's just it, Mrs. Jenkins. No one can steal it away from your brother because he's too good. You should see him. It's like he knows exactly what everyone's holding. I swear he can see the next card in his mind before it's even dealt."

Gary laughed. "It is kind of like that. I can just remember what cards have been played." He shrugged. "I think it's a gift from God."

"The Bible says nothing about God giving folks the gift of card playing," Susanna countered.

"Well, maybe it should." Gary laughed again. "I think you worry too much about what the Bible has to say, anyway. It's full of rules for everyone to follow. Too many rules, if you ask me."

"It's not just a book of rules, but the rules are important in order to keep us from making really bad mistakes. Look at how it might have helped our parents if Father had considered not associating and tying himself to someone who wasn't also a believer."

"You can hardly go around asking every businessman if he is a Christian."

"And why not? If you're going to have a business arrangement with them, shouldn't

you know their values and standards?" Susanna asked.

The four men exchanged a look, and each
one gave a shrug.

Herc got to his feet and put his knife away.
"I think we ought to go." Bill pushed away
from the table with a nod.

"Women tend to make things a lot more
complicated," Gary said. "As for the players,
I don't want to know their life story, I just
want to win their money." He laughed, and
the others joined in.

Just then there was a knock on the door.
The passageway was open, and Susanna could
see their mother standing there, dressed to
go out.

The men all came to attention as Gary
stepped forward. "Mother, these are some of
the men I work with." He presented each of
them, and Susanna watched as her mother
show little or no interest.

"I need to speak with Susanna. We had
an early supper, but there's still food left over
if you're hungry, Gary. Susanna, I thought
you might join me for some dessert at the
Harvey House. I need to speak to you on a
most important matter." Her expression was
unreadable.

"I suppose I could if Father is here to
watch over the hotel. Nearly every room has

a guest, so someone needs to be here to see to their needs."

"He's planning to be here shortly. He wanted to make a quick stop at the mercantile to pick up some foot powder. His feet have been hurting from standing on them so long."

Susanna nodded. "That sounds wise. Once he's here, I can join you."

"Can't Gary watch over things until he comes?" Mother asked, looking to her son. "You can keep the front desk until your father arrives, can't you?"

Gary looked at his friends and then back to Susanna. "I'll stay if you want to go ahead with Mother."

The situation made Susanna uncomfortable, but she nodded. Even though she was supposedly dead to her mother, Susanna felt she must try to bridge the chasm that lay between them. "Very well. Let me get my hat and gloves."

Susanna went to her little bedroom and wondered what her mother wanted. The fact that they were headed to the Harvey House at least suggested there wouldn't be any major scenes. Her mother had been careful not to make public displays of her emotions while still managing to garner as much positive attention as possible. Still, there was no telling what she would do.

After smoothing her hair, Susanna pinned her hat in place. The wide-brimmed straw hat had proven to be very useful in the hot New Mexico sunshine, and even though it was starting to cool off and the sun was close to setting, Susanna figured it was still her best bet. She toyed with the idea of leaving her gloves behind. Mother, however, was wearing hers, and Susanna didn't want to start off by insulting her. Gloves were still expected, even in San Marcial, New Mexico Territory.

Susanna finished pulling on her gloves, then picked up a small purse. She checked to make sure she had enough money. No doubt she would be expected to pay for dessert.

She emerged to find her mother was nowhere to be found. Gary stood by the door, and his friends were gone with exception of Herc.

"Father's arrived," Gary said, motioning toward the door. "Mother went to speak to him."

"I can well imagine." Susanna sighed heavily. "Thanks for being willing to wait. I have no idea what Mother wants, but I'm sure it won't be pleasant."

"You look mighty pretty, Mrs. Jenkins," Herc declared. "I don't suppose you'd like to accompany me to the dance hall on Saturday night?"

Susanna shook her head. "No. I'm not much into dancing, but thank you for the invitation." She gave him no time to respond and made a quick exit into the lobby.

Her parents stood whispering at the check-in desk. Susanna decided to say nothing and stood in silence until her mother concluded and patted Father's arm. No doubt she was reassuring him that she would get Susanna to cooperate with them one way or another. It was hard to imagine that they were unable to comprehend their responsibility in all that had happened, but Susanna believed they honestly thought themselves completely innocent of blame.

"Let's go," Mother said, coming to her side. "I heard there is some of the very best black forest cake ever made. A special recipe the new German cook is presenting."

Susanna forced a smile. "Sounds delicious."

They arrived at the Harvey House just moments later and were immediately seated and waited upon. Susanna loved the order and civility of the place. It was such a perfect eating establishment, and she'd heard that the hotel rooms were equally well-ordered. In her own life of chaos, Susanna found a deep appreciation for such harmony.

"Hello, ladies," the Harvey Girl greeted.

She handed them menus and then asked for their drink order. To Susanna's surprise, her mother ordered coffee. Susanna did likewise, then looked for something substantial to eat before indulging in the cake her mother was so eager to try. She settled on some chicken noodle soup and focused on her coffee as she waited for the food.

Mother was strangely silent even when Susanna prompted conversation. Thankfully the soup arrived quickly, and Susanna offered grace.

She removed her gloves, eyeing her mother the entire time. "I haven't yet had supper. I hope you don't mind."

"Of course not." Her mother's tone was curt but not overly annoyed.

Susanna decided to ignore it and began to eat the soup.

It wasn't long before the Harvey Girl brought the cake and a bowl of freshly whipped cream. She smiled at the two women. "The whipping cream really enhances the flavor of the cherries and chocolate. Chef recommends having a little with each bite of cake. I'm confident that you'll find this dessert quite enjoyable."

With that, she left them to their strange feast. Susanna ate her soup in silence while her mother spooned a dollop of the whipped cream onto her plate. Susanna tried to imagine what this meeting was about. Was her mother going to apologize? Or perhaps she wanted to further berate Susanna for her attitude. The latter seemed unlikely as they were in a public setting. Her mother would surely have saved such a thing for private. Whatever had motivated this meeting, Susanna couldn't quite shake a sense of trepidation. How she wished Owen might show up so she could invite him to join them.

Susanna finally sampled the cake and cream and agreed it was probably the best black forest dessert she'd ever eaten. "The cake is so moist, and the cherries are just the perfect combination of sweet and tart, don't you agree?"

Mother looked at her for a moment, then nodded. "I do. It is everything I hoped for."

After this exchange, they continued to eat in silence, which surprised Susanna. After all, her mother was the one to call for this meeting. She no doubt had something on her mind.

Lord, I don't know what she has planned, but I'm asking You to give me wisdom and clarity of mind. I don't want to react in a manner that will cause us both embarrassment.

The silent prayer helped calm Susanna as she waited to see what her mother would do or say. Finally, the waiting was over.

Pushing back her empty plate, Mother pulled her cup and saucer closer. "That was superb. I've never had better."

"It is quite delicious."

Mother put the cup to her lips and seemed to take a long sample of the coffee. Susanna couldn't help wondering if it was simply for effect, however. She'd never seen her mother drink much coffee, and now she nursed the cup as if it were a cure to save her life.

"I know you must wonder why I've invited you here tonight," her mother said, not even bothering to put the cup down.

"You did say that I was dead to you."

Her mother wasn't the least bit embarrassed. She simply nodded. "I want to apologize for that. Father said I let my nerves get the best of me, and I suppose he was right. I was just overwhelmed by the situation."

"Apology accepted." Susanna refocused on her cake. She didn't want to belabor the matter. There was more to this than her mother feeling the need for absolution, and the sooner this part could be done with, the sooner Susanna would learn what this was all about.

"In my condition, there is never any certainty of being able to apologize at a later date," Mother began again. "The Bible says that where it is up to us, we should live peaceably with all men. I'm sure that must be true for women as well. Especially mothers and daughters."

Susanna knew her mother expected her to ask about the implied condition, but she refused. If there were truly something wrong, Mother wouldn't hesitate to explain it in vivid detail. So rather than speak, Susanna added sugar to her coffee and sampled it. It was now too sweet, but she wasn't going to waste it. She took another sip, then put the cup back on the saucer.

"Susanna, you need to know that often-times things of a more serious nature interfere with my ability to show patience and even kindness. I'm afraid you caught me at a bad time the other evening. I had just learned some particularly worrisome news."

"I'm sorry that you were upset." Susanna picked up her fork and began to eat more of her dessert. She knew her mother's game. She would dole out little bits of information in order to coax Susanna into prying for answers. Usually Susanna cooperated so as to get the game over with as soon as possible. This time she simply wasn't in the mood. "For pity's sake, Mother, just say what you've come to say."

Her mother put her hand to her chest. "The doctor says I must have immediate tests and expensive medicines if I am to live."

Susanna stared at her mother, who continued rambling without pause.

"Of course, I'll need to go to a better doctor. Probably one in Albuquerque to begin with, but most likely a specialist in California. Your father is quite worried, and he won't hear of me doing anything in the way of work. We will probably need to hire Lia for longer hours, as I'm sure to need someone to help me."

"But I thought you were going to California," Susanna replied in a matter-of-fact manner.

Her mother nodded. "You're absolutely right. I will probably be in some hospital or convalescent facility. It is a grave worry, for I'm certain the cost will be exorbitant."

Susanna wasn't sure what to say or do. She felt confident her mother was making this up. It was probably the best idea she and Father had for getting Susanna to part with her money.

Susanna toyed with her remaining cake and then put aside her fork. "Well, there's only one thing to be done. You and I will go see the doctor who has diagnosed you thus far. We will talk to him about the best course of action—the best facilities to handle whatever it is that is wrong—and we will go there together. You can hardly be expected to travel alone, and Father must stay and run the hotel."

"No. You don't need to worry about that. Your father is certain Harrison would wish for him to accompany me. He felt that you could run the hotel in our absence."

Susanna shook her head. "I don't think I could rest easy without being at your side."

Her mother paled a bit and shook her head. "We can figure that out later, but there is the matter of the expenses for travel and for the doctors and medicine. We will be quite unable to pay for such things without your help."

"Well, I wouldn't feel comfortable without being there to speak to the doctors and hospital personnel myself." Susanna dabbed her mouth with her napkin. "It's such a worry to imagine that you might die without the proper help. I want to know that the doctors are doing everything possible. You know there are many great hospitals, and we must wisely consider which would be best. Now, what exactly is wrong?"

"Susanna, your father and I can manage this ourselves," Mother said firmly. "We just need to know that you can manage the hotel."

"Oh, I see. I thought you needed me to pay for it."

"We will," Mother replied in such a hasty

manner that even she was concerned at the urgency. "I mean . . . well, again, my nerves are completely exhausted by all that's going on."

"Mother, I don't want you to worry about a thing." Susanna reached out to pat her mother's hand. "That's why I intend to speak with your doctor in the morning. We'll figure out what he believes will be the best place for you to go for further diagnoses."

"No, that isn't necessary. I don't need you to take over the situation. Your father and I can manage those details."

"Yes, but as you've already said, your nerves are exhausted, and Father will be no better, knowing that his dear wife is ill to the point of possible death." Susanna shook her head. "I remember how hard it was when Mark was sick. You will thank me later for being there to manage the financial demands and stand as support. We will speak to the doctor tomorrow. I'll come and get you first thing in the morning." Susanna paused and looked at her mother. "By the way, who is your doctor? I've not had time to meet any of the medical folks in this area. I know there are doctors for the Santa Fe and that the railroad has its own little hospital, but I have no idea what is available to those not associated with the railroad."

"I have managed for myself, Susanna. I

don't need you to speak to my doctor." Mother's agitation was growing, and Susanna had taken all of the lies she was going to stand for.

"There is no doctor, is there, Mother?" Susanna signaled the Harvey Girl. "I'd like to pay the check." She handed the girl some money. "Will this cover it?"

"More than."

"Good. You keep the rest as your tip."

Susanna got to her feet while her mother watched with her mouth clenched tight and her eyes wide in fear. When Susanna headed for the door, she heard her mother's chair scaping across the floor as she hurried to follow.

They were outside before Mother called to her. "Susanna, wait!"

Susanna turned and shook her head. "How could you lie about something so important as being sick enough to die? Did you honestly expect that I would just hand over my money without checking into what was going on?"

"You don't understand. I simply don't want you in the middle of it. I have my pride, you know. My health is my business."

"Mother, you have always made your health issues the business of anyone and everyone who was close enough to hear your complaints."

Her mother gasped and put a gloved hand to her mouth. "That isn't true. Oh, you are a heartless child. It is hardly my fault that I am so weak and frail."

Susanna laughed out loud. "I know of no one stronger or healthier than you, Mother." She fixed her mother with a look and shook her head as she sobered. "And for that I am glad. I only wish you were."

Susanna looked around her rooms in disbelief. Everything was a mess. Drawers had been pulled out in the kitchen and at the desk. Someone had clearly gone through every corner of the living area. The bedrooms too showed signs of someone having rifled through their belongings.

Gary and his friends were nowhere to be found. Neither was Father. She had fully expected to find him at the front desk, but he wasn't there.

She drew a deep breath and wondered what she should do. It would probably be wise to get the local law officials involved.

She stepped outside the hotel and spotted a couple of boys playing kick the can. "Boys," she called, "could you come here a moment?"

They both looked fearful, as if they knew they were in trouble.

She smiled to reassure them. "I wonder if you might fetch the constable for me."

"Sure. He's just down the street."

Susanna nodded. "Thank you. Just tell him that I need to see him at the Grand Hotel."

The boys made a mad dash down the sandy dirt road, each trying to outrun the other. Susanna might have laughed had the situation not been so grave. She waited outside, glancing up and down the street, wondering where her father had gone. She had begun to pace when the boys returned with the lawman.

"Miss, these boys said you needed to see me."

"Yes, thank you, boys. Here's a nickel for each of you." Susanna smiled at the way their eyes widened. They nudged each other, then stepped aside for the constable.

"What seems to be the trouble?" he asked.

"Someone broke into our private living quarters here at the hotel. They went through everything." She led the way into the hotel.

"Is anything missing?"

"Yes. About ten dollars in coins and paper money. I kept it in my bedroom." She pointed to the open door across the room. "That one is my room. The other is my brother's. I'm not sure what he might be missing. I suppose if we can locate him, we can ask. I think he might be at my folks' house."

"The Medford place?"

"Yes."

"You think the money is the only thing missing?"

"Well, it was the only thing of any value." She looked around the room. "We haven't been here that long, and I haven't added any personal decorations. I don't have any jewelry to speak of since I've been in mourning—at least nothing that's worth money." She sat down at the table, suddenly feeling very shocked by this turn of events.

"Susanna?" a voice called from the front of the hotel. Owen looked into the room. He immediately frowned as he caught sight of the constable. "George, what's going on?"

"Owen, do you know this young woman?"

"I do. We go to church together—and we're friends." Owen came to where Susanna was sitting. "What happened?"

"Someone broke in and . . . well, you can see for yourself the mess they made."

"Where's your father?"

"I don't know." Susanna shrugged. "Mother stopped by and asked me to join her at the Harvey House for dessert. Father was here at the hotel to watch over things, and Gary and his friends were still here at the time but had plans for an evening of fun."

"Is anything missing?" Owen asked.

"We were just covering that," the constable replied before Susanna could speak. "Apparently some money but nothing else."

"Unless Gary had something of value in his room." Susanna shook her head. "Although I don't know what it would be other than money."

"There's been some other robberies of late. A few of the stores have been broken into as well. We figure it's probably the same folks responsible. It seems like they're clumsy and not all that good at this—probably kids or young men just getting started in a life of crime. Keep an eye out for anything unusual, but I don't think they'll be back. They know now that there isn't anything of value."

"But what about the hotel guests?" she asked. "I haven't checked to see if any of the rooms were broken into."

The constable nodded. "I'll swing upstairs and talk to whoever is here. I doubt the thieves would have risked it, though. They wouldn't have any way of knowing whether people were in their rooms or not, so taking that chance wouldn't have been wise."

"Thank you." Susanna forced a smile. "I appreciate that you came so quickly."

"I wish I could do more, but like I said, I think we're just dealing with kids. Whoever it was probably saw your father step out and decided to give it a go."

"We have some new boomers who started last week," Owen offered. "You could check in with them. A couple strike me as rather underhanded."

"I'll do that. I know there were some new cowboys too. Meanwhile, just keep things locked up and someone on duty. That is the best advice I can offer."

Susanna nodded. She'd thought they had someone on duty.

12

The weather turned rainy for several days, which seemed to take newcomers by surprise, but Owen knew it wasn't unusual for September. At least with the rain, the temperatures dropped. They would have a better time of it now. The fall and winter months would make for much easier work at the shops. Owen hoped it would even help Gary get a better handle on what he was doing. As it stood, the kid wasn't going to have a job much longer if he couldn't figure out what was required of him.

As Owen dressed for church, he wondered what he was going to do about Gary Ragsdale. The young man was wholly unqualified to do much of anything. His parents had spoiled and pampered him to the point of uselessness, and now he had trouble learning even basic new skills. Owen wanted to help Gary, but nothing seemed to work. Owen had even tried taking him aside after working hours to show him various things, but Gary's mind was less and less focused. Owen had tried to talk to him about it, but Gary wanted no part of such intimacy and only told Owen that he would try harder.

It was the same thing Owen's brother had pledged. Owen couldn't help but hear his brother's same childlike pleadings.

"Owen, I promise I'll do better. Just give me another chance."

"Give him another chance," their father had demanded. *"Everyone makes mistakes."*

"But most folks learn from their mistakes, and Daniel seems not to care enough to learn."

Owen remembered the conversation as if it were yesterday. Maybe because it was the last real conversation he'd had with his father and brother. He walked to church still hearing their voices.

"Just tell them it was your fault, Owen. The foreman won't fire you. You never make mistakes, and this will be no problem for you. If you tell them it was Daniel's doing, he'll lose his job."

"I'm not going to lie." Owen had looked at his father and then his brother. They honestly expected him to lie. The truth was in their expressions.

"If you don't, Daniel will lose his job."

If Owen was honest about Gary, the boy would lose his job. It wasn't an easy situation. Owen was starting to have strong feelings for Susanna, and Gary was her brother. If he fired Gary or let him be fired, would she be angry at him? Susanna didn't seem to be that kind of person, but then, Owen hadn't expected his father's reaction either.

"This is your brother, and you have to stand by him. Daniel will do better next time."

But he hadn't. In fact, the next time Daniel messed up on the job, it resulted not only his own death but also that of another man. Owen could still see the look on his father's face at their funeral. He blamed Owen. They never spoke about it, but the accusation was there in his father's eyes. Truth be told, Owen blamed himself.

That was five years ago, and the following year, his father had died when his engine derailed. When word came, Owen was almost relieved. Somehow, just knowing that his father was no longer alive to blame him for the death of his brother took a burden off Owen's shoulders.

What kind of man felt relief at the death of his father and brother? Owen had never been able to forgive himself. He had sworn he'd never again take the blame for someone else, that he'd never again let an employee pass on substandard work, yet he was in that position with Gary.

And it wasn't because of Susanna that Owen allowed it. The truth of it hit Owen hard. He was letting Gary get away with things as if it might somehow make up for his brother's death. Some part of Owen blamed himself for the horrible accident that claimed Daniel's life, and without realizing it, he was trying his best to right that wrong.

The congregation was already singing as Owen slipped into the back pew. He opened a hymnal and pretended to sing along, but the realization of what was going on troubled him in a way he couldn't understand.

Pastor Lewis took to the pulpit after two more songs and the offertory. Owen opened his Bible but found it impossible to focus. He'd been praying for answers, and all morning this was the only thing he could think about. He needed to do something about Gary, yet he found it impossible. How could he fire the young man?

"Sometimes God calls us to uncomfortable situations," Pastor Lewis began. "Sometimes we want to do the right thing, but it won't be an easy or popular thing. A lot of times, doing things God's way is an unpopular choice. The Bible is full of stories that show these kinds of situations. If you've spent any time at all in the Word of God, you know it to be true. Still, we wrestle with right and wrong as if there might be a third solution that will somehow get us out of making an uncomfortable choice." The pastor grinned. "I'm here today to tell you there isn't."

"God has always been pretty much to the point. He doesn't often veer off to the right or the left. As Mr. Bevins often says, 'There's a right way and a wrong way to do things. There's no sort-of-right or sort-of-wrong way.'"

Folks in the congregation chuckled at this, and Mr. Bevins, an older man who worked in the clerical offices of Santa Fe, nodded enthusiastically as the pastor continued.

"That could have been spoken from God Himself. In other words, God has a way, and God clearly shows us the way. For example, He doesn't make a mystery of how to be saved from our sins. He offers us salvation through His Son, Jesus. There isn't another way, and I feel compelled to talk about that today.

"See, in the old days, folks had to make a lot of animal sacrifices to make themselves right with God. They had to bring in all sorts of offerings to the priests. There were ceremonies and animal sacrifices, and stayin' on God's good side was hard. There were laws—

hundreds and hundreds of 'em that folks had to follow—and if you have ever stopped to read through Leviticus, you might be surprised to find that we break a lot of those laws every day. It was and still is impossible for us to be saved on our own behavior."

He smiled down on the congregation. "Thank God, He has a better plan. It's just one plan. One way. But it'll save us from eternal damnation and hell's fire.

"Now, I know some of you don't think that's fair. There ought to be options, some folks say. It ought to be that a fella could have a choice. Well, the fact is, you do have a choice. You have a choice to be saved or be condemned. It's pretty simple." He shrugged. "We try to make it hard, but the truth is the truth and never changes. We try to alter things so that we can get our own way. We try to maneuver around the rules and make exceptions for special situations. But there are no exceptions and no special situations. Even the thief on the cross beside Jesus knew that. He knew his time was short. He saw there were only two choices, and he wanted the one that would save him.

"Do you want that? 'Cause there is only one way. Turn to John fourteen." He waited a moment for people to reach that place in their Bible.

Owen knew the pastor was speaking of salvation, but he couldn't help thinking about his situation with Gary. There really weren't a lot of options. He could either keep Gary as he was and deal with the problems that created, or he could move him to another job. It was up to Owen to make a decision, and the longer he put it off, the harder that decision would be.

Pastor Lewis started up again. "Jesus has just told his disciples that he's gonna go away. He further tells them they know the way to where he's goin'. Thomas—the one who later doubts Jesus—tells him they don't know the way, and this is what Jesus says to him: 'I am the way, the truth, and the life: no man cometh unto the Father, but by me.'"

He stepped away from the pulpit. "Pretty plain and simple, and yet we constantly try to complicate it. Just like we do with most of the issues in our life. There's almost always a simple answer, but we don't want to take it.

"Jesus made a way for us to have eternal life with God the Father, but still we refuse to believe. A lot of folks think it can't be that simple. Some folks are still confused by what it means. I've been preachin' a lot of years, and I've learned in my lifetime that comin' to Jesus is as easy as believin' and confessin'. Turn with me over to Romans ten, verses nine and ten."

Again, he waited while folks turned the

pages in their Bibles. Pastor Lewis remained where he was, not bothering to return to the pulpit nor read from his Bible. "'That if thou shalt confess with thy mouth the Lord Jesus, and shalt believe in thine heart that God hath raised him from the dead, thou shalt be saved. For with the heart man believeth unto righteousness; and with the mouth confession is made unto salvation.'

"Did you understand that, my friend? It's as simple as confessin' with your mouth that Jesus is Lord and believin' in your heart that God raised Jesus from the dead—a death, I might add, that He accepted on your behalf. A death on the cross as one final sacrifice for sin."

Someone sniffed back tears, and somewhere up front a man blew his nose. Owen could remember realizing his own sinfulness and coming to God humbled by the truth of who he was without a Savior.

"It's not complicated, folks," the pastor said, softening his voice. "Jesus knew it couldn't be complicated, or we would never get it figured out. He's standin' here today with his arms reachin' out to you. He knows you're tired of trying to figure things out by yourself. He knows you have a lot of pain and sorrow. He knows this world can be a terrible place on your own. But, folks, you don't have to be on your own. He's waitin' here right now. Won't you come forward if you'd like to make your peace with him?"

To Owen's surprise, several of the men he knew from the railyards stood and stepped forward. A couple of other people followed suit. Here he was thinking about his own problems, and there were half a dozen people in need of a Savior.

Someone started humming a hymn, and it wasn't long until most of the church had joined in. Pastor Lewis nodded and began to pray with each person who'd come forward.

Owen bowed his head. *Lord, forgive me for focusing on myself and my problems. I know You'll see me through—I know You'll give me the answers I need. I'm thankful for my salvation, Lord, and glad to see others coming to You. Forgive me that I wasn't one of those who helped them along.*

Susanna had never seen people coming forward and getting saved like this. At their church back in Topeka, services were much more formal, and if a person wanted to discuss salvation or anything else with the pastor, they made an appointment for sometime later in the week. As Pastor Lewis prayed with each person, Susanna could tell her folks were more than a little uncomfortable, but the experience of watching people yield their lives to God touched her deeply. They were making their decision public—letting the entire church see that they were giving their lives to God. What a wonderful way of letting the truth be known. Susanna had never had such an experience, and something about it nudged at her until she got to her feet and made her way forward.

When Pastor Lewis looked her in the eye, she could very well imagine Jesus gazing at her. The old man smiled and leaned close to whisper, "And do you want to take Jesus as your Savior?"

"I thought I had," Susanna replied. "But this public confession seems important to me. I don't know why, but here I am."

He smiled and nodded. "Sometimes it's just nice to show everybody where you stand. Do you believe Jesus is the only Son of God— that He came to earth to save us and gave His life on the cross to take away our sins? Do you believe He rose from the dead and has prepared a place for us in heaven?"

Susanna nodded. "I do."

"See how simple that was?" Pastor Lewis grinned. He bowed his head, and Susanna closed her eyes. "Lord, bless this child of yours. She has publicly accepted your free gift of salvation. Direct her steps now and always as she chooses to live for you. In Jesus' name, amen."

"Amen," Susanna whispered.

He moved on to the next person and left Susanna to wonder in awe at how right this moment felt. She had done nothing more than admit to things she'd believed for most of her life, so maybe she hadn't needed to make this public confession, but somehow it seemed to be one of the most important things she'd ever done.

After Pastor Lewis finished praying with the others, he took his place at the pulpit and asked the congregation to pray a blessing on those who had come forward. Susanna bowed her head and smiled. She truly did feel blessed.

Later, when church had been dismissed, Susanna found herself surrounded by people. Some gave her hug, and others commented on being surprised by her actions.

"I figured you were already a Christian," one of the women from her quilting group said. "If I'd known otherwise, we would have gotten you saved at our sewing party."

Susanna smiled. "I've known Jesus was Lord for a long time, and I have always believed in God. I just never made a confession like Pastor talked about."

The old woman nodded. "I understand.

Sometimes we just sort of fall into a thing without really knowing what it's all about and what's expected of us."

Several other women came up, saying much the same, and Susanna felt obliged to explain herself to each one. She didn't want people thinking that she'd been a heathen. By the time Mrs. Lewis came to see her, however, Susanna was beginning to think that maybe an explanation wasn't so important.

"Isn't God a wonder?" Mrs. Lewis asked.

Susanna nodded. Finally, it wasn't about her. "Yes! I was just thinking about that. It's so amazing how He joins us all together through Jesus. People I've never known or only known a little have become family. All because of Jesus."

Mrs. Lewis nodded. "Indeed. All because of Him." She gave Susanna a hug. "I'm so glad you're a part of the family."

Susanna was still in awe as she exited the church. Her parents were nowhere to be found. No doubt they were humiliated and embarrassed by what she'd done. Gary hadn't even bothered to come to church today, but no doubt he'd hear all about it. She began walking toward the hotel.

"Say, you want to have some lunch with me over at the Harvey House?"

She turned and found Gary's friend Herc

behind her. She smiled. "No, but thanks for asking." She gave it no other thought and turned to go.

Herc, however, grabbed her arm and spun her back around. Instinctively, Susanna raised her gloved hand and slapped him.

"Let go of me."

He was surprised and stepped back, dropping his hold. "I didn't mean any harm. Just wanted to persuade you to go with me."

"Well, that isn't the way to do it." She felt her cheeks flush. "I'm sorry for hitting you. I don't know what came over me."

"Is there a problem?"

Susanna was relieved to hear Owen's voice. She looked at him and smiled. "I'm afraid I overreacted. Hercules was just asking me to lunch, and I told him no, but then my nerves got the best of me. I am sorry, Herc."

The boomer nodded. "Me too. Your brother wouldn't take kindly to me manhandling his sister. I don't know what got into me. Guess I was just excited."

She nodded. "Well, let's forget about it."

Herc glanced at Owen and then nodded. "Good idea. Nice to see you, Mrs. Jenkins. Owen." He quickly walked away.

"I don't know exactly what all just happened," Owen said, "but I wondered if you wanted to go to lunch with me."

She turned to face him. "I'd like that very much, but could we just grab a couple of sandwiches and go sit by the river? It's such a beautiful day, and the rains have stopped. I'd like very much to be outside."

"I think that sounds great."

"Oh, I'd like to change my clothes."

Owen nodded. "Why don't I go to the Harvey House and get us some food while you go change?"

"That sounds perfect."

He hesitated a moment. "I, uh, want to say something about you getting saved, but I'm not sure what a person should say."

She laughed. "Especially given the fact that I've already spent most of my life believing in God and Jesus and going to church. But somehow it just felt important to confess it with Pastor Lewis."

He shrugged. "No one can doubt your intentions now. Maybe it's a good thing to make it public so folks know what you stand for."

"That sounds right. Now they all know I stand for Jesus."

Owen pointed down the street. "It looks like they're getting quite the line at the Harvey House. I'd better get over there."

"No. I have a better idea." They were already close to the river. "Why don't we just take a walk? We can go back to the hotel afterward, I'll fix some sandwiches, and we can eat there. I have some other things Lia brought over too. We can have a veritable feast. Right now I just feel like walking."

"And you don't mind not changing your clothes?"

"I'm fine, if you don't mind carrying your Bible."

"It's not that heavy." Owen tucked it under his arm.

They walked for a while, enjoying the river and the picturesque way it cut through the desert. Susanna hadn't been this happy since Mark was alive and well. Owen gave her a feeling of joy and security that had long been missing. She knew without a doubt she was starting to have strong feelings for him.

"I'm glad you wanted to go for a walk," Owen said. "I like the way it makes me feel at peace."

"Yes." She looked over at him and found him watching her. She smiled and returned her gaze straight ahead. What must he think of her? She had suggested this time alone.

"How are things with your folks?" he asked.

"About the same. They're starting to be quite vocal about this all being my fault. At first it was Uncle Harrison's fault, but now it's mine because I could have helped them remain in Topeka and never let them know I had the means."

"How could you have kept them in Topeka?"

She smiled. "The money Mark left me."

"Oh, that. Of course." He shook his head. "I am sorry."

She liked the way he'd responded as if the money didn't matter. "Money changes everything."

"If it helps," he said, chuckling, "I have a sizable bank account myself. Without family or a wife to support, I've been able to put away most of my salary these last fifteen years."

She laughed. "Well, good. We can rest assured that we don't need each other's money." She paused and sobered. "Actually, that is very nice to know."

He nodded. "I suppose it is. Folks are always taking advantage of each other, it seems."

"Especially in my family. Money has corrupted everything." She shook her head and thought of how sad it was to admit such a thing. Her parents had never found contentment and probably never would. "As I said, at first my parents could blame Uncle Harrison, and now they can blame me. Mother has schemed to get me to give her large amounts of money, even telling me that she's ill and needs to go to California to see a doctor." Susanna shook her head. "Honestly, if I thought it would make things right for them, I would give all I have."

"But it won't fix the problem."

"No," she admitted. "I'm not sure anything will. Neither Father nor Mother will admit their part in their circumstances." She stopped and turned to face Owen. "I don't know why I'm telling you all of this. I suppose I just need a friend to help me bear the burden, but you certainly didn't ask for that."

He touched her arm. "I'm asking for it now. I've come to care for you, Susanna. I think you know that."

She gave a little sigh. "I know that I've come to care for you. I enjoy our talks and time together. I'm just sorry that you seem so intricately drawn into my family's problems. I know Gary isn't working out well. I can tell by the way he acts around you."

"It's true. He's a real problem, and I fear I will have to move him to another department. He's begged me not to do that, but I think it's only because he fears someone else wouldn't be as lenient."

"Most likely."

Owen glanced down at the ground. "I don't know what to do. There are times when

I think he's really trying, and other times he reminds me of my brother."

"How is that?"

"Daniel wouldn't listen either. Or if he did, he wouldn't do what he was supposed to do. He died in an accident at the shops, and it was because he wouldn't follow procedure. It killed another man too. My father blamed me, and when he died a year later, I'm ashamed to say I felt mostly relief. Relief that he couldn't go on blaming me."

"I'm so sorry, Owen."

"Daniel was so spoiled. Mom died when he was just two. Our grandparents raised us after that. Our father was a train engineer and gone most of the time. Daniel was allowed to do anything he wanted. I was already twelve and was expected to be helpful, to watch over him. I was angry at my mother's death and closed myself off from other people. No one had time to worry about it, so I just kept on being that way. When Grandma and Grandpa died, it only made me more determined never to be close to anyone. It wasn't until I came here and met Pastor Lewis that I learned to open up again. Even so, I don't make a lot of friends. Just a few at a time. It seems safer that way."

"I understand. Mark, my husband, was my only real friend for most of my life. A couple of girls befriended me, but their friendship was so superficial that I lost interest. It seemed wrong to invest so much time and energy in something that wasn't real."

"Yes, exactly."

They started walking again, but this time Owen shifted the Bible to his right hand and looped his left arm with Susanna's. She gave him a smile, hoping he realized just how much she wanted that connection.

"I hope," she finally said, feeling that it was important to offer Owen some assurance, "you won't worry about what you must do with Gary. At least not on my account. I have no say in the matter, nor will I beg for special privileges for him. If you recall, I was the one who warned you when you took him on."

They left the river and walked north toward the road that would lead them back into town. Susanna felt as if she'd finally found the peace her life had been missing. First with her decision about Jesus, and now spending time with Owen.

When Mark had first made her promise she would remarry after he died, Susanna couldn't fathom that possibility. And though she had promised him she would, she hadn't meant it. Not really. Now, after spending even these short few months with Owen, she could see the possibility. Owen made her feel safe and cared for, just as Mark had. He made sense in her otherwise senseless world. She could only hope he felt the same way about her.

"When we get back to the hotel, I'll fix us some lunch," she said. "If you aren't expecting anything too fancy, we should be able to put together a decent meal."

Owen laughed. "I never expect anything fancy, so have no fear of . . ." His words trailed off. "There's smoke up there. Something's on fire!"

13

The hotel's on fire!" one of the boys who'd fetched the constable for Susanna called out as they approached the hotel. "Hurry, Mrs. Jenkins!"

She frowned and looked at Owen. "A fire?"

They rounded the corner and made their way to the front of the building, where quite a few people had already gathered. The volunteer fire department stood around, discussing what had happened. Thankfully, the fire was already out.

Susanna went up to the group of men, finding LeRoy and Mr. Medford among them. "What's going on? Where's my father?"

"It seems there was a fire in the living quarters of the hotel," LeRoy told her. "A candle fell over and set the desk papers on fire, and that spread to the floor and cabinets. There's not a lot of damage, though. The desk contents and desk suffered the bulk of it."

Susanna shook her head. "But I didn't light a candle this morning. I had no need. The sun was so beautiful this morning that I opened all the windows instead."

Father had arrived early that morning as usual, and then they had left the front desk unattended after the last of the guests checked out. The hotel had been empty and locked while Father and Susanna were at church. Of course, Gary had still been sleeping when they left. What if he were still inside?

She started for the door. "My brother was sleeping in his bedroom."

LeRoy escorted Susanna inside with Owen at her side. "He was already out. He showed up with your father while the fire department was working and then left again." They made their way into Susanna's living quarters. "I don't know what you kept in the desk drawer, but it looks to have burnt up."

"There was money in the drawer, and the drawer was locked." Her voice was barely a murmur as she stared at the open drawer. Inside lay a pile of completely consumed papers. Only ash remained. "The hotel money. I kept it there because we don't yet have a fireproof safe and the bank is closed until tomorrow. The drawer was locked." She was repeating herself, but the shock of the situation had unsettled her.

She looked around the room. Much of the living quarters remained untouched, but the kitchen area and desk had suffered much. Someone had thought to move the table and chairs so they escaped being consumed, but the counters and cabinets had smoke and fire damage. Everywhere soot and ashy remains mingled with the water used to put out the flames. Her area rug was tracked and soggy. It would take a lot to clean up everything and get rid of the smoky smell.

Susanna sat down on the closest chair, shaking her head. "What in the world could have happened?"

LeRoy shrugged. "Like I said, it looked to the fire chief that a candle fell over."

"Maybe Gary lit it when he woke up. I had pulled down a couple of the shades, so maybe he felt the need for more light." Susanna sighed heavily, fighting tears. "I can't believe this has happened. I must get in touch with Uncle Harrison. I should send him a telegram." She thought of the lost money. Had it truly burned up?

"Don't you imagine your father will do that?" Owen asked.

She shrugged. "I thought my father would be here after church. It's his job, and yet where is he? Why isn't he here even now?"

LeRoy spoke up. "He and Gary did show up for a while. The fire chief sent someone to the Medford house to get them. Your father came and gave things a cursory look. He said you had no reservations for the night, so he'd keep the place closed for cleanup. After that, he left."

"No doubt he figures you'll take charge of making things right," Owen said, looking at Susanna. "Don't worry, I'll stick around and help you."

"Lia and the boys and I will come over too," LeRoy added. "We'll have the place whipped into shape in no time."

"You're so kind to offer," Susanna said, still feeling weak, even nauseated, from the sight of the room.

"I'll help too," a new voice said.

Susanna looked up to find Gary standing in the doorway. She shook her head. "I was so afraid you had been hurt."

"Nope. I was up and out." He glanced around. "It sure made a mess."

"Did you light the candle?"

"What candle?"

"They said a candle started the fire. I didn't light a candle before I left for church.

I don't know who would have, other than you or maybe Father."

"It wasn't me." Gary's voice was tight. He turned away. "Look, I said I'd help you clean, and I will."

Susanna thought his response strange. "Where's Father?"

"Back at the house." Gary seemed to compose himself. "I think he plans to close the hotel for a while."

"Close it for a while?" She got to her feet. "There's hardly any need for that. I agree to keeping it closed today and maybe tomorrow to get the smoky smell out of the rooms, but there isn't so much damage that we need to worry about safety. Do we?" She looked to LeRoy.

"Oh no. It's perfectly safe. The fire didn't damage the structure at all. The walls are good. It mostly just burned the desk and counters and the floor. We can pull all of that out of here." He stepped closer to the origin of the fire. "See, the candle fell on the desk and set the desk and papers on fire. That fire traveled onto the floor. The floors probably caught fire and in turn lit the curtain you had hiding the area under the counters. Then the flames traveled up the curtain and set the counters on fire. But the damage is really minimal. It's mostly the smoke damage and the water used to put out the fire that made all this mess. You'll see, though—it'll clean up pretty easy. Why don't you and Owen come to our house for lunch, and then we can come back and tackle everything? You can come too, Gary."

"Thanks, but we ate at the Harvey House. I'll come back later." Gary left without another word.

"He's acting strange," Susanna said, not meaning to say it aloud. She looked at Owen, who nodded.

"There, I told you it wouldn't be so bad," LeRoy said as they gathered the last bits of sooty debris. "Susanna, we'll get rid of this stuff while Lia shows you how to make things smell better. You'll be able to sleep here tonight without any trouble."

"I hadn't planned to sleep anywhere else," Susanna admitted even though Gary had mentioned sleeping at the house with their parents.

Once the men and her brother had gone, she turned to Lia.

"You're such an answer to prayer. I had no idea how I was going to get things back in order, much less make the hotel smell better."

"We'll finish cleaning with the vinegar

while the oranges and lemons boil. I think you'll be surprised at how much odor is eliminated just by doing this. Lastly, we'll use orange oil to rub the furniture in each of the rooms upstairs. It will take away any lingering smells and leave the room smelling fresh."

"It was smart to open all the windows in each room. Such a simple thing, but I know it helps."

"That and washing all the bedding and curtains. That job is laborious but will finish things out nicely. It was so kind of the church ladies to take over that duty for you, and with all of them helping, you'll have fresh bedding and curtains by tomorrow."

"I really appreciate the help. I couldn't have managed by myself." Susanna gave Lia a grateful smile. "You have been such a good friend to me. Thank you for arranging for the extra help."

"I'm glad we can be friends. I think you'll find the people here, especially at church, are good folks. They have hearts of gold and are eager to help one another."

"I wish my mother could see how good they are. I wish she could stop with her pretenses and desires to be something she's not and appreciate the people around her. I think her entire life would change if only she could do that one thing."

Lia shrugged. "Sometimes people can't see the blessing that is right in front of them."

Susanna thought of that later when Gary came to check on her. He looked so tired—weary from something more than the fire.

"What's going on with you? You look like you've lost your last friend."

Gary shook his head. "I'm fine. Just tired. Tomorrow I have to be at the shops by six, so I need to go to bed. I was going to sleep at the house, but then I figured it might not be safe for you here by yourself."

She stopped him as he trudged toward his bedroom. "I have some food if you're hungry."

"Yeah, that might help." He looked at the table and chairs. "I'm glad the place didn't go up completely."

"It's amazing the fire wasn't much worse. We are very blessed. Uncle Harrison could have lost the entire hotel."

"Yeah." Gary plopped down in a chair and shook his head. "Do you suppose he has fire insurance?"

"I don't know. I haven't even sent him a telegram. I wasn't sure if Father was going to do that, and since it's Sunday, I figured I'd wait and ask him in the morning. Did he say anything to you about the fire?"

"Like what?"

Susanna brought him a sandwich she'd made earlier. Ham and cheese with butter. It was one of Gary's favorites since their arrival in San Marcial. "I just wondered if he knew anything about the candle and what had started the fire."

"Why would he?" Gary snapped. He grabbed the sandwich and took a big bite.

Susanna was taken aback by his attitude. "You don't have to be so angry with me. It's just a question. We need to figure out what happened. Someone was careless, and it could have ended in complete tragedy. As it is, it burned up all the money we made from the Saturday and Sunday guests, and had a passerby not seen the smoke, it might have burned more than the hotel kitchen. The whole block could have caught."

"But it didn't. And I'm sure Uncle Harrison can afford the loss. Besides, he probably has insurance. No one will suffer." Gary took another bite. "You got something to drink?" he asked with his mouth full.

"I can make some tea or coffee."

"Water's fine. Don't bother to make anything."

She nodded and got him a glass of water. Whatever was eating at him, Gary wasn't at all himself. Perhaps he knew more about the fire than he was letting on.

Owen was awake long after he'd gone to bed. He couldn't help but wonder what had actually set the hotel on fire. He remembered Herc being unhappy that Susanna wouldn't go to lunch with him. Could he have done it to get back at her?

LeRoy had mentioned the casual way Susanna's father acted about the entire matter. He hadn't said much in front of Susanna, but when he and Owen were alone, he'd voiced his opinion without hesitation.

"I think Mr. Ragsdale and his son know more than they're letting on," he'd told Owen as they washed up for supper. *"Mr. Ragsdale wasn't all that interested when we sent someone to let him know the hotel was on fire. Mrs. Ragsdale was even worse. She actually said she hoped the place burned to the ground."*

Had one of the Ragsdales set the fire, hoping to eliminate their responsibility to run the hotel? Owen rolled onto his stomach, then raised up to punch the pillow into a more comfortable form. It would soon be time to get up, and he hadn't slept a wink. He sighed and did his best to relax.

Susanna had been gravely concerned by the situation. She had worked throughout the day and evening to see that the hotel was put back in order. She'd obviously had nothing to do with the fire, but someone had deliberately set it, and that knowledge made Owen furious. They could have caused the entire block to burn down. Fires were nothing to play around with. San Marcial had lost a portion of the town just a few years back due to a fire.

When he opened his eyes again, it was just starting to lighten up outside. He checked his clock and found it was time to get up. He couldn't have had more than two hours of sleep. He yawned and sat on the edge of his bed. Today he had to decide what to do about Gary, but there still didn't seem to be a clear resolution.

He dressed and headed over to the Harvey House rather than take time to make his own breakfast. He ordered a big meal, knowing he'd burn through the calories before lunchtime. While he ate, Owen contemplated what was to be done. He knew Gary was ill-suited to boilermaking and repair but couldn't honestly say that he'd shown a proclivity toward anything else.

"Looks like you're eating for an army," Timothy Payne said, stopping by Owen's table.

Owen looked up and nodded. "There's

plenty here, if you want to join me. Help yourself to the extra toast."

"I believe I will. I came to get my thermos filled with coffee, but toast sounds good. They have the best strawberry jam. Just don't tell Sylvia." He grinned and took the chair opposite Owen. "I told her that her jam was better."

When the Harvey Girl arrived, Mr. Payne handed her his thermos. "Fill 'er up, please, and put it on my tab."

She smiled. "Mr. Payne, you don't have a tab."

"Well, maybe I should." He grinned and flipped her a dime. Next, he took a piece of toast from the rack and slathered it with jam. "You looked troubled, Owen. What's going on?"

"It's a lot of things. I didn't sleep well last night. There was a fire at the hotel, and I helped with that all day and into the evening. Then, when I tried to sleep . . . well, there was a lot on my mind."

"Such as?"

Owen wasn't eager to discuss his concerns about the fire, so he focused on Gary. "I need to find another place for Gary Ragsdale."

"I wondered how long you were going to keep covering for him."

Owen swallowed some coffee along with

the lump that had suddenly formed in his throat. He had never meant to let things go on as long as they had. "He's a good kid. He wants to learn, but he's never in his life had to be responsible. It's hard to turn someone into a man overnight. His father and mother never prepared him for life. Not this kind of life, anyhow."

Payne nodded. "I think you've gone above and beyond. There are other things we can try him at. He won't just be fired."

"I know. I think he's worried about that happening, though. I think he feels that since I'm interested in his sister, I'll go on overlooking his shortcomings. Then there's the influence of the boomers. Those three he hangs around with haven't helped him at all. They got him interested in playing poker and blackjack in the backroom games. Apparently he's good enough that he's won quite a bit of money."

"That's just their way of getting him good and hooked. They'll convince him he's some sort of card sharp, and he'll end up losing all of his wages. And if he does happen to be good at playing, they'll do what they can to recruit him to take advantage of others. I heard there's even a bible of sorts that they pass around to those who work for them. It's a book of tricks you can play in order to win big."

Owen shook his head. "So much corruption in the world."

"To be sure." Payne got to his feet. "I tell you what. I'll come by and relieve you of the need to fire Gary from your area. One of our parts runners left for California. Gary could take his place, and the work isn't that hard—just finding the right part and takin' it to the right person." He smiled. "I'll come for him as soon as I can this morning. That way it won't have to come from you."

"He'll still blame me, I'm sure."

"I can't do anything about that." Mr. Payne picked up his filled thermos. "A man's gonna think what he wants. We'll know the truth."

But that was just it. The truth was that Owen didn't want to work with Gary any longer. He was dangerous and seemed unable to learn. Owen wanted him out of his area before someone got hurt . . . or killed. Gary would know that the minute he looked into Owen's eyes.

Owen sighed and pushed back from the table. Hopefully he could figure out some way to explain it to the boy.

14

Gary had barely started work when Mr. Payne showed up. He called them all together, then made an announcement. "I'm moving Gary to parts. One of our best men has headed off to California, and we need a replacement. I believe Gary would be perfect for the job, and there will be a small increase in pay."

The news came as a surprise, but Gary tried to show little reaction. He knew things had been difficult with Owen. He wasn't able to work as fast as the others, and he was still making a lot of mistakes despite having worked in the department for over two months.

"Gary, I'll show you where you'll be working and what you'll be expected to do," Mr. Payne declared. He looked at Owen. "Sorry to rob you of a man, but for now I think this is best."

"And you get a pay raise," Herc said to Gary. "You get all the breaks. You won't work nearly as hard in parts."

Gary couldn't tell if Owen was in on this or not. He had a frown on his face as if this were news to him and he wasn't sure how to make do without his man, but on the other hand, Gary knew changes had already been suggested.

Gary followed the shop supervisor out of the building, crossing his arms against his chest as he often did when things grew tense.

"I know you've been trying your best, Gary," Mr. Payne said, "and I want you to know that's the only reason I'm keeping you around. I don't think you're lazy, just misplaced."

Gary looked at the older man. "I really like working for the Santa Fe, but I don't seem to have any talent for working with my hands."

"You've never had to. Most of these boys have worked with their hands all their lives, either on farms or ranches or construction. You can't be blamed for not having been brought up that way, but you have to understand that we don't have all the time in the world for you to learn. The train boilers are too critical to have someone there who doesn't know what he's doing. Two and a half months is long enough to learn the job. We like you well enough to move you to another department, so don't get angry because you're not with Owen and the others."

"I'm not angry. Just, well . . ." Gary shook his head. "I guess I just wonder if I'll ever be good at anything."

Payne stopped and looked him in the eye. "You're the only one who has any say over that, son. If you want to be like those boomers, never having any purpose but to get what you want and move on, then that's all you'll ever be. I suggest you figure out what you really want in life. Maybe working for the Santa Fe isn't where you belong."

"That's the trouble. I don't seem to belong anywhere."

Owen looked for Gary after the whistle blew at the end of the day, but the boy was nowhere to be found. Owen hoped the change to parts had been a good one for him. The mood of the boomers had been far more negative after Gary left, but Owen couldn't help that. The other men who worked for Owen were glad for the change, even though they liked Gary. They were tired of having to redo the boy's work and told Owen they hoped Gary fit in with the parts department. Owen hoped that as well. Above all, he hoped that Gary knew Owen didn't wish him any harm or ill will, and that was partially why he planned to go to the hotel after getting cleaned up. He wanted very much to see how Gary's day had gone and to let him know that he was still there for him if he needed anything.

He also wanted to see Susanna and learn how she was doing in the aftermath of the fire. He knew she'd been very upset, even suspicious. She'd mentioned at one point that she wasn't convinced it had been an accident. Neither was he.

Owen made his way to the Grand Hotel about half an hour after the evening train arrived in San Marcial. He hoped that was enough time for any passengers who wanted to check in to the Grand to do so, and that Susanna would now be free for the evening.

She looked up from the check-in desk the minute he walked through the door. For a moment she did nothing but watch him, but finally she straightened from where she had been making notes in the registry book and smiled. "Good evening, Owen. To what do I owe this visit?"

"I came for a couple of reasons. One, I wanted to check on Gary."

"I haven't seen him. He must have gone to the house or off to eat with his friends. Why did you want to see him?"

"Mr. Payne moved him from my department today. I wanted to make sure he wasn't mad at me or upset."

She looked concerned. "Where did they move him?"

"Parts. We have hundreds of parts for the repair work we do. Invoices come in for parts, and the runners fill the orders and deliver them. That's what Gary will be doing."

"It sounds a lot easier than welding boilers." She smiled and brushed back a wisp of honey-brown hair.

"It should be. I think it will suit him well. Mr. Payne just showed up, however, and took Gary away without warning. I wanted to make sure he knew no one was mad at him."

"You mean you wanted to make sure he knew that *you* weren't mad at him."

Owen smiled and looked at the floor. "Yeah, well, when you put it that way . . ." He let the words trail off.

She understood. "Like I said, I don't know where he is, but you're more than welcome to wait for him."

Owen looked around. "Where's your father?"

"Good question. He hasn't been around much since the fire. He told me yesterday that Mother is much too upset for him to leave her side. She apparently went on and on about how if they'd been living at the hotel, they would have all been killed."

"Or they would have been there, and the fire never would have happened," Owen countered.

"That's exactly my thought. Come on back. I'll fix something to eat, if you like. It won't be anything fancy. I haven't been to the grocer for a while."

"Why don't I take you to a little café I know? They have the best Mexican food you'll ever try."

"Spicy?" she asked.

He laughed. "Not for the *gringos*. The food they serve gringos is much milder. They learned they had to prepare it that way. Besides, they're cousins of Lia. You'll like them. A man and his wife run the place, and sometimes their children wait tables. They're up in Old Town."

"It sounds interesting, but I don't know that I should leave the hotel. The rooms are full tonight. What if someone needs something?"

"Get Manuel to watch the desk. He can handle it." He could tell she wanted to say yes. "Better still, I'll go find him while you get your hat and gloves."

When she agreed, Owen made a hurried exit, eager to spend the evening with her. He easily found Manuel and gave the boy fifty cents. Manuel's eyes widened at the sight of the coins. Owen shrugged. "The worker is worth his wage."

They walked back to the hotel and found Susanna ready to go. Owen liked that she hadn't bothered to worry overmuch about her appearance. Susanna always looked perfect, as far as he was concerned.

"We won't be long, Manuel. Just watch the hotel and make sure everyone has what they need, all right?" Susanna pointed to the desk. "I put out some homemade cookies on the desk for you. There's milk in the icebox if you get thirsty."

"*Gracias, Señora.* Gracias." Manuel eyed the cookies with enthusiasm.

Owen looped his arm through Susanna's. People were beginning to recognize them as a couple, and he wanted it that way. He might not yet be ready to ask for her hand, but he liked folks knowing he had a claim on her. Even if it was just an unspoken one.

"My uncle is coming next week," Susanna said as they walked the road to Old Town.

"Because of the fire?"

"Yes. He wants to speak with Father, but he's not telling him he's coming. Just me. I'm not sure what he hopes to gain. Father is hardly speaking to anyone, and Mother spends most of her time crying. At least that's what Gary told me. He's not saying a lot either. Ever since the fire, he seems to have very little to say. I know it's only been a day, but it worries me."

"You think he had something to do with the fire?"

She shook her head. "I don't know what to think. He just isn't himself. I suppose it's possible someone he knows was responsible, but we both know my father had the most to gain. If the place burned down, Uncle Harrison would have to take pity on him and provide a different solution."

"Or not. He could just ignore him and let him fend for himself."

Susanna considered this for a moment. "I don't think that will ever happen. There was some sort of agreement between Uncle Harrison and my grandfather to take care of my father. I think he's stuck with it. And worse, I think my father knows it. That's why I don't think he'll ever change."

They arrived at the little café and made their way inside. The man running the place came and embraced Owen as if he were a son. "We have missed you. Where have you been?"

"Working, mostly." He looked at Susanna. "And making new friends."

The man laughed and slapped Owen on the back. "I think your *amiga* takes up most of your time, eh?"

"Juan, this is Susanna Jenkins. She helps with the new hotel in town. Her uncle owns it."

"Ah, sí. Welcome, señorita."

"Señora," Owen corrected. When the man's eyes widened, he quickly added, "Her husband is dead."

"*Lo siento*, señora." Juan frowned.

"It's all right," Susanna replied. "It's been over a year and, well . . . it's been over a year." She seemed uncomfortable trying to explain.

Owen quickly jumped in. "We're starved and thought you might have some gringo food for us."

"Of course. Come, I'll put you at the corner table—that way you can talk." He led the way through the small, busy café and took them to a tiny table in the far corner of the room. "I'll bring you food and lemonade."

"It's a very interesting place," Susanna said, looking around. "It smells wonderful— like chiles cooking and fresh tortillas. Lia sometimes comes over after she's been at Mother's and brings me tortillas. I love the way they smell."

"I think you'll love the food. They use a lot of different sauces. Some are definitely hotter than others, but they're all good. I think you're going to enjoy it."

"I already am," she replied, giving him a hint of a smile.

She looked so weary and tired, and Owen wanted to help. "I have an idea. You need to get away from here."

"A vacation? Who has time for that?"

"Well, maybe not exactly a vacation, but a week from next Monday I have to go to Albuquerque to oversee a boiler repair. Why don't you come with me? I'll find you a nice hotel room while I stay with the Santa Fe workers. We can explore the town when I'm not working."

"I . . . well, that seems rather . . . inappropriate." She sounded nervous, and only then did Owen realize how the proposition must have sounded to her.

"I'm sorry. I hope I didn't, ah, offend you," he stammered. "I didn't mean anything inappropriate."

"I know you didn't. I just know what others might think."

He chuckled. "I didn't think you cared what other people thought."

"I don't. Not really. I mean, goodness, I live at a hotel practically by myself." She shook her head. "The trip sounds lovely. So

I'd just stay at the hotel and read while you worked—is that it?"

He felt relieved that she wasn't angry. "You could do whatever you liked during the day. I'll have to be there a couple of days. I just thought you might enjoy getting away. We can ride the train there and back. There won't be a charge for that. I'd even pay for your room at the hotel, but that really does sound inappropriate."

This time she was the one to laugh. "Oh, listen to us."

"We can explore Albuquerque in the evening hours and enjoy some time away. Doesn't it sound good?"

"It does," she said with a wistful expression. "I don't know who will manage the hotel."

"Your uncle is coming the Friday before. I'm sure he'll put the fear of God back into your father and get him working again. Besides, just tell them you're going to be away. Don't let them keep you from enjoying your life."

Susanna knew her feelings for Owen were growing each day, and she wasn't sure what to do about it. He hadn't spoken of being in love, just that he cared. Did that caring extend to something more permanent than mere friendship? Did she want it to? Owen was a good friend, and she enjoyed their time together. Could she fall in love with him?

This is silly. I barely know him, and yet here I sit, thinking about spending the rest of my life with him. What kind of fool am I?

Marriage was far too important a thing to decide after just a few months of friendship. Mother would say it was highly irresponsible even to allow such thoughts, and Susanna would have to agree. She would have to guard her heart.

But it wasn't the action of someone guarding their heart to agree to go to Albuquerque unchaperoned—not that she really needed a chaperone as a widowed woman. Still, she didn't want to ruin her reputation, but the idea of going away with Owen appealed to her in a way she couldn't dismiss. She couldn't ignore the way she thought about him most of the time, nor the way his appearance always seemed to quicken her heartbeat. It was much too late to guard her heart.

By the time they made it back to the hotel, Gary was there, and Owen took the opportunity to have a few minutes with him alone. Susanna busied herself in the kitchen. LeRoy and Owen had promised her some new cabinets, but so far there had been no time, and she was keeping her pans and canned food items in wooden crates. She wondered when the men might actually get around to remaking the place, since they worked full-time, and LeRoy had a family who needed him as well.

"I'm heading home now," Owen said, returning with Gary. The two had taken a walk at one point, and Susanna wondered what they'd discussed. "LeRoy wanted you to know that we'll be here on Saturday afternoon to work on the kitchen. Neither of us have to work overtime, so we'll come and install the cabinets."

"You've already made the cabinets?"

"Yup. We both worked a little after work each night. That's where I'm heading now, actually. We don't want you to have to wait long."

She shook her head in wonder. "You two are much too kind, but I don't want to cause problems for LeRoy with his family."

"The boys want to help and will probably come on Saturday. They love to help their dad."

"That would be fine. Lia can come too, if she wants. I don't mind if they're all here, although this room isn't big enough. The boys have a way of filling a room."

"That's for sure."

"Maybe Lia and I should go to her house and leave you all here to work." She laughed.

"That might be a good idea. Maybe you and Lia could fix a big supper feast. Wouldn't that be grand?" He headed for the door. "I'll mention it to her. For now, I'll say good night."

"Good night, Owen."

Susanna watched him leave, then turned to find Gary staring at her. He frowned and shook his head.

"What's wrong with you?" she asked. "I've hardly seen you, and you look at me with such disgust."

"I don't like you getting all mushy over Owen."

"What's wrong with getting all mushy over Owen?" she asked.

Gary plopped down on the sofa and shook his head while Susanna went to the door and closed it for privacy from their hotel guests. There was a bell on the front counter that they could ring if they needed help.

"You don't even know him," Gary protested.

"No, not well," Susanna admitted. "That's why I like seeing him. I'm getting to know him."

"He probably just wants to spend time with you because he knows about your money."

"What do you know about my money?"

Gary shrugged. "I overheard Uncle Harrison say you're a wealthy woman."

"And you told Father. So that's how he knew."

"I didn't mean to cause trouble for you, I just didn't want him nagging me to give him *my* money. I figured it wasn't that big of a deal."

"Oh, you figured that, did you." She stood at the end of the couch and put her hands on her hips. "And do you see now just how much of an ordeal it has turned into? I purposefully didn't say anything to anyone because I didn't want my money being the focus of anyone's relationship with me. But for your information, I told Owen myself that I had money."

"Then of course he's gonna want to marry you." Gary shook his head. "That was stupid."

Susanna squared her shoulders. "My money and my relationships are my business. Stay out of it, Gary. All of it."

"So you are in love with him."

"I didn't say that. But even if I was, it would still be none of your business. Honestly, I don't know what's gotten into you. You never used to act like this. Why don't you tell me what's really upsetting you lately? You haven't been at all happy the last two days."

"I don't have to tell you anything." His tone was bitter.

Susanna softened her voice. "No, of course you don't have to. I just thought you might feel better if you did."

"We had to move to the middle of nowhere, and I have to work a dirty job, and there's nowhere to go for fun except a few pool halls and cardrooms. What's to tell that you don't already know? I hate it here. I can't even try to go to college."

"Do you want to go to college, Gary?"

He got up and started to pace. "It doesn't matter what I want. Everyone has made that abundantly clear. I don't even get to pick the department I work in."

"I'm sorry to hear that. Is that why you're considering going off with your boomer friends?"

Gary stopped. "Did Owen tell you that?"

"He didn't have to. I heard you talking to Herc about it."

Gary turned around and crossed his arms. "I don't know. The guys want me to go with them. They're gonna leave next month. They're tired of being here and tell me there's a lot more going on in some of the other towns. Albuquerque, for example, and it's not that far away."

"I see. Well, do you really think that kind of

life is going to make you happy? Roaming from town to town, never settling down to build relationships and get to know people? There are some really nice folks here in San Marcial."

"Yeah, but they aren't interested in me." Gary shook his head. "I don't matter to much of anyone."

"That's not true. You matter to me, and I know you matter to Owen. He wouldn't have taken time tonight to talk to you if he didn't care."

Gary frowned, then headed for his room. "I'm going to bed. Morning will be here before I know it."

Susanna wanted to say more, but she could see that her brother's mind was made up. Gary was in such turmoil. She knew he blamed their father for the problems they had, but he also blamed her and felt anger at Owen. Gary was always willing to blame anyone but himself when things were going wrong. She sighed. Maybe she'd talk to Pastor Lewis about him.

The next morning, after checking out their guests, Susanna went about her work gathering the sheets and pillowcases. Thankfully the hotel owned enough sets to change out every bed and still have one extra, but it was still necessary to tend to the wash every day, especially if the rooms had all been rented. Since Father hadn't shown up again, she had made an arrangement with Manuel to stay for the time it took her to go to the house, do the wash, and get things hung up to dry. Later, Lia would take the linens down, iron the sheets and pillowcases, and leave them stacked and ready in the basket for Susanna. Often, Father had brought the basket with him when he'd returned after supper, but lately he'd so rarely come to work that Susanna wasn't sure what she was going to do.

"Mrs. Jenkins," Pastor Lewis said as she came down the stairs to the lobby with her basket stuffed to overflowing.

"Pastor Lewis." She smiled. "I just decided last night to seek you out for a conversation, and here you are."

He smiled and gave her a nod. "I always like to visit new believers."

"I'm here, Señora Jenkins," Manuel announced, coming through the door. He saw Pastor Lewis and gave him a nod. "Papa Lewis." Manuel continued in Spanish, and the pastor replied in kind.

Susanna waited until their conversation was completed before motioning toward the door. "Would you care to walk with me? I'm going to take the laundry to my folks' house, where I can wash it. It's easier than trying to heat up water on the stove and wash it in the sink or tub here at the hotel."

"I'd be happy to walk with you, but only if you let me carry the basket."

"No need. I have a little wagon I pull. You can take over pulling that, if you like," she replied.

"I will do exactly that." He smiled again. "It's been a long time since I pulled my children in a wagon, but I think I recall how it's done."

She put the basket in the wagon and let him take the handle.

"You know," Pastor Lewis declared as they crossed the street and headed out, "Manuel lives with us."

"I heard. He's such a nice young man."

"His family died during an epidemic. He was just fourteen, and we encouraged him to come and stay with us. He didn't want to, but then he got sick as well, and Mrs. Lewis nursed him back to health. After that, it was natural for him to stick around. He's a good boy." The pastor's Texas drawl left Susanna relaxed and at ease.

"He's very helpful. I think I'm going to have to hire him on full-time if my father doesn't return to the hotel to work."

"Is there a problem?" the pastor asked.

Susanna found herself wishing she hadn't

said anything. "He's just been upset since the fire. We're still not sure what caused it. My uncle is coming here next week to check up on things." She decided to change the subject. "I want to talk to you, but it's about my brother. I'm worried about him."

"Then, by all means, tell me why."

Susanna nodded. "I don't know what you know about our family, but a lot is wrong." She heaved a heavy sigh. "This isn't a short story, but I'll try to make it as abbreviated as possible."

She launched into a short history of all that had happened to bring them to San Marcial, ending with the fire. "I don't know if Gary or maybe one of his friends had anything to do with it, but he hasn't been himself since it happened."

"It sounds like he hasn't been himself since you moved here, but that it might not be all bad. Changes can be good."

Susanna motioned for him to follow her to the back of the house once they reached the adobe structure. Her mother and father were used to her routine and wouldn't question her being out back. Thankfully, Lia had already gotten the water on to heat, and the cauldron was ready to receive the wash.

"My folks are angry with me, and I think that's made Gary angry too. They know I inherited enough money from my dead husband that I could have saved them from having to leave Topeka."

"But it's not your job to take care of them. You owe them honor and respect, not a wage."

"I've tried to provide different comforts." She glanced toward the laundry. "More for myself, I'm ashamed to say, than for them."

"You are a good person, Susanna. Don't be so hard on yourself."

"I just fear what will happen to Gary if he doesn't get some direction. He might end up like our father, floundering around, trying to find another get-rich-quick scheme to bring him fortune. Right now he's working for the Santa Fe—driven by anger at Father. He doesn't want to be anything like him, so he's doing manual labor. But the boomers, his friends from the railroad, got him involved in playing cards for money, and they want him to leave town and go with them to a larger city where he can make more money. I'm afraid he'll go."

"Sometimes you have to let people make their own mistakes, Susanna. You can't live Gary's life for him."

She met Pastor Lewis's concerned expression. "Then what do I do for him?"

The pastor smiled and patted her shoulder. "You pray."

15

Uncle Harrison arrived the next Friday. Susanna was the first to cross his path, since she was walking back from the ladies' aid meeting at the church. She saw him making his way to the hotel and headed him off so that they might speak privately.

"I hope you had a good trip," she said.

"It was tolerable. I was so livid over the fire, I cleared my calendar in order to deal with this. How bad is the damage?"

"It's nearly all repaired."

"Make sure to give me the receipts, and you will be reimbursed."

"Well, the repairs . . . we all pitched in and did them together." She shrugged. "So very little money was spent."

His expression changed to disbelief. "Truly? Your parents helped?"

"No, not them, but different folks—yes. The ladies at the church helped by washing out the bedding and draperies, Owen and LeRoy—two friends from church—have done the hardest work of taking out the damaged parts of the kitchen and replacing them. They made some new cabinets, so we can find out what that cost, but I doubt they'd let you pay them." She paused and smiled. "Even Gary helped."

"But not your father or mother?"

Susanna knew she couldn't lie. She bowed her head. "No. Father has scarcely even come to work since it happened. I'm not sure what's going on."

"So he's not been doing his job?"

"No. I'm afraid if I were gone, he'd lock the place up and leave it to die."

"We'll see about that. I've had all I'm going to take from him. The fire chief here feels the fire was deliberately set."

Susanna nodded. "I think so too. It was too obvious that someone broke into the desk and took the money from Friday through Sunday morning before the fire started. I think they were covering up the theft. We were packed full Friday and Saturday nights, and there was quite a bit of money, but because the bank was closed, I locked it in the desk. Unfortunately, the hotel ledger and bank book were in the desk drawer too, and they burned as well."

"To eliminate the record of how much was actually there, no doubt." Uncle Harrison glanced at the hotel. "The fire chief didn't think the ashes looked like paper money, and coinage wouldn't melt unless the fire was much hotter."

"I wondered about that myself. I have no way of knowing what burned money should look like, but I didn't think the coins would burn, and even if they did, I figured we'd find them maybe melted together. There was no sign of them."

"That's what the fire chief said. Do you have an idea of who might have set the fire?"

"Not exactly. I wondered about Gary and his friends, but I really don't think they had anything to do with it. However, Gary's been very upset about it and . . . well . . ." She fell silent for a moment and raised her gaze to his. "Gary was here sleeping when I left for church. Everything was fine then. Gary says it was fine when he woke up around eleven and headed out for something to eat. Mother and Father were also at church that morning. I took a walk with Owen Turner after the service. We probably returned to the hotel around one o'clock. By the time we arrived, the fire had already been put out."

"What are you trying to say?"

"It could have been anyone, I suppose. Gary admits to leaving the hotel unlocked. He doesn't have a key. I do. Father has the only other one."

"So anyone could have walked in and gone in search of money."

"Yes." Susanna tried not to blurt out what she was thinking, but she couldn't stay quiet. "I think . . . . I'm horrified to say it, but I think maybe Father was responsible."

"So do I."

"Why do you think it?"

"Because he made a small investment with one of our friends. Unless you gave him the money, he had to find it somewhere else."

Susanna gave a slow nod. "I see. No, he didn't get the money from me. I haven't given them anything extra, although they've tried to get all of my money. They found out I am well off. Mother feigned being sick, telling me that she and Father needed to go to California so she could see a specialist. She said she'd need a lot of money because they'd have to stay there. I knew she was lying but offered to make arrangements to go with her so Father could remain here to run the hotel. She had a fit. She felt I should give them the money, then remain here and run the hotel. I've no doubt in my mind that, had I done so, they would have continued to ask for money from California."

"No doubt." Uncle Harrison thought for a moment. "This really is getting us nowhere. If Herbert is going to steal from the hotel and set fires to hide his guilt, I can hardly keep him here."

"Well, we don't know for sure that he did it."

"Don't we? Where else would he have gotten the money?"

"Mother still has some jewelry. She hid it when they were forced from the house. He could have sold it. There are a few wealthy families in the area. He might have sought them out or maybe gone to one of the Santa Fe top men."

"I suppose that is a possibility."

Susanna knew they both wanted any excuse that didn't involve her parents. Sadly, they both knew that wasn't likely.

Inside the hotel, Susanna spoke with Manuel, then asked him to go let her father know he needed to come to the hotel but to say nothing about their visitor. Once Manuel was gone, she glanced at the journal she'd purchased in order to keep track of the hotel guests since the original guestbook had burned. "We have two gentlemen who will be with us through Saturday, checking out

Sunday morning. They're with the Santa Fe offices. Very nice men. Otherwise, the hotel is empty. I'll set you up in room 101, if you like."

She led him into the family quarters to show him their progress on the repairs.

Uncle Harrison looked around. "Room 101 will be fine. You should also know that I'm arranging for a fireproof safe to be installed. You will be the only one to know the combination."

"I don't think that's the way to go. Make Father the only one to know. Make a big announcement of it. He will see that he's the only one who has the information, and he won't be able to take money from the safe without everyone knowing it must be him."

"All right. We'll try it your way. I'm skeptical, however. He had no concern about teaming up with our friend in Kansas City for this new venture. He had to know word would get back to me."

"Is it a good venture?" She couldn't keep the hopefulness from her voice.

"It has its possibilities, but I don't think it will last. I believe they'll make some good money up front, but then within a few months it will all fall apart."

"Will you speak to Father about it?"

"No." Her uncle finished his inspection.

"This looks quite nice. I'd like to thank the men who have been doing the work."

"I can arrange that. If you can stay more than a day, we could have dinner together tomorrow."

"I can stay. Look, I think I'd like to rest before I meet with your father." He sounded so weary as they made their way back to the front desk. He was probably just as troubled and disappointed as she was.

She grabbed the key for his room. "Here you go. I doubt Father will hurry over. If he comes at all. We may have to go to him."

Her uncle nodded and took the key. "Come for me at four, if you would be so kind. Unless, of course, your father shows up before then."

"I will."

She watched him go, feeling sorry for the older man. He seemed so dejected. If her father was the one who set the fire and stole the money, Uncle would have to make some very important decisions. And how could it not have been her father? Perhaps that was why Gary was so upset about the whole thing. She would have to catch him after work sometime and see if she could get the truth out of him.

"*Hola*, Susanna."

Susanna looked up to find Lia in the lobby. "Is everything all right?"

"I thought I would come by and see how things went at the ladies' aid meeting."

"It went well. We're gathering blankets and quilts for winter to give to some of the poorer families. I wish I knew how to quilt so I could be working on one."

"Come on over to my house tonight. I'm putting together a tied quilt. It's much faster. I sewed large simple blocks together, and now I'm using yarn to tie it. It's a fast way to make a quilt."

"I'd like to come over, but my uncle is in town."

Lia's face sobered. "Is this because of the fire?"

"Yes. He's here to see my father." Susanna sighed. "Not that it will do any good."

"Never lose hope. God has changed people who were even more difficult." Lia smiled and put her arm around Susanna's shoulder. "God can work through you to change your parents. You must be strong."

"I just don't know that I can endure that long. So many things are wrong."

"And God can help with all of it." Lia squeezed Susanna in her embrace, then let go. "You must believe and trust Him for the answers."

"Uncle Harrison is here," Susanna told her brother when he came home from work. "He's come to talk to Father about the fire."

Gary looked at the floor. "What about it? It happened, and the damage has been repaired." He glanced back up. "Are you heading over to see the folks now?"

"Yes. I wasn't sure if you wanted to come with us. It might help you to share in the discussion."

"The arguing, you mean? No thanks. I've had enough of that. I'm going to clean up and go play poker. I have tomorrow off and plan to play all night if the games go on that long."

"Be careful you don't lose all your money."

"I won't. I have most of it in the bank. I'm not as stupid as Father."

"Gary, that's hardly called for. Just be patient. I'm sure in time Father will come to his senses and see that Uncle Harrison has been right all along. It's hard, as we both know, to see our own folly."

"You always think the best of everybody, but there are people out there who just want to hurt you. They don't care about your well-being."

"You talk like someone who knows."

"We both know. We were both hurt by Father and Mother."

"But they are our parents, and we should honor them as the Bible says."

Gary gave a loud huff and headed for his bedroom. "I think even God would agree they don't deserve honor."

"Why won't you tell me what's bothering you?" she pleaded.

He looked at her and started to speak, then closed his mouth and shook his head. "It won't change things, so why bother?" He walked away, not waiting for her reply.

Susanna watched him until he closed the door. When she turned, she saw that Uncle Harrison was standing in the open doorway of her living quarters. She didn't know how long he'd been there.

"Are you ready to go to the house?" she asked.

He frowned and nodded. "I presume your father never showed up."

"No. But I didn't mention that you were here, so he probably thought I just wanted him to watch the hotel."

Uncle Harrison shook his head. "I fear this has all been in vain."

"I was reminded earlier that we must have hope—that God has changed even more difficult people."

"I suppose that's true, but I'm not sure I'll live long enough to see it. I may have to let

Herbert fail. We may both have to let them go their own way."

Susanna frowned but knew her uncle spoke the truth. Unless she was prepared to lose everything she owned, she would have to let them do things their own way. Could she do it? Could she watch the parents she loved make bad decisions and do nothing to help?

Susanna and her uncle walked to the little adobe house. It was nearly six o'clock, and she knew her parents would just be sitting down to supper. What would they do when they saw Uncle Harrison? Would her father confess what he'd done, or had he even done it? Were they misjudging him?

Susanna knocked lightly, then opened the front door. "Mother, Father, it's me, and look who I've brought to visit you." She stepped into the open area where her parents sat at a small dining table. "Uncle Harrison has come."

Her mother looked up and scowled. "What do you want?"

Susanna's father said nothing and stared at his plate of food.

"We thought we'd join you for supper. Lia said there was plenty. Here, Uncle Harrison." She pulled out a chair. "You sit, and I'll get some plates."

"We didn't invite you to stay," Mother protested.

"Perhaps not, but we must insist," Susanna's uncle declared. "There is much we need to discuss."

"I have no desire to discuss business over dinner," Mother replied, turning her nose up in a smug manner.

"Then we'll eat first and then talk," Susanna said, placing a plate in front of her uncle and another at the empty spot between her mother and father. She dished up pot pie and salad for both Uncle Harrison and herself. She noted her father drinking coffee and her mother's glass of iced tea. "Would you like to have coffee or iced tea, Uncle?"

"Coffee would suit me well."

Susanna nodded and went to pour him a cup before her mother could make a comment. The tea was already on the table, so for herself she merely brought a glass. She placed the cup and saucer to the left of her uncle, then took her seat and poured herself a glass of iced tea.

"Why didn't you let us know you were in town?" Father asked as he began to pick at his salad.

"I tried. We sent a boy to tell you to come to the hotel."

Susanna nodded. "Didn't Manuel find you?"

"He did, but I was busy with something else."

"So busy that you haven't been doing your duty at the hotel?" Susanna's uncle questioned.

"A variety of things have needed my attention. Susanna was able to manage without me."

"That wasn't our agreement, Herbert."

"I thought we were going to wait until after dinner to talk business," Mother interrupted. She put her hand to her head. "I simply cannot take this added stress. Susanna, please bring me a tray to my room. Make sure it has cake on it."

"Yes, Mother."

They all watched as Mother made her getaway. She didn't even bother to look back at them as she closed the bedroom door. Would she always run away from her problems in such a manner?

"I expect you to put aside any other distractions and be to work regularly from now on," Uncle Harrison said. He sampled the pot pie and smiled. "This is delicious."

"Lia is a very good cook. She's helping me learn some of her traditional meals."

Still Father said nothing. Susanna wondered if he would ever bother to answer. She decided to tell Uncle Harrison about her upcoming trip. She'd already told her parents, but the reminder wouldn't hurt.

"Father will have to take over, because Monday I'm taking a short trip and will be gone until Wednesday evening."

Uncle Harrison nodded. "I'm sure you've earned some time away. Where will you be going?"

"Albuquerque. I'll do some shopping and hopefully get a few things for the hotel. We could use a picture or two on the walls." She smiled and ignored the panic on her father's face.

"Well, that settles it, then, Herbert. You will be the only one around to keep things running. I'll expect you to be at the hotel first thing tomorrow so we can go over the new procedures the insurance company has asked for."

"Insurance company? You mean there was fire insurance?" her father asked, sounding more than a little hopeful.

"There was. However, the company feels confident that the fire was deliberately set. That makes it impossible to pay out until they have a done a complete investigation."

"Investigation."

"Yes. They are going to send a man down here to look over things. However, since the repairs have been made, I imagine he'll simply interview the staff and fire crew."

"Interview us about what?" Father asked.

"What you know about the fire, of course. Where you were and why you weren't on duty. Things like that."

Susanna thought her father might be sick. He looked so pale and uncomfortable. She took that opportunity to see to Mother's tray. It broke her heart to imagine her father guilty of setting the fire, but his appearance and fearful voice left her little doubt that he had done the deed. What would happen now?

16

On Sunday, Uncle Harrison took them all out to the Harvey House for lunch. Susanna took the opportunity to remind her parents that she'd be leaving for a few days.

"I'm taking the train in the morning."

"Where are you going?" her mother asked.

"I told you last week. I'm taking a few days off and going to Albuquerque. I'll be back on Wednesday. You'll have to see to the cleaning and laundry, Mother. Father will have his hands full with running the hotel."

"What?" Her father looked at her as if she were speaking in Spanish.

"I told you last week that I was taking this trip and that the responsibility for the hotel would fall to you two."

"They can manage it," Uncle Harrison

said, motioning for the waitress to bring more coffee. "This was their responsibility to begin with."

"I know nothing about cleaning a hotel and doing its laundry," Mother said, shaking her head. "I cannot learn it now—certainly not in time for your trip. You'll have to cancel."

"No, she won't. I've been after you to accept your responsibility, Gladys, and now you will have to."

"I'm much too weak to do so. I feel I'm coming down with something."

"Well, that is a pity, but the rooms will still need to be cleaned, and the hotel is fully booked tonight. All of the rooms will need attention tomorrow and the days after that."

Mother began to sniff and then to cry in full. "I want to go home," she said, pushing back from the table.

Susanna's father got to his feet and helped her from her chair. He glanced at his brother, then at Susanna and Gary. "I'm sorry. I must see that she gets home safely."

They walked away before anyone could speak.

Susanna watched them weave through the crowded dining room. She felt her anger stir. "I knew they'd do something to ruin this for me."

"No. You will go on your trip as planned," Uncle Harrison said. "I will see that everything is taken care of. I can hardly force them physically, but I can punish them financially." He pointed a finger at Susanna. "But you cannot interfere to make it ineffectual."

"What do you mean?"

"I mean, I plan to cut back on your father and mother's monthly stipend. Money seems to be the only thing they respect, and since your father has hardly been at work the last two weeks, he won't be paid for it."

Susanna knew they would be after her to make up for the loss. Her mother was still busy ordering finery from her favorite stores via catalogues, and Father went through money like nothing had ever changed.

"I don't know if I can be strong enough, Uncle Harrison. They nag, and Mother whines in such a way that it's hard to ignore."

Gary nodded. "You've no idea. I was glad to join Susanna at the hotel and escape it. I didn't even realize how bad it had gotten until I left."

"That's often the way it is. You don't know what you have until it's gone. That's what I wish your father and mother could learn. They've lived a life of wealth and comfort, and if your father had only listened to me—

come to work for me—he could still be living it. Instead . . . well, they have this."

The Harvey Girl brought dessert. Susanna asked her to prepare her parents' dessert to take back to the house. It would be simple enough to wrap the apple pie in waxed paper. The thought brought to mind her picnic along the river with Owen. She took a bite of her pie and smiled at the flavor and memory.

Uncle Harrison all but inhaled his piece. Gary, too, was quick to devour his, even though he'd eaten his entire meal and half of Susanna's.

When his pie was gone, her uncle sighed. "Look, I don't have high hopes when it comes to your parents, but I feel I have to try this last time to reform them. Especially your father. If I can at least get my brother to see right, I will happily put him back on his feet."

"You will?" Gary asked. "Does he know that?"

"I told him if he proved himself to me by changing his ways, I would use part of my own inheritance to see him re-established."

"You told him that and still he's making a mockery of this?" Susanna had known her father was being stubborn about things and her mother . . . well, Mother was impossible. But for her father and mother to know that things could be so different if they'd just mend their ways . . . it made no sense that they should continue to be so defiant.

"I've explained it to your father many times since he lost everything in Topeka. He simply will not receive correction, nor advice." Uncle Harrison shook his head and looked more sorrowful than Susanna had ever seen him. "I'm afraid to say this might well be the end of our family as we know it. I told your aunt that it broke my heart, but I might have to give your father what's left of his inheritance and cut all ties."

"No!" Susanna shook her head emphatically. "I couldn't bear for that to happen. We've so little family as it is."

"But I cannot help your father go on making those unwise decisions. Even your Aunt Helen agreed it was foolish. You might as well know that I've cut your father from my will. I'm leaving everything to Helen and to you two."

"What?" Gary perked up at this. "You're not leaving Father anything?"

Uncle Harrison sighed. "How can I? It would be foolish, Gary. He would have it squandered in less than a year at the rate he's going."

"You can't take Susanna to Albuquerque," Lia protested. "It's a dirty town with nothing of interest for her. It's much too wild. You cannot leave her to wander it alone—even during the day."

"But she's already planning to get away. She needs this time away from her parents," Owen said.

"There's not even a Harvey House there yet. I know they have plans for one, but it hasn't been built, and the hotels around the railroad aren't that great. Let her come with me and the boys. Since LeRoy is going with you to Albuquerque, we're going to the ranch. Susanna could come too. She'd have a lot more fun with us than sitting in a hotel room in Albuquerque."

"That does sound better. Especially after hearing about how unsafe it might be for her." Owen considered whether Susanna would be open to going with Lia. "I think she'd enjoy being with you. I'll talk to her tonight and see what she has to say about it."

"If you want, I can ask her myself. I could tell her all about what we'll be doing and entice her to come. While I do that, why don't you boys see about taking a couple days of vacation to tack on to the days you'll be in Albuquerque? Obviously, the shops here can spare you right now."

Owen laughed. "I think they can. I'd like a couple of days at the ranch. All right. You talk to Susanna. I'm sure you can convince her. While you do that, we'll go talk to Mr. Payne."

The next morning, they all boarded the train for Albuquerque with it settled that the ladies and boys would be staying at the Mendoza ranch.

"I'm so glad you agreed to come with us," Lia told Susanna. "I want so much to introduce you to my family and have you learn to make some of our traditional dishes from my mother and grandmother. They are the best cooks in the world."

"And we'll get to ride horses," Emilio told Susanna. "That's the most fun of all."

"I like helping Uncle Enrico with his tiles," John admitted. "I want to learn how to make them all by myself."

"John is the artist in our family," LeRoy said, smiling. He tousled the boy's dark hair. "I hope he makes us some new tiles for the patio. Every time he goes, he and Uncle Enrico make more. Little by little, we're expanding our patio."

"I'll make as many as I can. How many days will we be there?" John asked, eyes wide.

"A total of four," Lia said. She looked at Susanna. "I know you were planning to go back to San Marcial on Wednesday when Owen was going to head home, but the guys were able to get a couple of days of vacation time. I hope you and Owen will stay at the ranch."

"We'd head home on Thursday evening instead of Wednesday morning," Owen said, smiling. "I can send your father a telegram from Albuquerque to let him know about your change in plans. Please say yes."

Susanna didn't even think twice. "Yes."

They all laughed and cheered.

The ride to the Mendoza ranch wasn't far, and it had its own small station of sorts. The boys pointed out the sheep and horse pens to Susanna and told her about her uncle bringing the livestock there to wait for the train when he was shipping them out for sale. They seemed to know all about the routine of roundup and loading, and Susanna found it very fascinating.

"See," John declared as they stepped from the train, "look there. The pens have chutes so the sheep come up right into the boxcars."

"That must be very convenient. I figured the men had to pick them up and put them onto the train one by one."

The boys laughed hysterically at that and ran to share the news with their grandfather. *"Abuelo! Abuelo!"*

Susanna could hear them talking in Spanish and laughing. No doubt they were telling him about her silly notions. She knew better about the sheep but thought the boys would find it funny.

The train stayed just long enough to drop off Susanna, Lia, and the boys before continuing north to Albuquerque and the Santa Fe shops where Owen and LeRoy would spend the next couple of days working. Susanna immediately missed Owen's presence despite the excitement of meeting Lia's family, who'd come to bring them home.

Emilio Mendoza, Lia's father, stepped forward and welcomed Susanna graciously. "We are very honored to have you come and stay with us."

"I assure you, the honor is mine. How kind of you to take in a stranger at the last minute."

"You are Lia's good friend, so you are no stranger," Lia's father said. Then he added, "You are family."

Several others had come to welcome them. Mostly young men who Susanna found out were Lia's cousins, though one was her older brother, Javier. They managed the horses that had been brought for the boys to ride. Emilio and John squealed with delight at the sight of the saddled mounts.

"You brought my favorite horse," Emilio declared, going up to a brown-and-white paint. He gave the horse's nose a gentle rub.

Lia's father helped Susanna and his daughter into the wagon he'd brought, while a couple of the men loaded the luggage in the back.

Susanna gazed out across the open landscape. It looked like scrub and sand—nothing that would suggest a healthy environment for raising animals. But the farther they moved toward the river, the more things changed. It was clear that the Mendoza family had cultivated the ground and worked with the land to encourage grass and other growth. As they approached the large hacienda and other buildings, Susanna was amazed at the colorful ways they had painted the walls. The large hacienda was still adobe coral but had beautiful arches and walkways that bore colorful tiles and white trim. Beyond the main house were smaller adobe houses that had been painted yellow and blue or green and orange, with broad purple bands around the windows. Susanna had never seen anything like it.

"What do you think?" Lia asked.

"It's beautiful. I can hardly take it all in. It's like an oasis in the desert."

"That's exactly what it is. We have plenty of water, and Papa found ways to irrigate, so we have hay for the animals and fields where they can roam."

Susanna looked beyond the houses to the stables and outbuildings. There were more than a dozen large pens filled with horses.

"We just sent the lambs to market," Lia's father explained. "Next week we have a herd of horses headed to California. Real beauties. I think the new owners are going to be very pleased."

Lia nodded. "People come from all over the country to buy Papa's horses."

Mr. Mendoza brought the wagon to a halt and rattled off orders in Spanish. He helped Susanna down from the wagon and then Lia. He held his daughter in his arms for a couple of extra moments, laughing and saying something to her that sounded endearing. Susanna found herself jealous. What must it be like to have such a father?

Before she could take a step, the hacienda doors opened, and a flood of people rushed out to greet them. Susanna knew she'd never remember all their names, so she tried to focus on just a few.

"This is my *abuela*—my grandmother," Lia introduced. The old woman grinned up at Susanna. She was so petite, and her weathered, wrinkled face bore a hint of Lia's youthful looks.

"I'm pleased to meet you, Mrs. . . . ah . . ." Susanna looked to Lia, wondering what to call the old woman.

Before Lia could speak, however, the old woman spoke in English. "You call me Abuelita, just as Lia does. I will be your grandmother too."

Susanna smiled. "Thank you, Abuelita. That makes me very happy. I have no grandmother yet living." She felt so much a part of the family with that simple gesture of love.

"This is my mother," Lia said, drawing a beautiful black-haired woman close. She was surprisingly youthful. "Mama, this is Susanna. She is my dear friend."

The woman embraced Susanna. "I'm so glad you are my Lia's friend. You are very welcome here. You must make yourself at home."

"What should I call you?" Susanna asked as she stepped back from the hug.

"Call me Anna," the woman said, smiling. Lia's father had already instructed Susanna to call him Emilio, so it only seemed right that she would call Lia's mother by her first name as well.

They moved inside the house, with everyone talking at once. Susanna heard a mix of English and Spanish and had to laugh to herself. If she were to remain in San Marcial, it would serve her well to increase her Spanish lessons with Lia.

~

That evening, Owen and LeRoy walked to the company housing area. One of the small employee houses had been readied for them, and they were both ready to drop. Lucky for them, the house had an outbuilding with indoor plumbing as well as showers. They both took advantage of the facilities, then fell into their beds without even the slightest interest in doing anything else.

"I'm glad Susanna went with Lia. I couldn't any more walk around town with her right now than run a race. I'm so tired."

"Well, we worked ten hours straight. We didn't even stop for lunch—wouldn't even have had lunch if the boss hadn't taken pity on us and brought us those tamales."

"True." Owen yawned and rolled over. "Did you set the alarm?"

"Yeah," LeRoy murmured.

"What time are we getting up?"

"Too early. That's what time."

Owen smiled and let his mind drift. He imagined himself with Susanna at the Mendoza ranch. Maybe he'd propose to her there. He waited for that thought to shock him, but when it didn't, he smiled. He was in love with

Widow Jenkins. Who would have thought? He'd known her only a few months, yet he was ready to spend the rest of his life with her.

I love her, he mused. *I really and truly love her.*

"Did you say something?" LeRoy murmured.

Owen grinned. "Nothing. I was just thinking."

"Well, don't think so loud. I was nearly asleep."

Owen smiled all the more. Just wait until he told LeRoy what was really on his mind.

17

Susanna didn't know when she'd enjoyed life more. Even her days with Mark, although a blessing of love, were never as full of life and festivity. Lia's family seemed to make every day a day of celebration. If ever a family loved one another, it was this collection of people, and Susanna found herself wishing she were a real part of it.

Sitting in the shade of the courtyard, Susanna marveled at the variety of potted plants and enjoyed the coolness of the morning. The house spilled out into this oasis from every angle through large doors that folded back. It was an amazing way to bring the outside in or take their indoor areas out. Upstairs, her bedroom had beautiful double doors that opened onto a large porch that wrapped all the way around the second floor and looked down on the beautiful courtyard. It was an incredible place, and Susanna couldn't help falling in love with it and the family who lived there.

Lia appeared to disrupt her reflection. "Susanna, come now. Abuelita is going to teach you to make tortillas. She is the best of all of us. Of course, she's been making them for eighty years."

There was an outdoor kitchen area set up with tables and a long cast-iron griddle. It was clearly a homemade grill where the women could do a lot of cooking at one time. They brought their tins of lard and bags of flour and masa, as well as salt and baking powder. Susanna watched as the group fell into an easy rhythm of mixing dough and separating out little balls to use in the press. Abuelita liked to roll her tortillas with her hands and took the little balls of dough and very quickly rolled them into a thin circle. Susanna had only ever made a pie crust on two different occasions and was certain she'd be no good at this. Still, no one seemed to mind her mistakes.

As they worked, they laughed and told stories from their childhoods and lives on the hacienda. Lia's cousins told tales about how they would sneak off with Lia and swim in the river. Once they encountered a snake that they were certain was going to bite Lia, but her papa showed up out of nowhere and shot the beast. That was when they learned that even though they thought they were sneaking away, the adults knew what they were doing and took turns standing guard over them in case something happened.

To Susanna, it was wonderful to imagine that someone might care enough to watch over her that way. Then she had to smile. That was what God was doing. Pastor Lewis said God was always watching over them—taking care of each need for safety and protection.

Susanna preferred the press for making tortillas, but the ladies kept insisting she practice rolling the tortillas by hand. She wasn't very good at it, and Lia's mother teased her that if she couldn't roll a tortilla, she would never catch a husband. For some reason, that made Susanna try all the harder until she had a nice thin circle to put on the griddle.

They spent hours making stacks and stacks of corn and flour tortillas. Lia said they did this every few days because, with all the people who lived there, the tortillas never lasted long.

"It's no different than the mother who has to bake bread every week," Lia said as they sampled some of their efforts. The flavor was wonderful.

Next the ladies showed Susanna how to work with the chiles. There were many different kinds, and Susanna wasn't sure she would ever get them all straight. She paid special attention when Lia's mother showed her the long, skinny red chiles and told her these were some of the hottest.

"You will find we use a lot of these three," Lia said, pointing to a funny-looking collection of dried pieces. "These are ancho chiles. They are a little fruity and not very hot."

"They look like a dried prune."

The next ones Lia pointed out looked much the same, with their dark appearance. "These are mulato chiles. They are hotter and have a sort of smoky taste. And last, these are pasilla or chile negro. They are very much like the ancho chiles and not as hot as the mulato."

Susanna studied them. These were longer and skinnier. "I don't know how I'll ever learn to tell them apart. Are they always black?"

Lia laughed. "No. If you look closer, you'll see the ancho were red. They start out green and turn red. We grow them here in the courtyard."

"What about the others?"

"The mulatos are black—sometimes more of a dark brown—and the pasilla are black as well. That's why they call them *chile negro—*

black chiles. We will soak them and steam them to make them soft again in order to cook with them. These three chiles are very popular. So much so that Abuelita had Uncle Enrico make many trips to Mexico to bring them here. Finally, Papa said we should just grow our own, and so we do. Come, I want to show you something."

Susanna followed Lia to a part of the house she'd not yet been to. Lia opened large double doors and ushered Susanna inside. Overhead were lattices from which hundreds of bundles of chile peppers hung to dry. The room smelled glorious. Susanna looked around the large pantry. Shelves lined the walls and were filled with homemade canned goods, rows of dried herbs, and chiles that had been ground into powder form.

"This is amazing. How wonderful to have your own store."

"Papa even sells some of the dried and ground peppers. Not everyone has time to grow their own." Lia smiled. "Now you know why my food is always so good. We have done it this way for generations. Even before my great-grandparents came to America."

"It's wonderful. I love how you all work together." Susanna leaned back against one of the posts that held up the roof. "I have to admit I'm envious. There are so many of you all together, and you love each other. That much is clear."

"Don't envy. We have our problems, just like other families. When there are more people, there are just more problems. Uncle Enrico and my father fight all the time." She smiled. "But you are right. They love each other."

After the tortillas, John came to tell his mother that Uncle Enrico had invited him to work on the tiles.

Susanna couldn't help but get excited. "Oh, may I watch?"

Lia giggled. "Of course. I'm sure my *tío* wouldn't mind."

They left the house and walked past the smaller houses and the barns until they came to a large building at the far north end of the complex. The large sliding doors were open, and inside was such a variety of stuff that Susanna couldn't take it all in at once.

"Over there is where the tiles are drying," John told Susanna and his mother. "And over here is where all the painting is done. Down there," he pointed, "are the ovens."

"Lia, you have brought your beautiful friend," Uncle Enrico declared, coming from behind a tall drying rack. "I'm honored."

"I'm sorry to impose. I just wondered if I might watch you for a while." Susanna continued trying to see everything at once.

"We're going to paint designs today," John said, his voice animated. "This is my favorite thing to do with the tiles."

"That's because you are very good at it," Uncle Enrico told him.

The older man led them to the place he had prepared and found a couple of stools for the women to sit on. He and John had their own special chairs and claimed these at the table.

Susanna was fascinated as Enrico showed her the templates he had made for the designs. They were carved out of thin wooden sheets. She watched as he placed a tile and template together. Once they were positioned as he wanted them, he took a sponge dabbed it in black, then touched it to the template and tile. He did it so quickly that it only took a couple of seconds and the entire tile was done. He took off the template, and the clay tile beneath was decorated with intricate patterns.

"That is how I get the outline on the tiles. But today, John and I are painting. I just wanted to show you that because I was certain you would wonder how the design was drawn so perfectly."

She looked at the stack of tiles that had been stenciled and dried. "Yes. I would have."

"Much happens to the tiles before they

reach this place. The clay has to be mixed to just the right consistency. Then it must be pounded and kneaded and rolled out on the table."

"Just like tortillas," she said, laughing.

"Sí. These are my tortillas." Uncle Enrico chuckled and nodded to John, who had been waiting patiently for something. The boy picked up a paint brush and a tile as his great-uncle continued to explain.

"Once the clay is spread to the proper thickness, I cut the blocks. I created a cutting tool so that I can just press it into the clay and cut many blocks at once. When this is done, I let them dry. Eventually they will be baked and glazed and baked again, and finally they will be painted."

"They're truly so beautiful. I love the ones at Lia's house."

"I did the ones inside, and Juan has made the outside ones."

"Yes, he told me on the trip here. He was so excited to come and work again."

"I probably shouldn't have taken the boys from school, but this is school too," Lia said, smiling at her son. "I think these are things they should learn. Emilio works with the horses, and my father has taught him so much. He's a better rider than any of us and knows how to handle so many problems."

"At such a young age, that is amazing," Susanna said, marveling, as John was already focused on painting certain areas of the tile a beautiful blue.

"Papa always said that children can learn as well as adults," Lia continued. "They might not be as big or strong, but they are smart. The girls learn all about cooking and sewing when they are still quite young. We learn about horses too, even tiles if we are interested, or farming or building. Whatever it is, my papa always said it was important to be always learning."

After a horseback ride that afternoon and supper that evening, several of the family brought out instruments and serenaded the group with wonderful Spanish songs. Susanna couldn't understand the words but loved the rich baritone of Lia's father.

As she reflected on all the fun she was having, she realized she hadn't thought even once about her own family or the problems that awaited her in San Marcial.

When Owen and LeRoy finally arrived, the party was well underway, and Susanna was ready to forget her own people and beg to stay with Lia's.

"I've never felt more love and affection.

Not just for each other, but toward me," Susanna told Owen as they stepped into the courtyard. "I never thought family could be like this. Even Mark's mother and father were very staid and sober. Mark and I enjoyed each other's company, but it wasn't the same as what I have here with Lia's family and . . . you."

"I'm glad you included me," Owen said, taking her hand. "My family was no better than yours. In fact, worse. My mother died when I was twelve, and my grandparents finished raising my brother and me. Our father was a train engineer and never home—at least not for long. I could never do right by any of them, and I was a difficult child at times. I was so angry to have lost my mother. She was a good woman."

"So you were close to her?"

He nodded and looked up into the sky. "We were. She's the one who first told me about Jesus. No one else in the family even seemed to care. I can't honestly say what they cared about, except maybe my brother, Daniel. He was only two when Mama died, and my grandmother found her comfort in losing a daughter by spoiling her grandson. Daniel was never made to account for anything he did. I suppose that's why he didn't think he should have to own up to his mistakes as an adult."

Susanna shook her head as they paused to gaze into each other's eyes. A light rain had begun to fall. Owen pulled her along to the covered walkway and put his arm around her. He held her close. It felt so right, and Susanna couldn't help but sigh.

She laid her head on his shoulder. "I'm sorry you weren't loved."

"I always felt so alone. When my grandparents died, I didn't even cry."

She nodded. "I understand. I didn't either. We weren't at all close. I hate to admit it, but I'm not even sure I would cry if my mother died. Isn't that horrible? I feel like a terrible person."

"But you aren't," Owen said, turning her to face him. "You're the kindest and most generous soul. You've been a blessing to them, and whether or not they see it, I do." He pushed back stray strands of her hair as the rain fell a little harder. "You are an amazing woman, Susanna. You're all I can think about." He touched her cheek. "I've never known anyone like you."

"Nor I you. I have to admit that you've been on my mind a lot lately. I guess realizing that a family could be like this has made me reconsider how I feel about a lot of things."

"Like getting married again? Not just being friends?" He leaned in, and Susanna was certain he would kiss her. She closed her eyes and raised her lips.

"Owen! Susanna!" John called from the arched walkway that led into the house.

Susanna didn't think he could see them, but she pulled away all the same.

Owen answered. "We're here." His tone was irritated.

"We're having dessert. Mama says to come or you'll miss out."

The magic of the moment was gone, and Susanna knew the kiss would have to come another time. She started walking toward the house as Owen called back to John.

"We're coming. Tell her we're coming."

～

The next day Susanna enjoyed a long leisurely ride with Owen. Of course, young Emilio had to come along to show them where it was safe to ride and to point out all of his favorite places. They spied the large herd Lia's father had cultivated. The horses were beautiful.

She thought of her and Owen's impending departure and felt sadness wash over her. She wanted to stay here forever. She loved these people. How could it be that she could spend a lifetime with some people and not feel as much affection for them as she did for these in just a few days?

She and Owen had very little time alone. The men seemed eager to take him and LeRoy off to do things that only the men were invited to do. When they were able to steal a few moments, there were always dozens of people around, and slipping away was impossible. Before Susanna knew it, it was evening, and people were talking about them leaving in the morning. She pushed those thoughts aside, however. She didn't want to go.

After supper, the family once again brought out their guitars, violins, and other instruments and played. Several of the men, including Lia's brother, Javier, helped move the furniture back so that they could dance. Javier and his wife did a particularly attractive dance that Susanna had never witnessed.

Lia joined her as they watched. "It's a dance of courtship and love," she told Susanna.

"I could guess that for myself. It's beautiful. I always wished I could dance better than I do. I'm all right with a reel or slow waltz but not very graceful."

Lia laughed. "I love to dance. LeRoy, however, has two left feet. Big left feet. He is always stepping on me. So I dance with the girls. You'll see. We dance very well."

And they did, wearing beautiful dresses from their Mexican heritage. Susanna marveled at the skirt of the gowns, which were cut so full that the girls could raise them from side to side up over their heads to make a full circle.

It was a wonderful party, and Susanna found herself wishing it might never end. She thought briefly of what awaited her back in San Marcial. Her parents and Gary had probably been fighting the whole time with Uncle Harrison. If he was still there. Susanna wouldn't blame him if he'd left them to face their problems alone. They had asked for it in their bad attitudes and unwillingness to cooperate.

She could imagine the welcome she had waiting. Mother would whine and probably give Susanna a good dressing down. She would accuse her of deserting them and self-ishly considering her own needs over theirs. Father would probably make himself absent again, and the hotel and all of its work would once again fall on her shoulders.

She sighed as the ladies concluded their dance, and she gave serious thought to volun-teering to be a maid on the Mendoza ranch.

Owen sat beside Susanna, and all he could think about was asking her to marry him. He'd thought about it the entire time he was in Albuquerque, and his time on the ranch only increased that desire. He couldn't stop thinking about it and knew he had to ask her tonight, no matter what interferences or interruptions popped up.

A couple of Lia's cousins continued to play guitars and even sang a little from time to time. Others finished their dessert and cleaned away the remnants of the evening. One by one they left the house, and the number of people dwindled down to just LeRoy and his family, Lia's parents, and Owen and Susanna. With a romantic fire burning in the fireplace and a gentle rain falling outside, Owen thought there would never be a better time to propose.

He waited until everyone else had gone to bed, then drew Susanna to the sofa in front of the fire. "I thought we'd never have another moment alone. I know we won't tomorrow."

"No, that's almost certain." She sighed. "I wish I could stay here forever. I love it here. I loved it before you came and even more now that you're here."

He put his arm around her and pulled her closer. "I can't give you a hacienda like this or the big extended family, but I want . . . I want to give you myself."

She looked at him and smiled. "And I want to give myself to you. I never thought I would want to love again, but I really have no say over it. My heart has chosen to love, and it has chosen you."

He smiled and lifted her chin ever so slightly. "And my heart has chosen you. Marry me?"

Her smile widened. "Of course."

Their lips touched ever so lightly in a brief kiss. Owen wanted more than that, but he knew it was important for them not to get carried away.

"I love you, Susanna. I think I have since we were bound together by a jump rope at church."

She laughed and put her head on his shoulder. "There was something very special about that moment."

They gazed into the fire for a while. Owen wondered what she was thinking. He knew she was as content for the moment as he was, but both of them knew trouble and problems awaited them in San Marcial. This time he was the one to sigh.

Susanna pulled away and looked at him. She touched his cheek and smiled. "I love you, Owen. No matter what we have to endure, I know I can face it with you by my side."

He smiled. "I was just thinking that very thing. As long as we have each other and God, I believe we can manage anything that comes along."

18

Susanna's absence proved one thing to her father. He couldn't run the hotel without her. She was the one who kept it all together. Despite his brother's presence and ever-watchful eye, Herbert knew he would never be able to make do without help. Gladys certainly couldn't be counted on. She'd never worked a day in her life and wasn't about to start now. No, Susanna was key, and unfortunately, Harrison knew this too.

That night after eating supper at the Harvey House with Harrison, Herbert decided he would have to approach the matter. As they walked in the darkness back to the hotel, Herbert tried to work up his gumption, but Harrison started talking first.

"That girl who cooks for you certainly does a better job than the Harvey House.

Although I will say their food is without a doubt the best in restaurant quality."

"I agree. I've often thought about approaching Mr. Harvey and discussing the idea of expansion. I could help him to take his restaurants to other railroad companies."

Harrison huffed. "And what makes you think you're the first one to think of this? Don't you know he's been approached by every railroad in the country? He has some of the best people working with him and for him. Honestly, Herbert, I sometimes wonder about your ability to reason."

"You don't have to be cruel. I simply thought it an idea worth discussing with him. I suppose I should have known others would think of it too."

"That's the problem. You think you're so much wiser than everyone else, yet if anything you are more ignorant. You have only to look at your current situation to see the truth of what I say."

"Speaking of my situation, I feel there are things we must discuss before you leave."

What was the best way to approach the matter? Should he tell Harrison that Gladys was just too sick and the doctor had told her not to work? Perhaps if they could convince him of that, as they had hoped to convince Susanna, Harrison might let them both off the hook. Or if not, maybe he could convince Harrison to give him more money in order to hire more staff.

Manuel greeted them as the bells hanging over the hotel door rang out to announce their presence. The bells had been Harrison's idea to allow the staff to be busy elsewhere but hear whenever someone came into the hotel or left. Herbert had to admit it was a good idea. He just wished that he'd thought of it.

"Good evening, Manuel. Did we receive any more guests?" Harrison asked.

"No, señor. It's been a very quiet night."

The young man smiled and talked with Harrison while Herbert made his way back to the private rooms. Harrison had chided him for being unwilling to live at the hotel even for these few days, but Herbert had reminded his brother that he could hardly leave his wife at home alone. This was a wild town, and who knew what might happen. They'd had a terrible fight about it until finally Harrison stormed off, muttering that he'd stick around and man the hotel at night until Susanna returned.

Herbert had felt like he'd won the round until Harrison announced he would deduct four nights' pay from the stipend he gave them. He'd already docked a large portion for Herbert's admission that he'd been away more than he'd been there. That, added to the fact that Gladys wasn't helping in any way, left his brother quite angry and very vocal about them having their wages cut.

Of course, there was Susanna. Surely she would take pity on them. His brother had made it clear that she would be paid in her mother's stead. Herbert just needed to find a way to get her to turn her portion over to the family. They'd been having enough trouble trying to exist on the small stipend Harrison provided. A reduced salary was simply impossible. Susanna would have to understand and give them the money.

Herbert considered how it might be accomplished but couldn't help remembering the way Gladys had tried to fool Susanna into giving them money to go to California for a doctor. Herbert had thought his wife's idea was a good one. Susanna was quite tenderhearted, and he honestly thought she'd willingly hand over the money. Instead, she'd wanted to go with her mother to the doctor. It might have been different if they'd been able to talk to the doctor first—maybe cut him in on some of the money. But instead, realizing the doctor had no idea what they were doing, Gladys had known she would be found out. Of course, then she was found out simply by refusing to let Susanna do as she suggested.

Harrison came into the private quarters with Manuel on his heels. "I'm heading home, Mr. Ragsdale," the young man announced.

"Very well." Herbert gave him a nod. "Thank you."

"The hotel has four guests, Mr. Ragsdale," Manuel told him as he headed for the front doors. "They are all in their rooms. Good night."

"Good night, Manuel. Susanna should be back tomorrow."

"Thank you for your help, and I'll arrange for your pay, just as we talked about," Harrison replied.

Harrison watched from the door and gave a wave. Herbert could see no reason to be so friendly with the help. The minute you acted like a friend instead of an employer, they took advantage of you. And what did Harrison mean that he'd arranged for Manuel's pay?

The bells rang melodiously, signaling the boy's departure, and Herbert got to his feet. "What arrangements did you make with him?"

"I learned what you were paying him. I wonder how you would like it if I paid you the same." Harrison sat down at the dining table and picked up the newspaper.

"He's not responsible for all that I have to take care of," Herbert argued. Then he forced himself to calm down. He needed to figure out how to convince his brother to move them away from San Marcial to a better place. Perhaps now, with Susanna and Manuel, Harrison would realize he could send them elsewhere.

Herbert joined his brother at the small dining table. He leaned his elbows on the table and folded his hands. He pressed his chin against his hands, wondering what he could say to convince his brother that this punishment wasn't the answer.

"Harrison, we need to talk about this arrangement."

"What's to discuss?" his brother asked as he turned the page.

"It's not working out. My wife is sickly and miserable living in the desert. I'm unhappy myself."

Harrison dropped the paper and looked at him. "That misery is born of your own mistakes."

"All right, I made a mistake in my investment," Herbert admitted. "But it doesn't mean I should be punished for the rest of my life."

"I have no intention of punishing you for the rest of your life. I want you to learn a lesson. Unlike all the other times before, when you learned nothing and went on to do it again and again. There are consequences for your actions, Herbert, but all your life you have avoided them. Now you must answer for what you've done."

"I've learned my lesson. I have. I know that I should have listened to your counsel." Herbert knew what his brother wanted to hear and was ready to lay it on thick. "I was foolish. I realize that now. I've made my family miserable and unhappy. It's a wonder they're still with me. I think Gladys would have left me by now were she healthier."

"There is nothing wrong with your wife that a little honesty wouldn't cure."

"Well, I cannot say for sure that is true, but I know I have made mistakes, and that is all I can confess to. I know what you want me to understand now. Money is hard-earned, even amongst the wealthy. I haven't appreciated the mental work that has gone into securing decent investments and am ready now to accept that I was to blame for all that happened."

"I'm glad to hear you confess that, but I'm sure there's more that you might say on the matter."

Herbert shifted uncomfortably. "I'm not sure what else you want me to say, but I am sorry. I've told you that and am truly remorseful for my lack of wisdom. I am a changed man. I assure you. Losing everything has taught me a valuable lesson."

Harrison studied him for a moment, then frowned, as if disappointed in his reply. "You haven't exactly made good choices here."

"No, not always," Herbert admitted. "I'm not proud of my attitude, but I am working to do the right thing and to listen to your counsel."

Again Harrison looked at him as if waiting for something more. Finally, he shook his head. "I'm sure in time you will be much better at making decisions, but for now this is an important time of learning."

"But I *have* learned. It was never my desire to hurt you or our father." Herbert's mind raced to figure out what Harrison wanted to hear. "I was prideful and thought I knew best. I see that now. I was a disappointment to you both, but I just didn't realize that my ways were so flawed." He continued to ramble about his poor choices and how he wished he'd allowed Harrison and their father to teach him, all while watching his brother's face for any sign that he'd finally hit upon the right topic.

What did Harrison expect of him? Nothing Herbert said seemed to move him. Nothing seemed to prompt his own apologies for having forced this lifestyle change on Herbert and his family. Instead, Harrison sat there looking quite unconvinced.

"I'm glad you are finally starting to understand," Harrison said, putting the paper aside and getting to his feet. "I'm off to bed. My train is tomorrow, and I still want to write a letter to Susanna. I'll see you in the morning. Make sure you're here early just as we discussed."

"I . . . ah . . . who will watch the front desk tonight?"

"I will," Harrison replied. "There doesn't seem to be any other choice, does there?"

"Well . . . I could stay." A thought suddenly came to him. "I could stay here and send Gary to the house to keep his mother safe." Herbert smiled. Surely this would impress his brother. "That way you can get a good night's sleep and be ready for your trip."

"That's decent of you. Thank you. I'll retire to Susanna's room, then. Good night."

Herbert wanted to say something—anything—to stop his brother from leaving, but he remained silent. He had made clear his acceptance of his mistakes. Why couldn't Harrison in turn absolve him and return him to his rightful place? How long did he intend to leave Herbert and his family here in this hideous excuse of a town? He'd even made this grandiose gesture, and Harrison still seemed unimpressed.

With Harrison off to bed, Herbert at least felt free of his accusing stare. The constant expression on Harrison's face was disapproval, and Herbert could bear it no more. Perhaps the answer was to continue with the card games. He'd been able to win a nice amount on several occasions.

"How's it going, Father?" Gary asked, coming in for the night. He hung up his hat and jacket just inside the room, then sat down to pull off his boots.

"Wait!" Herbert smiled. "What about going with me to play a game of cards?"

"I've been playing pool all evening, and I'm tired. Dawn will come soon enough, and I'll be expected at work." He frowned. "Besides, do you have any money to play?"

"I have a little, and that's all I'll need. Come join me. We don't have to be long at it, but Harrison has taken up all my time today, and I need to put him from my mind. A game or two of cards will be just the trick."

Gary looked at his father and shook his head. "You don't need me to play, and I'm tired. I'm going to bed."

"Look, I know things haven't been right between us. Harrison and I had a good talk tonight, and I'm starting to see all the mistakes I've made. I want things to be better between us, son." He was quickly forgetting all about his offer to watch over the hotel to-night.

Gary sighed. "I suppose a couple of games will be all right, but no more. I don't want the night to get away from me, and I refuse to lose all my pay just so you can have a companion."

"You won't lose, Gary. You almost always win." Herbert gathered his hat and coat as Gary got to his feet to reclaim his.

"What about the hotel?"

"Harrison's here. Besides, we'll lock the front door. No one will be coming for a room."

An hour later, Herbert looked at what little money he had left. He had been so certain of that last hand, but instead, one of the other regulars pulled a straight and dashed Herbert's hopes of a big kill. Now he had another really great hand—a sure winner. He contemplated what he could do. He needed more money. He looked at Gary, who was folding.

"Gary, can I borrow ten . . . no, twenty dollars?" he asked, leaning close to his son.

"No." Gary looked at him like he'd lost his mind.

Why did everyone always have to be so judgmental? Gary. Susanna. Harrison. They all thought so lowly of him. Why couldn't they be supportive?

"Well, Ragsdale? You gonna call?"

Herbert looked at his resources. He didn't have enough to call. Maybe they'd take an I.O.U. But what could he place under lien? He owned nothing of worth. Gladys had a few pieces of jewelry left, but most were paste and not the expensive gemstones she thought them to be.

"Ragsdale?" The dealer gave him a hard look.

"I'm trying to think. I don't have the cash and was considering an I.O.U." There, he'd said it. Now he'd see what their reactions might be.

"What do you have that's worth anything?" the dealer asked.

"I . . . well, I was just thinking . . ."

"He has a house," one of the men declared. "A nice little place."

"You have a house?" the dealer asked, his hard look softening. He smiled. "Of course we'd take an I.O.U. on the house."

Gary poked his father in the ribs. "You can't do that. Think of the risk."

Herbert leaned in close to Gary. "But I have a good hand."

"But it's not your house," Gary replied in a whisper.

The words hit Herbert like a slap in the face. He stared at his son for several seconds.

Gary got up, shaking his head. "I would think having done this once before would teach you a lesson. I'm out of here."

A sick feeling bubbled up in Herbert's stomach. He knew he had little choice. He threw his cards facedown on the table. "Too steep for my blood. I fold."

The men grumbled and called him a chicken and other names, but Herbert followed his son out of the saloon like a whipped pup. How could he have honestly considered putting a lien on Susanna's house? He truly was as much of a fool as they all thought him to be. He was no good. No good at anything. He'd stolen from Susanna once before and he'd been ready to do it again . . . and all because he was certain he could make a killing on his cards.

"I'm glad you came to your senses," Gary said. His tone betrayed his disgust.

"I don't know what got into me." Herbert felt overcome with guilt. "I don't know what ever gets into me. I feel certain I have the upper hand on a thing, only to lose it all."

They reached the hotel and went inside as quietly as possible. Thankfully, there was no sign of Harrison having learned of his deception.

Herbert breathed a sigh of relief. He'd been concerned that Harrison might have gotten up and come to check on him, but there was no sign of his brother.

In the family living quarters, Gary quickly rid himself of his hat, coat, and boots and headed for his room. He paused at the door. "Don't ask me to play cards with you ever again. I am deeply ashamed of what you nearly did. You aren't to be trusted."

"But I didn't do it, Gary. Isn't that a good thing?" Herbert asked, hoping to smooth things over with his son.

Gary shook his head. "I wouldn't have let you do it. I would have told them the truth, and then they would have beat you to a pulp." He left his father staring after him in surprise.

Herbert didn't move for several moments. No one understood him or cared. No one. Gladys had only married him for his money, and over the years they had learned to tolerate each other and accommodate each other's needs, but not out of love. Without money in his pocket, Gladys would no doubt find a way to walk away from him. She would suddenly remember a cousin somewhere who needed her or arrange to respite in some distant sanitarium.

He sank to the table and buried his face in his hands. What was he to do? His own brother wanted little to do with him, and why not? Tonight he had nearly put his daughter's house at risk. He had known it was wrong, but he'd hardly been able to stop himself. If not for Gary, he would have done it. And lost everything once again.

There was no doubt in his mind that he would have lost. Nothing ever went his way. It didn't matter that he'd held a full house in his hands. Someone else would have had the winning hand. They always did. He was nothing but a loser.

＿＿＿＿＿

Guilt over how he'd treated his father made Gary uncomfortable as he tried to get ready for bed. He hadn't said anything that wasn't true, but anger had motivated him. He finally stopped fighting his conscience and went to apologize.

He found his father at the table, face buried in his hands, weeping. Gary had never seen his father cry and found it disturbing. He pulled a chair close and put his arm around the older man. He didn't know what to say or how to help him. It was clear he was broken and perhaps even contrite.

Gary whispered a prayer, although he'd never been much about praying. He wasn't even sure he was doing it right.

Help me, God. Help me say the right thing.

"I'm sorry I hurt you," Gary said.

His father raised his head. "I'm sorry I ruined your life. It's all my fault, but I don't know how to fix it. I've ruined everything."

Gary had never felt more awkward. What could he say? His father's words were true. He could hardly push aside the confession as unimportant. He was glad Father was willing to recognize his part in the matter. It made Gary feel better just knowing he was finally willing to admit his part. Yet at the same time, Gary felt as if he should say something.

"You . . . you made mistakes. We all do." Gary sighed. Those words felt woefully inadequate.

"But my mistakes have caused problems for so many people . . . people I care about . . . deeply."

Gary met his gaze and nodded. "They have, but it doesn't mean you can't try to make things right."

"But don't you see? I can't make things right. I can't. Nothing allows me to go back in time and do things the way I should have—to be the son my father wanted—the husband and father you all needed me to be."

Gary realized the truth in what his father said. A person couldn't go back in time and couldn't change anything that had already been done. What was the answer?

"I guess . . . well, the only thing you can do is . . . ask to be forgiven and start new. Start again and show yourself to be a changed man."

"But not everyone will forgive me. Not everyone will be willing to give me another chance."

"No, I don't suppose they will. But then, that's between them and God, and it's their choice. You can't make people trust you again, Father. You can't make them forgive you, and that's the consequence of what you did. Some will forgive you and give you another chance, and others won't. You'll just have to find a way to be all right with that."

Father looked at him for a moment, then shook his head. "When did you get to be so wise?"

"I don't think it's me," Gary said, feeling sheepish. "I asked God to help, and I think He just did."

His father wiped his eyes. "It's going to take His help to make this work. I know I don't have it in me anymore."

Gary nodded. "Owen once told me we have to come to the end of ourselves. Maybe that's what this is all about."

The older man nodded. "Maybe."

Gary started back for his room, and his father called out. He turned. "What is it, Father?"

"I know I don't have a right to ask this, but I'm trying to be responsible and keep the hotel tonight so that Harrison can rest for his trip tomorrow. Could you . . . would you mind spending the night at the house so your mother isn't alone?"

He seemed sincere, and Gary knew this was one way he could start to heal their broken relationship. "Sure. I'll go."

"Thank you, Gary. Thank you."

19

Susanna watched the desert landscape pass by the train window. She hated leaving the Mendoza ranch and the people there. The time away had given her a sense of family that had never existed with her own parents and Gary.

Owen had been snoozing in the seat beside her, but when she turned from the window, Susanna found him watching her.

"What?" she asked.

"Nothing. I'm just watching you and thinking how blessed I am that you're mine. What were you thinking about?"

She shook her head. "How I wish I never had to leave the Mendoza ranch. How I wish I'd grown up with that kind of family."

He nodded. "I've felt that way myself many times. They treat LeRoy like he was born to them, and when I started coming with him, they treated me the same way. My own father never had that kind of interest or love for me."

"Exactly." Susanna looked across the aisle to where the boys slept nestled against their mother and father. The train had been so early that rousing the sleeping boys had been nigh on impossible. Even Lia and LeRoy had their eyes closed as if trying to catch any last moments of rest before their day truly began.

Owen squeezed Susanna's hand. "Don't worry. We'll have our own family, and we'll make it special like that."

"But we don't have the extended family they have."

"Maybe we can borrow them from time to time," Owen said, grinning.

Susanna laughed. "Maybe. I just can't get over how wonderful their life on the ranch is and how happy they all seemed."

"They still have their issues and problems, I'm sure. We saw what they wanted us to see."

"Yes, but there was such a sincerity about them that I truly think we saw it all. Yes, they have troubles," she admitted, "but they deal with them openly and without malice and bitterness. My family only seems to know how to act in meanness and contempt. Even Uncle

Harrison's actions are out of selfish frustration to teach my father a lesson."

"Well, the Mendozas do love the Lord. That makes a difference. We might not all attend the same church, but I know Mr. Mendoza believes quite faithfully in salvation through Jesus Christ. His kindness and good works flow naturally out of his love for God. I think the rest of the family feels the same way."

"I hope we'll always put Jesus first." Susanna met Owen's gaze. "My family never did. We had our church pew bought and paid for and our faithful attendance record, but God's true presence has never graced our home."

"It will ours. You need to stop fretting." Owen smiled and put his arm around Susanna. "Oh look, it stopped raining. That doesn't mean there can't still be a flash flood, though. A lot of times the river will get a deluge up north, and it will come racing down here and overflow its banks. When the season is particularly rainy, you need to be prepared, because when a flash flood comes, there's no time to arrange for anything."

"It seems so frightening the way you describe it."

"It can be," Owen replied. "It's dangerous, to be sure. We had a bad one a few years back that left two feet of water all over town. Of course, it receded fairly quickly. Desert land has a way of absorbing the slightest bit of moisture. Just make sure that if we have more than a couple of days of steady rain, you get all the important stuff up to the second floor and then keep watch. That's pretty much all you can do."

"What do you do at the shops?" The train moved over a rough spot and threw Susanna sideways. Owen held on to her, however, making her feel safe and protected.

"There isn't always much we can do. If we have warning, we load up as much of the expensive equipment as we can and get the trains out of there. We definitely move out all of the engines that can run. If something happens, likely it will be fast, and there will be no time to let each other know that we're all right. Usually they'll telegraph from up north if the water breaks and heads this way, so sometimes we can get the women and children to safety up on the hill past Old Town, up by San Geronimo."

Susanna leaned her head against him, not caring that this public display was probably completely uncalled for. "You should talk to my father about it. I know I'll be the one to do the work, but he should at least have an idea of how to protect Uncle Harrison's hotel."

"And your house."

"I'm praying that maybe it could be *our* house." She sat up. "Uncle Harrison still wants Mother and Father to live at the hotel. If he insists and manages to get them to move, the house could be ours . . . at least until we can buy a hacienda." She grinned.

Owen chuckled. "It's good to know you've got this all planned out."

"Well, not all . . . but I've thought about it a lot in the last few hours."

He laughed all the louder, causing Lia and LeRoy to stir.

LeRoy looked over at Owen and Susanna. "Are we there?"

"Just about. Close enough to start gathering our things," Owen said, moving away from Susanna.

Lia stretched and yawned as John opened his eyes and scooted closer to the window. LeRoy gave Emilio a shake. "Time to wake up, son. We're almost home."

Emilio grunted and tried to curl up closer to his father.

LeRoy laughed and pulled Emilio onto his lap. "We're gonna be there in a minute, and I won't be able to take you to the Harvey House if you're not awake."

"You'll miss out on your favorite pancakes with berries and whipped cream," Lia added.

This perked up the boy considerably. He slid off his father's lap and joined his brother at the window. "We're almost there," he declared, glancing back at his parents.

Susanna laughed. "That got him awake."

"Works like magic," Lia said.

"Are you gonna join them at the Harvey House?" Owen asked.

"No. I need to check in with my father and make sure the hotel is still standing. Besides, the breakfast Lia's mother and grandmother fed us wouldn't allow for another bite."

"Best cooking in the territory." Owen leaned closer. "I hope you were taking notes."

"I did and then some." Susanna shook her head. "I could cook a few things prior to this, but not much. I've never been properly trained until these last four days. Goodness, I learned so much. I think I could even kill and dress my own chicken."

"Abuelita thinks every girl should learn that first," Lia admitted. "I could do it when I was just six."

"I can't imagine, but the next time you kill one, let me know. I want to come watch so I don't forget."

"Watch nothing. I'll make you do it."

They all laughed at this.

San Marcial appeared unchanged. The river was up, but the hotel and town were safe and free of floodwaters. Susanna sighed as she bid her friends good-bye on the depot platform. She wished they could all remain together, but everyone had their own jobs to do. Now would come the hours of accusations from her parents that she had deserted them and forced them to endure more than anyone should ever have to endure.

"Susanna."

She turned to find her uncle approaching. She smiled. "I see you're still alive and in one piece."

He smiled in return. "It wasn't easy, but to tell you the truth, I think we've made headway."

"What happened?"

"Your father is changed. At least somewhat. He hasn't admitted to stealing or setting the fire, but he did tell me, with no small degree of sincerity, that he can see how he failed and is trying his best to make amends."

"Well, that is encouraging."

Her uncle extended a letter. "I wrote you more in here. Feel free to write me with suggestions for the situation after you assess it for yourself."

"All aboard!"

"That's my train."

"You're going to El Paso?" Susanna knew the train would continue southward.

"Yes. I have business there. I'm considering another hotel. This time I'll make it out of adobe."

She laughed. "I told you so."

He kissed her cheek, then hurried toward the same passenger car she'd been on just minutes ago. She waited until he appeared in one of the open windows and gave her a wave. She returned the gesture, picked up her suitcase, then started through the depot just as the train began to strain forward.

She supposed it might be wise to read the letter before she saw her father, so she sat down in the tiny depot to open the envelope. Quickly scanning the lines, she was surprised to hear her uncle speak in a more hopeful manner, though he admitted the change in her father had only been present since he'd awoken that morning. When she'd left for the ranch, her uncle wasn't at all encouraged, but now he seemed to have a different outlook. What a relief. Perhaps her father had realized he couldn't continue going down the same road.

The last part of the letter explained that Uncle Harrison was headed to El Paso and would probably be back through in a few weeks. Susanna tucked the letter into her purse and headed for the hotel, feeling a little lighter than she had. If Father truly had seen the error of his ways, she might finally be able to reason with him.

That would just leave Mother to contend with.

~~~~~~

Herbert Ragsdale was waiting when Susanna entered the hotel. He actually smiled at her—something he hadn't done in a long time.

"Good to see you're back, Susanna. Did you see your uncle?"

"Yes. We passed on the platform. He tells me he's headed to El Paso. He's thinking of building a hotel there. Right on the border."

"I think him quite mad. El Paso has nothing more to offer than San Marcial does. I think he could make a great deal more money by choosing a larger town elsewhere, but I wished him well."

She smiled and put down her suitcase. "That was kind of you."

"Do you suppose we will have new guests this morning?" he asked.

"No. I saw no one getting off the train but us. LeRoy and Lia took the boys to the Harvey House for special pancakes, and Owen headed off to his place before work."

"Good. That will give us some time to talk. The guests I have here now aren't leaving for several days, so I don't think they'll need anything from me. Tina, the girl who helped in your absence, put out plenty of towels and washcloths, so I think they'll have everything they need."

"And if not, we'll just be a few feet away." Susanna picked up her case again and walked through the open door to the private quarters.

Gary was finishing some toast and ham. "I see you made it back," he said, then continued to eat.

"Yes. You look well-rested."

Gary swallowed as he shrugged. "I spent the night at the house so Father could tend the hotel last night. I came home for breakfast because there's nothing decent to eat over there." He picked up his toast. "Did you enjoy yourself?"

"I did." Susanna deposited the case once again and came to the table. She grabbed a clean coffee mug and poured herself a cup before sitting down across from her brother. "Life at the Mendoza ranch is different from anything I've ever known. Their concept of family is working together. They have the most amazing meals, with the women all cooking to create them, and then everyone eats and talks and laughs. After supper there was music. Lia's family is quite musical. Several play violin and guitar. It was really wonderful to be part of a family who loves each other so much."

She glanced up to see her father in the doorway. He looked so sad for a moment that she wished she'd said nothing. She decided not to make a big deal of it.

"Lia's uncle makes the most amazing tiles from clay," she continued. "It's a huge process, and Lia's son John is quite an artist. He can paint intricate designs on the tiles, sometimes from templates and sometimes freehand. I think he'll go far. Emilio, on the other hand, loves horses and plans to move to the ranch when he's finished with school so he can learn everything about having his own ranch. They have sheep too, but they were in a far pasture, and I didn't see them."

"It sounds like you had a good time," her father said, taking a seat at the table beside her.

"I did. It was good to get away. How did things go here? Uncle Harrison was in a very good mood when I met him at the station."

Gary tossed down the rest of his coffee and got to his feet. "I'm going to be late if I don't get a move on."

"Have a great day. Do you have a lunch?" Susanna asked.

"No." He stopped and turned around, a look of frustration on his face.

She smiled. "I'll bring you one."

Relief washed over him. "Thanks, sis."

He made a dash for the door and was gone. Susanna chuckled. He'd never called her *sis* before. It touched her in a way nothing else could have.

She glanced at her father, still feeling guilty for the happiness she'd felt with Lia's family. "So, you wanted to discuss something?"

"Yes." He picked up Gary's coffee cup and refilled it with coffee. After a long sip, he put the cup down and drew a deep breath. "I have a confession to make to you."

"All right." She tried not to sound too eager.

"I stole that money from you when it looked like someone had broken in. I was desperate for money." He paused and fixed her with a gaze she couldn't quite read. Was it remorse? "I also set the fire and stole the hotel money."

Her eyes widened, and she hurried to take a drink of coffee to keep from blurting out something she might regret. It had taken a lot of courage for her father to make this confession, and she didn't want to ruin it by saying the wrong thing.

The hot liquid calmed her a bit. She set the cup down and nodded. "Did you tell this to Uncle Harrison?"

"No. But I will. I think Gary knew, and I'm sorry to have burdened him with that knowledge. I'll apologize to him. But I felt like I owed it to you first."

"Why?"

"Because that wasn't all I did. Well, it wasn't all that I considered doing."

Susanna shook her head. "I don't think I understand."

"I was in a card game last night, and I nearly wagered the house."

She blinked. "*My* house?

He glanced downward, then back up to meet her gaze. "Yes. I was like a man possessed. Just like when I put our Topeka house in jeopardy. It's like a sickness, I suppose. I am determined, however, to beat it. If Gary hadn't been there, I'm not sure I could have stepped away, but I did. Because of it, I see myself in a new light, recognizing the horrible things I've done."

"I have to say, I'm not completely surprised."

"Oh, I'm sure you aren't. I think you've always figured me for the fire. I honestly hoped the place would burn to the ground and free your mother and me from this prison. I don't know what Harrison will say when I tell him. I'm hoping a few months of proving myself will soften the blow."

"He's gone to El Paso and will back through here in a few weeks. Maybe you can show him how much you've grown. Of course, he probably won't believe it unless you and Mother both are living here at the hotel."

"I know. That's my next step. I have to break this news to her and get her to understand that she must live here and help me."

"I can still help with the hotel," Susanna promised. "I don't mind."

"I know you don't, but the truth is that my brother is cutting our pay because your mother isn't doing her part. We barely made it on what he gave us as it was. If your mother is doing her part, then perhaps he'll give me back the full stipend." He got to his feet. "I'm heading over to tell your mother now. I hope you'll pray for me."

"Of course. I'll also take care of things here while you're gone."

"The guests who are here won't require any cleaning, and of course we don't change their beds unless they're here longer than a week. So you should be able to take it easy."

Susanna nodded. That was the one concession she could allow. If the same guests were to have the same room for a few nights, there was no need to change the sheets. "I'll be praying, then. I can give my full attention to it."

Herbert made his way home, anxious to speak to his wife while at the same time dreading it. Gladys would never understand, nor would she ever agree to do her part. He knew her mind would be completely set against it—and him—as she always was. No matter how much Susanna prayed, it would take an outright miracle to get Gladys to change from the spoiled woman she was.

He entered the house and was greeted by nothing but silence. They'd not been able to hire anyone to cook and clean for them in the short time Lia was gone, so they'd mostly been eating cold foods or getting their meals at the Harvey House.

The clock on the wall chimed seven. His wife was used to sleeping until ten and then taking her tea and breakfast. Sometimes in bed, when things were particularly difficult. Herbert knew that waking her to tell her how things had changed would not bode well, but he had no choice. He needed to get back to the hotel soon, and no matter when he told her, she wasn't going to like the news.

"Gladys?"

He found her still sleeping. For a moment he stared down at her, trying to remember a reason, any reason, they were still together. It certainly wasn't love—at least not the kind of love that promoted happiness. No, he didn't think it was love at all, but more merely being used to each other. The main thing they had in common was the last twenty-six years. There was little else. But folks didn't easily divorce. The world didn't encourage such things.

She stirred, and Herbert touched her shoulder. "Gladys. Wake up."

She opened her eyes. "What? What's going on? Why have you awakened me?"

"We need to talk."

"What time is it?"

"A little past seven." He pulled up a chair and sat down. "I know it's early, but it's the only chance I have. Susanna is watching the hotel for me."

"She's back? Oh, thank goodness. Hopefully that means Lia will be here soon."

"Probably after she gets her boys off to school." Herbert twisted his hands. "Look, I have to tell you something. Something has happened that has changed me."

"Changed you?" She looked at him as if he'd lost his mind. She scooted up in the bed. "What in the world are you talking about, Herbert?"

"I was responsible for the fire at the hotel. I haven't told my brother yet, but I took the money from the desk and knew it would be missed, and so I set the fire, hoping to cover up what I'd done. That was the money I used to invest in that project I told you about."

"Frankly, I don't care. I wish the entire place had burned to the ground." She shifted to make herself more comfortable. "I certainly don't want you telling Harrison. He'd probably have you thrown in jail to teach you another lesson."

"And he'd be right to do so. Look, I've been wrong. I've been foolish to believe I knew better than everyone else. We are going to accept responsibility for what we've done and do right by Harrison."

"What *we've* done? *I've* certainly done nothing wrong." She folded her arms against her body. "This is madness."

"We're going to move to the hotel and live there. We're going to take care of the place and prove to Harrison that we've changed—that I've changed. Then maybe he will reestablish us as we desire. It's our only chance to make things right."

"You're mad. Completely mad. I'm not going to live in the hotel, and I'm certainly not going to do manual labor. I wasn't born to that and won't start now. You do as you wish, but I'm staying right here. At least until I can figure out a way to leave."

"But don't you see? If we do as Harrison has asked and do it well, we *can* leave. He said that if I learned to manage things properly, he would set us up elsewhere. We hold the solution in our own hands."

"I've seen how much work goes into that hotel with the laundry alone. I cannot manage it."

"Well, maybe we could pay Lia to handle the laundry, but you could strip the beds and clean the rooms. Then, when the laundry has been returned, you could remake the beds. That wouldn't be so bad, would it?"

She looked at him as if he'd suggested she shoot the pastor. "You are mad. I think perhaps I will send a telegram to my dear friend Harriet in Denver. Perhaps I can reside with her for a time."

Herbert reached out to touch her arm, but Gladys jerked away. He frowned. "I know we haven't had a good marriage, but I'm hoping we can figure our way through this and get back on our feet again. Gladys, you're my wife, and if you want to return to the kind of life we had, you'll have to do your part."

"You have lied and failed to provide for me as you promised. Perhaps a divorce is a better solution."

His shoulders sagged. "Perhaps. I had hoped it wouldn't come to that."

Herbert got up and cast a glance over his shoulder. Gladys seemed surprised by his comment. Maybe she didn't really mean it.

He gave her a nod. "I suppose you'll do as you please. You always have."

20

Susanna was impressed by the change that had come over her father. He was spending longer and longer hours at the hotel and only occasionally asked Manuel to watch over the place. To Susanna's greatest surprise, her father had even taken to helping her strip the linens from the rooms and air out the bedding. She found she had less and less to do, which gave her more time to ponder her future.

Even now, her father was upstairs sweeping out the unoccupied rooms while Susanna ironed sheets and pillowcases. She imagined it wouldn't be long before Uncle Harrison came back through San Marcial and she could report the way her father had taken over his duties. Maybe then she would make the announcement about her engagement to

Owen. He didn't want to wait much longer to marry, and neither did she.

They spent most of their free time together now, and she wasn't sure why she hadn't told her family about their plans. Often they sat at the hotel, talking in hushed whispers. Her family had to be curious about what was being said.

Telling her parents about her engagement was difficult, however. She knew her father had guessed at their situation. After all, they spent every free hour together. Her mother, however, still wanted very little to do with Susanna. She made it clear that Susanna had wronged her greatly by refusing to fix all of their problems with her money. Susanna had tried to talk to her about Father and the change in him, but it was only one more thing her mother blamed on Susanna. Mother had even mentioned the possibility of leaving San Marcial and her marriage, and had told Susanna in no uncertain terms that if it happened, it would be her fault. Telling Mother that she planned to marry Owen and would need the house back would never set well. It might even completely end Mother's relationship with any of them. Susanna didn't want that.

"Hello?"

It was Lia, and Susanna put the iron on

the stove and called for her to join her in the family quarters.

"How nice to see you again," Susanna teased. "It's been, what, a whole day?"

They laughed. Lia had become a sister to Susanna in every way, even handing down wonderful Mexican-style clothes to her.

"I tried on those blouses you sent. They're wonderful. So much cooler than anything I brought with me."

Lia nodded. "They are wonderful. The cotton is so light and fine, and the design so much looser than most American clothes. It lets the air cool you so much better."

"I'm sure my mother will be offended that I'm wearing such bright colors." Susanna had put away her mourning clothes when they moved to San Marcial several months earlier, but her mother still thought it completely inappropriate. "She'll be even more offended by the plans I have with Owen."

"You haven't told your family that you plan to marry?"

"No." Susanna left her ironing and came to the table. "Why don't you sit, and I'll get you some tea?"

"I can't stay. I just wanted to pick up the bedding, since I finished up at your house and am waiting for a casserole to finish baking. I thought it'd be just as easy to come get it as to have you bring it. That way I can go ahead and get the laundry started."

"It's in the wagon under the stairs. I wanted to finish the ironing in the cool of the morning. Despite how much the days have cooled down, I'm afraid that's one habit that remains."

"So, when do you plan to tell them about you and Owen?" Lia asked. "I want to host a party for you."

Susanna considered this for a moment. "I don't know. I suppose I'll talk to Owen about it tonight. I think Father and Gary already know where it's headed, but my mother . . . well, she's an entirely different matter. What's her mood today? Maybe I should go tell her when she's alone and in a decent frame of mind."

"Oh, that's the other reason I stopped by. Your mother hasn't been well these last few days, and she's getting worse. She's been coughing a lot. I don't know if she should see a doctor or not, but she's been quite congested, and she's not eating as well as she usually does. She keeps telling me it's nothing."

"Hmm, maybe I should speak to Father about it."

Lia glanced around the room, then lowered her voice to a whisper. "They are sleeping in separate rooms at the house. He's taken Gary's old room."

"When he's not here," Susanna countered. "I was surprised when I found him asleep on the sofa a couple of nights ago. He said he just sat down to adjust his shoes before heading home and fell asleep, but I wondered at the time if something was wrong." She frowned and pulled off her apron. "It seems I'd better go speak to Mother. Come on, we can take turns pulling the laundry wagon."

Susanna and Lia put the sheets and pillowcases to soak and then made their way inside. Lia went immediately to tend to her baking, while Susanna wondered if her mother would receive her visit.

"I'll get the sheets washed and on the line before I leave," Lia told Susanna. "The casserole is for lunch and supper. It's egg noodles and chicken. I thought it would be easy on your mother's stomach. I also left chicken broth in the pan at the back of the stove in case she can't really eat."

"You're always so thoughtful, Lia. Thank you."

Lia smiled. "It is I who thank you. I'm glad for the extra money. LeRoy makes good money working for the railroad, but we have many dreams."

Susanna nodded with a wistful sigh. "Don't we all?"

Once Lia had left the house, Susanna made her way to her mother's bedroom. She thought again of the fact that her folks were sleeping apart. She supposed it wasn't that unusual. Her folks had had separate bedrooms back in Topeka, but she knew they had slept together unless one or the other was sick. Perhaps since her mother had a cough, she had sent Father to Gary's room.

"Mother?" Susanna tapped on the door, then opened it slowly. "Mother, it's Susanna."

Her mother was lying in the bed and looked flushed.

Susanna came to her side and frowned. "Mother, you look ill." Without thinking, she reached out and touched her mother's forehead as she had done with Mark when he was dying. "You have a fever."

"I know." Mother didn't open her eyes but pulled the covers to her chin. "I've been so chilled that . . ." She coughed, and Susanna could hear how bad the congestion was.

"Don't try to speak. You'll just cough all the more. I'm going to fetch the doctor. You need to be seen."

There was no argument from her mother. Not that Mother had ever protested when someone wanted to send for the doctor. When extra attention was involved, Mother was more than happy to accommodate.

Susanna found Lia behind the house, working with the sheets. "She's burning up, and that cough sounds terrible. I need to get her a doctor."

"Dr. Sanborn is a good one. He has taken care of us in the past. He's on Railroad Avenue just across from the depot."

"Yes, I've seen his sign. I'll go there at once and return as soon as I can."

"I'll be here."

Susanna hurried down the street, making her way toward the depot. Her mother was always complaining about one health issue or another, but this time it was real, and her father hadn't even mentioned it. Perhaps he didn't know.

She made her way into the doctor's office and found an older woman managing a small desk. The front room was decorated in a rather homey yet businesslike manner.

"May I help you?" the woman asked.

"I've come to see if the doctor could make a house call. It's my mother. She's very congested and has a fever."

The old woman nodded. "The doctor is out right now making rounds. When he returns, I'll have him come to her. What's the address?"

Susanna gave her the number and directions.

The woman nodded and smiled. "The old Medford house?"

"Yes." Susanna returned her smile. "I'm the woman who purchased it. Susanna Jenkins. My mother's name is Gladys Ragsdale."

"And your father is running the Grand Hotel with your help. I know all about you folks. I keep meaning to drop in to say hello and let you know about Dr. Sanborn. You know, just in case you had need."

"Lia Branson told me about the doctor. She said he was their physician and had always done right by them."

"They're such a great family. Those boys have impeccable manners."

Susanna laughed. "They do. They're precious."

"Doc delivered them both." The woman sounded quite proud of this fact. "He's my husband, you know. I'm Lilly Sanborn."

Susanna extended her hand. "It's so nice to meet you. I hope we shall meet again under better circumstances."

Mrs. Sanborn gave her hand a squeeze. "We shall. I'm already determined we will be good friends. Perhaps you and Lia could come see me some afternoon. We live just upstairs."

She pointed to a closed door. "Right through there."

"I'll check with her, and we'll send you word. For now, however, I'd better get back to my mother. She sounded terrible."

"Probably bronchitis. People often think you can't get such things in the desert. They're always coming to the southwest to cure tuberculosis and think nothing else can unsettle the lungs here. But we have all the illnesses the rest of the world has. Start boiling some water on the stove. That will help her breathe easier. The dry air is sometimes very irritating when it's bronchitis or pneumonia."

Susanna nodded and headed home. She stopped at the hotel just long enough to let her father know what was going on. He thanked her for getting the doctor and promised he'd get Manuel to watch the desk and be home when he could. Lia was already hanging the sheets on the lines when Susanna returned to the house.

Her mother was sound asleep but wheezing terribly. Susanna remembered what Mrs. Sanborn had said and put some water on the stove to boil. It was just starting to boil when there was a loud knock on the door.

She opened the door and found a man with a thick white mustache. He pulled off his hat to reveal equally white hair and smiled. "I'm the doctor."

"Dr. Sanborn. It's a pleasure to meet you, although I wish it were under better circumstances." Susanna ushered him into her mother's room. "Mother, the doctor has come to examine you."

Her mother opened her eyes and began to cough. She could barely get her breath, and Susanna hurried to help her sit.

"You shouldn't be lying flat," the doctor admonished. "That just allows all the mucus to settle in the lungs. Prop her up. At least forty-five degrees."

Susanna grabbed a couple of pillows from the other bed. "My mother's name is Gladys Ragsdale," she offered as she helped her mother get comfortably arranged at the new angle.

"Mrs. Ragsdale, I am Dr. Sanborn. I'm going to listen to you breathe and see just how bad this is." He pulled a stethoscope from his bag and put it against her back. He barely listened to her before declaring a diagnosis. "She has pneumonia. This is quite dangerous. I can hear it in both lungs."

"What can we do?" Susanna couldn't hide the fear in her voice.

"It will be important to keep her warm and propped up. Also strong black coffee.

She'll need to drink strong black coffee several times a day. The hot liquid will help, but moreover the coffee has properties in it that will speed up the blood and help open the lungs."

Susanna nodded. "I can see to that for certain. Is there any medicine she might take?"

"I have some cough syrup if the strain gets to be too much, but we want her to cough out the mucus so she clears her lungs. You can give her willow bark tea for the fever."

"I will." Susanna looked at her mother, who looked so helpless. She'd never witnessed her sick like this in all the times her mother had made a fuss about her health.

"I'll come check on her this evening," the doctor said.

"Thank you. What do I owe you?"

He smiled and put away his stethoscope. "We'll settle up when this is done with. The missus and I will be praying for her." He glanced down at Mother, who had already fallen back asleep. He gave a little nod and picked up his bag. "Keep her comfortable. Try to get her to take some broth later. She needs to keep up her strength. Chicken is best, but oxtail is a good alternative."

Susanna saw him to the door and then went to tell Lia what the doctor had said. Lia was so understanding and helpful. She promised to be there as much as possible.

"The boys will be home from school at four. I'll need to be there until LeRoy gets home around four thirty. After that I can come over for a few hours."

"I'd appreciate that. Just until we get some sort of routine figured out. I need to let my father and brother know what's going on too. We'll have to find a way to take turns taking care of her, but having you to help us will make all the difference." Susanna gave Lia a hug. "You truly are like a sister to me."

Lia nodded. "We'll be praying too. I know pneumonia is serious. Would you allow me to let the ladies from our quilting club know? They will get the word out to pray."

"I would love that very much. Thank you, Lia."

Susanna made her way back to her mother's bedside. She pulled up a chair and took hold of her mother's hand. She hadn't expected this simple movement to wake her mother, but it did.

"Susanna."

"I'm here, Mother."

The older woman struggled to breathe. The wheezing was terrible, and Susanna couldn't help but think back to Mark. He had been sick like this. His fever had raged, and his breathing had been so labored. Willow bark tea hadn't helped. Neither had the mustard plaster, nor the peppermint tea. Nothing had helped. Would it be that way again?

Her mother opened her eyes. "I'm afraid."

Susanna could see the sincerity in her eyes. "I am too. I'm praying for you, however. And Lia and I are going to nurse you the best we can. I'm going to make you some strong coffee. The doctor said it will help."

"What if . . . I don't get well?"

"Oh, don't talk like that. I'm sure you'll recover."

Her mother shook her head. "I'm . . . not healthy."

"You're better than you think. The doctor is coming back to see you tonight, so let's show him what we can accomplish. I'll get you some strong coffee, and after that some willow bark tea. We need to keep you drinking fluids. It will help bring down the fever."

Mother grabbed at Susanna. "But . . . what if God . . . is punishing me?"

Taking her mother's hand, Susanna did her best to offer comfort. "He's here for you, Mother. Just put your trust in Him."

"I was . . . cruel. Said things . . ." She gasped for air. "I'm not . . . good."

"No one is, without Jesus."

"Send for . . . the preacher . . . and your

father. I need . . ." She fell into a coughing fit, and Susanna helped her sit more upright until the spasms were over.

"I'll send for them, Mother."

She helped her mother lie back and then hurried to where Lia was finishing the laundry. "Mother wants Pastor Lewis and my father to come. Do you want to stay with her while I go get him?"

"Of course." Lia pinned the last sheet on the line. "I'm done here."

Susanna drew a deep breath and let it go slowly. "Dr. Sanborn said to get her to drink strong, black coffee. Would you make some and, if I'm not back when it's done, try to get her to drink it?"

"I will." Lia smiled. "Try not to worry. You've said yourself that she is a strong, healthy woman. We'll see her through this."

"I just keep thinking of Mark—my husband. This was how it was with him."

Lia took Susanna's hands in hers. "This isn't Mark, but if the worst happens, we'll all be here for you. You won't face it alone."

"I know that, but what I don't know is if Mother has made her peace with God. I think that's why she wants the pastor. I think she knows she may die."

Susanna went to find Pastor Lewis only to learn he was out at one of the ranches and wouldn't be back until late. Susanna considered finding another preacher but went back to the house instead. She had a strange feeling about her mother's condition. She'd had the same feeling when Mark died.

Father had come to check on Mother and then gone back to work, according to Lia. There was also a visit from a couple of women from church. They had heard that Mother was sick and wanted to help in any way they could. Susanna was touched by their kindness. No one in Topeka from their large church had bothered when Mark was ill.

The evening wore on, and Susanna continued to check her mother's condition and to wipe her brow with a tepid cloth.

"I'm going to . . . die," her mother whispered.

Susanna touched the cloth to her cheek. "No, you aren't."

"I've been such . . . a terrible person, Susanna. I'm going . . . to hell."

"Not if you put your faith in Jesus. You know what the Bible says. You've listened to the pastor's sermons. God doesn't want you to be afraid and alone. He's always been here for you."

"I don't deserve . . ." She began to cough, and Susanna helped her sit up for a moment.

"Mother, none of us deserve anything good. We're all sinners, the Bible says. You can put your trust in Jesus, though, and He will save you from hell. He openly welcomes each of us to seek Him—to trust and love Him."

She helped her mother ease back against the pillow. "You don't have to be afraid, Mother. Just pray and tell Jesus that you believe in Him and that you repent of your sins."

"But my sins . . . are too many. I've been . . . terrible."

"Your sins are no worse than anyone else's, and God forgives them all. You mustn't tax yourself on this. Simply pray and be saved."

Her mother looked at her for a moment as if trying to ascertain the truth of the matter. Susanna wished she could ease her mother's fears. She prayed silently for God to reassure her mother that this was the only way to be saved, and that He very much wanted to save her.

It was nine o'clock when the doctor returned. Pastor Lewis and Father came with him, as well as Gary.

Susanna collapsed on the sofa in the living room while the others were with her mother. She hadn't meant to fall asleep, but she couldn't help it. When she woke up a few hours later, the house was dark except for a single candle burning on the table.

"Mother!" she exclaimed and jumped to her feet. She hurried into the bedroom and halted just inside.

"I promise, if I live . . . things will be . . . different," her mother said in a raspy voice.

Susanna's father sat at her bedside with his back to the door. Neither had apparently heard Susanna approach.

Father held Mother's hand. "I promise you the same. I've learned my lesson. Losing everything, and now possibly losing you . . . I'm not the same man. I'll never be that man again."

Susanna smiled and backed out of the room. She curled back up on the sofa and closed her eyes. What a peace it was to know that God was in control.

21

Owen learned from Gary that Mrs. Ragsdale was sick. He hadn't seen Susanna the night before, and Manuel had told him she had business with her family. He wanted to be with her, but he thought perhaps her uncle had returned. He was expected at any time, and Susanna had been hoping to talk to him.

"I know Susanna would appreciate seeing you," Gary said. "She's hardly done anything but take turns with Mother. Father hired a girl to do her work at the hotel, and he's done plenty of it himself. I've never seen my father clean before, but he's doing it now."

"I guess a man does what he must when times demand it," Owen replied. "Do you think Susanna would mind if I dropped by the house?"

"I think she'd be hurt if you didn't," Gary said, smiling. "You two set a date yet?"

Owen was surprised by his question. "Did Susanna tell you we were engaged, or did you just guess?"

"Not much of a guess. You two seem so natural together."

"The sooner we marry, the better." Owen thought he saw apprehension in Gary's expression. "I love your sister. I hope you know that, Gary."

"I do. I wasn't sure I wanted you as a brother-in-law, back when you were my boss."

"And now?" Owen looked at the younger man. He'd grown up a lot since coming to New Mexico that summer.

"Now I know what kind of man you are. You're honorable and kind. You're patient, and that's something a lot of folks can't say. Not that Susanna has ever been one to try patience in anyone." Gary shrugged. "I guess it's something I notice because I've needed it a lot."

"So you would agree to letting me marry your sister?"

"She couldn't find anyone better. I'm sorry I didn't want her to marry you at first. I didn't want you to take her away from us. Susanna's the only one of us who has any sense."

Owen chuckled. "Was she always around, even after she got married?"

"No, not exactly. Mother and Father had them come to dinner a lot, so we saw them all the time. But, well . . ." He fell silent. After a moment, he shrugged. "I guess living in Topeka was something we all took for granted. Not just being rich but also knowing how things worked. Down here we know nothing, and yet Susanna seems quite comfortable. We've all relied on her since our arrival, and knowing that you took to her right away made me worried that we wouldn't be able to get through this without her. I only just figured that out."

"We will always be here for you. Susanna and I have no plans to leave the area. At least not right now. We'll help in any way we need to."

"If my mother dies, it's going to be really bad for Father."

"I'm sure it would be. Do you really think your mother is that bad off?"

Gary nodded. "The doctor says she's very sick and he doesn't know if she'll make it."

Owen frowned. "I had no idea. What are you even doing here? You should be at home with your father and sister."

Gary shook his head. "I feel better being here. I can hardly bear to just sit around watching and waiting. I need to be busy. Working in the shops keeps me so busy I can't think of much else. Especially if I'm going to get the right parts to the right people."

"Well, just know that if you want, I'll talk to Mr. Payne for you. I'm sure he'd give you time away."

"Thanks, Owen." Gary gave him a weak smile. "No one's been better to me than you."

When work was over, Owen hurried to clean up and get to Susanna's house as soon as possible. He was hungry but didn't want to take the time to eat. It was a good thing he hadn't, because the minute he walked into the house, he could see that the ladies of the church had been busy. There were food dishes lined up all over the kitchen.

"Hungry?" Susanna asked.

"I am. I was so anxious to get over here and see how things were going that I didn't eat."

"Well, we have plenty. The church women have been stopping by all day. I knew they did this when someone died but wasn't expecting it for us. However, Mrs. Lewis told me that when the wife or mother of a family was sick, this was their routine. I think it's a very nice one. Poor Father could hardly cook for himself." She handed Owen a plate. "Just help yourself. Gary's already been through here, so there's a spoon in a few of the dishes. Just use the same one for the others. It won't matter."

"How's your mother?" Owen asked, dishing up what looked like creamed chicken pie. If it was Mrs. Payne's dish, he knew it would be incredible. He'd eaten it at many a church covered-dish dinner.

"I really don't know how Mother is doing. The doctor says so little. I don't think he knows either."

"I'm sorry to hear that," Owen said.

By the time he finished gathering food, Owen's mouth was watering and his stomach was growling. Susanna had cleared off a place for him at the table and had even brought him iced tea to drink.

"You'll make someone a good wife," he teased.

"I already got me a fella picked out," she countered with a wink.

As Owen took his first bite, Mr. Ragsdale came out of his wife's sickroom. His eyes were red, and it looked as if he'd been crying.

Susanna stiffened. "Is Mother . . . did she . . ."

"She's still alive," her father replied. "It's just so hard to see her like that." He sat down opposite Owen at the table. "Your brother is talking to her now, but she's barely conscious.

Fades in and out. I don't think she knows we're here."

"I'm sure she knows." She turned to Owen. "Would you mind if I ran over to the hotel for a change of clothes? I'll be right back, and it will give you time to eat."

"Yes, of course," Owen said, and Susanna smiled and hurried from the house.

Owen ate in silence, not wanting to be a nuisance to Mr. Ragsdale. The man obviously had a lot on his mind.

"What are your intentions toward my daughter?" Ragsdale asked out of the blue.

Owen had just taken a mouthful and nearly choked. He managed to wash it down with the iced tea, then wiped his mouth. "I hope to marry her." He smiled. "If we can have your blessing, that would make us both really happy."

Ragsdale nodded. "I can see how much you care for her. I haven't seen her this happy since before her husband got sick and died. It happened pretty quickly. I don't know if she told you or not."

"She did. A terrible thing to go through."

"Yes." Ragsdale nodded and toyed with the edge of the tablecloth. "They'd been good friends since childhood. It was almost impossible to separate them."

"She said as much. I asked her to tell me all about him and their time together."

"Does it bother you that she was married before?"

"Not in the least. She's an amazing woman, and I'm just happy to have her in my life now. You said you hadn't seen her this happy for a long time. Keeping her happy is my desire and goal. I want to make a good life for her—give her children, grow old together."

Ragsdale glanced toward the bedroom door. "I loved Gladys from nearly the first moment our parents brought us together."

"I'm sure she must have felt the same." Owen continued eating.

"No." Ragsdale shook his head. "No, she didn't. She was angry. She didn't want to marry me, but my family had money and power. Her father was a politician—popular with the people, but he didn't have a lot of money. Gladys always wanted to belong to the elite society in our town and elsewhere. She wanted people to admire her. To look up to her."

"Well, certainly she has come to love you over the years."

"I'm not sure I can even say that," Susanna's father said, shaking his head slowly. "She's never been very happy. She was happy to spend my money and attend all the parties that my name opened up to her, but love was never a topic of discussion. But then, now that I look at myself, I don't see a man worthy of love."

Owen heard the sadness in his voice. He wished he could say something that might help, but frankly, Owen had never known much love himself. It was what had always drawn him to God. God was said to be love, and Owen craved love. His father and grandparents favored his brother, and Owen was pretty much left to raise himself. There was never even the slightest word spoken about love. His mother offered love freely to him, but that ended when she died.

"If I knew God better, perhaps I wouldn't feel this way, but I doubt even God would love me if He really knew me."

It dawned on Owen that this was something he *could* say, something to share that might change everything. "But He does know you. Do you know that the Bible says God knew you in your mother's womb? He told this to Jeremiah, but it seems it would be true for each person. I'm pretty sure God knows everything about everything and everyone. I feel confident He knows everything about you."

"You really suppose God knows about my

cheating and lying? About my unwillingness to receive wise counsel to the ruination of my family? And still He would want anything to do with me?"

"We're all sinners, Mr. Ragsdale. There's no one who is righteous. Not even one. Everyone needs to be forgiven and to make peace with God, and the only way that can be done is through the blood of Christ. He's the only way to God. The only way to love."

Ragsdale put his face in his hands and began to weep. Owen had no clue what to do. He prayed silently and waited for some sign, some thought to come to mind.

"I want to put my trust in God," Ragsdale finally said, lifting his tear-streaked face. "I just fear He won't accept me."

"The Bible says He's willing that none should perish, but all should come to repentance. It says that in second Peter, chapter three. *All* includes you, Mr. Ragsdale."

"But I feel so worthless." He met Owen's eyes. "I *am* so worthless."

"We aren't worthless to God. He sent his only Son to die for us. That makes us pretty special. So, what do you have to lose in repenting and accepting Him as your Lord and Savior?" Owen couldn't help but smile.

Ragsdale nodded. "Will you pray with me?"

Owen's smile widened into a grin. "Of course. I'll start out, and then you finish by confessing you're a sinner and that you want Jesus as Lord."

They prayed together in the stillness of the house. Owen had never felt so overcome with joy. Of all the things he had expected to feel this day, the intense joy that filled his soul was not one of those things. Praying with a lost soul—someone who was hurting to the point of death—and seeing them give their life to God was better than almost anything else Owen could imagine.

"I'm sorry for the mistakes I've made," Herbert Ragsdale prayed. "I'm even sorrier for the things I've done on purpose that I knew weren't right. Forgive me, please. Forgive me and be my Lord and Savior, amen." He looked up. "Was that good enough? Am I saved now?"

Owen nodded. "God hears the prayers of His children—especially when they are seeking Him."

The door opened, and Susanna returned. She looked at her father and then at Owen, and clutched a bundle of clothes to her breast. "What's wrong? Is Mother gone?" She rushed toward the room, but Owen caught her hand as she passed.

"Nothing's wrong. Everything is very

right. Your father just accepted Jesus as his Savior."

Susanna's mouth fell open. She looked at her father. "How wonderful! Oh, Father . . ." She placed the clothes on a chair and went to him. She put her arms around his shoulders. "Now things really will be different."

He pulled away and nodded. "I hope you know how sorry I am for all the wrong I've done."

She nodded. "I'm sorry if I've hurt you or wronged you, Father."

They hugged again, and this time as they pulled away, Ragsdale looked at Owen. "You have my blessing."

Susanna sat at her mother's bedside and prayed. She thought of all that had transpired earlier with her father and Owen. The peace she felt was like an assurance that things would finally change. She only prayed that her mother's heart had been transformed as well. Mother was so afraid of dying, but Susanna had tried to share all that she could to give her comfort. She couldn't force her mother to accept Jesus or to have a change of heart about life, but she knew God could encourage her mother in both areas.

She wished Owen was still with her. The

moment he had left, she felt his absence, like a part of herself had departed. She had fallen so deeply in love with him that she could hardly comprehend the way she felt.

Thinking of this brought to mind Mark and her marriage to him. She had loved him so dearly, but this was like falling in love for the first time. How could it be that way? Was it just because it was a different man—a different time and place? She used to talk to Mark from time to time, not knowing if people in heaven ever heard the things people spoke on earth about or to them.

Now, as she watched over her mother, she remembered their last conversation. Mark had been so weak, barely able to speak to her. Like Mother, his lungs were congested and full of fluid. But unlike Mother, he wasn't at all afraid. He knew exactly where he stood with God and had no doubts about his future.

Susanna smiled. "I'm glad you were so certain. So at peace," she whispered. "You didn't depart in fear but in celebration. It made all the difference for those of us left behind."

The clock on the dresser revealed that it was midnight. Susanna had already told her Father that she was going back to the hotel to sleep for the night. She was exhausted and would be of no use to anyone tomorrow if she didn't get some rest. Father had assured her that he and Gary would keep watch, and that if anything worsened, he'd send Gary immediately.

Susanna felt Mother's head one more time. It seemed cooler, and she seemed to rest more peacefully.

"Please, God, heal her," she prayed.

She headed into the living room only to find her father and Owen talking once again. She smiled at her fiancé. "I thought you were gone for the night."

"I couldn't let you walk to the hotel alone."

"Gary would have walked with me."

"Gary went to bed," Owen said, getting to his feet.

Susanna went to her father and kissed the top of his head. It wasn't a usual gesture, and it surprised him. He looked up at her in question.

"I love you, Father. Never forget that."

His eyes grew damp. "I did forget it, but now I won't." He stood and wrapped her in his arms. "I won't ever forget again."

Susanna knew if she stayed much longer, she'd break down, and they'd all be having a fit of tears. She pulled away and looked around for her shawl. It was hanging over the back of one of the chairs.

"I'll be here early," she told her father.

"Not too early, child. Unless something

changes, I won't need you until later. Get some rest. You've earned it."

"She will, even if I have to sit watch outside her door," Owen promised.

Susanna pulled her shawl around her shoulders and smiled. "I promise I will sleep until I awaken."

As they walked back to the hotel, Owen put his arm around her shoulders and pulled her close. "Your father said I could marry you."

"I heard."

"So once your mother is well, I think we should tie the knot."

"I agree." She gave him a drowsy smile. "Even if Mother doesn't make it, I still want us to marry soon."

He stopped and bent to kiss her. "I'm glad you agree. I don't know what I would have done if you had disagreed."

They continued walking toward the hotel.

"You should be home sleeping," Susanna said. "It's midnight, and your shift is just a few hours away."

"I talked to Mr. Payne, and he's given me the day off. In fact, I've got a room at the hotel. Manuel fixed me up. That way, if something happens and Gary comes for you, you can send Manuel upstairs to get me. I won't be far at all."

This time Susanna was the one to stop. She looked up in gratitude. "I love you, Owen Turner. You are the kindest and most thoughtful man, and I am so blessed to have you in my life."

"And I love you, Susanna Jenkins."

22

Susanna woke with a start. She could smell bacon frying. What an odd thing to smell at the hotel. If anyone used the kitchen here, it was almost always her. Gary might make coffee or toast, but he wouldn't fry bacon.

She got up and quickly cast her nightgown aside. She dressed in one of the Mexican blouses Lia had given her. It felt so light and loose that Susanna almost wondered if she'd be properly dressed. She pulled on a navy serge skirt and tucked the blouse in carefully. She drew on stockings and shoes, still unable to free herself enough to go bare-legged and wear sandals. Finally, she was ready to tend her hair. She braided her honey-brown hair into a single plait and tied it off with a dark blue ribbon. Some day she might try pigtails like Lia wore from time to time. Susanna had never had her hair braided in such a manner, even when she was a child, and she thought it looked rather youthful and fun. Still, wearing her hair down instead of precisely pinned in an orderly bun was a step she hadn't thought herself brave enough to make. Propriety was always expected of her, especially by her mother, and married women—including widows—didn't wear their hair down.

Opening the door to the family living area, Susanna was surprised to find Owen in the kitchen. She closed and locked her bedroom door, as had become her habit since the break-in, and crossed to where he was handling a cast-iron skillet full of bacon.

"So you're the culprit," she said.

"I was hungry and didn't want to go to the Harvey House for fear you'd wake up and find me gone."

"No word from Father?"

"No. I take that as good news, don't you?"

She considered it for a moment. "I suppose so. He might have thought it not worth waking me if Mother had already passed, knowing I'd find out soon enough." She frowned. "Why don't you go ahead and eat, and I'll head over to the house?"

"I made this for you as well. You have to eat to keep up your strength."

"There's plenty of food at the house, or did you forget?"

"I didn't, but I would like to have you to myself for a few more minutes." He put down the skillet and turned to face her. Smiling, he pulled her into his arms. She automatically raised her head to see him better, and Owen took advantage of it, soundly kissing her before she could speak a word.

Susanna melted in his arms and sighed. She was so happy to have Owen in her life. When he pulled away, she didn't want to leave his embrace.

"The bacon's going to burn if I don't get it out of there," he said.

She laughed and reached for an apron. "Let me finish, and that way we can get to my folks' place all the faster. What time is it?"

"A quarter past six."

She nodded and began drawing the bacon from the skillet. She arranged it on the plate Owen had ready, then put the cast-iron skillet to one side.

"I have buttered toast all ready. And coffee," he said, barely suppressing a yawn. "I was going to fry eggs once you got up."

"This is enough," Susanna declared. "Why don't we make little bacon-toast sandwiches and leave the coffee for Manuel and Tina? I really want to see how Mother is doing, and I won't be able to enjoy a leisurely breakfast."

"I understand."

Susanna took a piece of the buttered toast and tucked a couple of pieces of bacon in the middle. "There," she said, folding it all together, "the perfect breakfast on the go."

Owen took two pieces of toast and twice as much bacon and made a sandwich. "I guess I'm ready."

They opened the door to the front lobby and found Manuel sitting at the check-in desk. He smiled. "I see you got your breakfast."

"Yes," Susanna said, holding it up. "There's some leftover bacon and plenty of coffee if you'd like some. We're heading to the house."

Manuel nodded. "A quiet night is a good night, sí?"

"I like to think so." Susanna headed for the door. "I promise one of us will be back to relieve you."

"Don't worry. I'm happy to stay. I slept a little on the sofa. Mr. Harrison said it was all right to do when I had to be here all night." He quickly added the latter explanation.

"I'm completely fine with that idea," she assured the boy. "I sleep in my room when it's my turn to keep the hotel at night. Uncle Harrison put that bell in place," she said, pointing to the pull, "for that very reason. It's quite a loud bell."

Manuel smiled. "I'm glad you do not mind my sleeping."

"Do you have a lot of people to tend this morning?" Susanna noted it was nearly six-thirty.

"No. There are only two guests, and they're staying until Saturday."

Susanna nodded, feeling relieved. "I'll be at my parents' house. Just send someone to us if you need anything."

He nodded. "We will be fine. You'll see." He smiled, revealing crooked teeth. "Tina and I are praying for your family."

"Thank you, Manuel."

Owen opened one of the double doors and ushered Susanna outside. The day was pleasant, with clear blue skies overhead. All around them, the town was waking up and coming to life, and Susanna couldn't help but smile. She really liked this little town. The summer heat wasn't so very bad—at least not if one could escape into a nice adobe house. Of course, she hadn't tried the winter here, and others had warned her it could get quite cold. But surely no worse than Kansas.

"You're awfully quiet," Owen said as they approached the house. "Are you worried about what you'll find?"

"I suppose I'm anxious, not really worried. I just want to know for myself how things have gone. When Mark was dying, I would fall asleep on the fainting couch in the corner of the room. Each time I woke up, it was with that same sort of anxious curiosity. I wasn't really worried about knowing the truth. I just wanted to get it over with."

They knocked on the door, and then Susanna walked inside.

"Father, it's me."

He sat at the table, drinking black coffee, as Susanna knew he had done most every morning. He looked surprised to see her.

"You should still be sleeping. You've hardly been gone six hours."

"I know, but I wanted to see how Mother was doing."

He smiled. "The doctor was here at five thirty. Blessed man, I didn't know anyone made house calls that early. He said her fever has dropped considerably. He believes she's turned a corner and will recover if we are devoted to getting her through this."

"Of course we are." Susanna was almost offended that the doctor would even question such a thing. Then again, maybe it had been whispered around town that their family was enduring a difficult time with one another. Susanna hoped not.

"That's exactly what I told him."

"I'm going to see her," Susanna said, looking to Owen and then her father.

"Go. No one will stop you," Father replied. "I'm sure your presence will be good for her."

Susanna passed into the room and listened to her mother's labored breaths. Perhaps they were a little easier, but she was still very sick. Sitting in the chair beside the bed, Susanna took her mother's hand and pressed it to her cheek. She had never felt close to her mother. Was it too late? Could they rekindle their relationship and make a fresh start?

"Susanna," a barely audible whisper sounded. Her mother's eyes opened.

"Mother! How are you feeling?"

"Tired."

"Of course. Your body has been fighting off the pneumonia. The doctor says you've taken a turn for the better. Isn't that wonderful?" She smiled as she lowered her mother's hand back to the bed. "You still have a long way to go to fully recover, but we will be here to see you through."

Her mother offered a weak smile. Her entire countenance seemed different to Susanna. It suggested Mother really had made her peace with God.

A coughing fit started, and Susanna

quickly raised her mother forward and began pounding on her back with the flat of her palm. The doctor had mentioned that it could help loosen the mucus, and Susanna wanted to do whatever she could to make matters better.

Father came into the room. "Do you need help?"

"No, I'm fine. Mother woke up, and the coughing started."

"The doctor is bringing something over today if it arrives. It's something to put out medicine for your mother to breathe."

Susanna shook her head. "How is that done?"

"It's some sort of steam machine. I can't remember what the mechanism is called, but apparently there's a way to heat the water in the container, which then sends the steam into another chamber where the medicine is kept. Then the patient breathes in the steam. He said this will open her lungs and let her breathe easier. He ordered it several days ago, even though I said I wasn't sure I could pay. It's very expensive."

"You needn't worry about that, Father. I'll pay whatever it costs."

"And if she can't, I will," Owen said from the door. "We're family now, or very nearly."

Mother stopped coughing and signaled

Susanna to let her lie back down. Susanna first plumped the pillows, then eased her mother back.

"Is that better?" she asked.

"Much," Mother replied with another cough.

"I think, since things are better, I'll head over to work," Owen said. "You should have some time together as a family, without other people around. This was a real close call, and it makes a person rethink things."

Susanna nodded. "It does. Thank you, Owen, for being here for my family and for me. I'll walk you to the door."

"No. You stay here with your mother. I'm just fine."

Susanna didn't protest. She remained at her mother's side. Father brought a chair in from the other room and sat beside Susanna.

Gladys gave a very slow shake of her head. "I've made . . . such a mess . . . of things. I'm sorry."

Father nodded. "I've made terrible decisions, and my mess is just as big. I'm sorry, as well."

Susanna almost felt like an intruder. Her parents were fixated on each other, but given the placement of her father's chair, she couldn't get up and leave. With no other choice, she sat with her head bowed, quietly looking at her folded hands. That they were admitting their past mistakes gave Susanna hope, and she found herself praying for them both.

~~~

Owen began working on the latest project at the shops. He found it impossible, however, to keep his mind on his work. He was blessed to know that Mrs. Ragsdale was better. That would raise Susanna's spirits and, in turn, raise his own.

He suppressed a yawn and went in search of the stays he would need to repair this particular boiler. That would be just the first part of this job. They would also need to replace the firebox. It would definitely require his complete attention, so he needed to clear the cobwebs from his head now.

"Owen, you looked exhausted," LeRoy told him as they crossed paths.

"I am. I was supposed to take today off. Susanna's mother has been quite ill, as you know, so I was up until past midnight. I had a room at the hotel but couldn't sleep much."

"How's Mrs. Ragsdale doing?"

"She was better this morning. The doctor thinks she'll make it now."

"That is good news. Lia was heading over there once the boys were off to school." LeRoy looked Owen over and shook his head.

"You look done in. Why'd you come to work if Payne gave you permission to take the day off?"

"They need this boiler fixed."

LeRoy shook his head. "There are others who could manage it. You need to learn to let folks earn their keep."

"I know." Owen yawned and shook his head. "I thought I'd sleep well enough last night, but I kept waking up at every creak and footfall. I kept thinking someone was coming to get me." He yawned again.

"I think you should head home and get a decent sleep. The boomers can manage this. I saw the boiler. Most of the work is gonna be reaming and taping out those stays and replacing them. Hundreds of them are cracked, and you know it's gonna take a lot of time for each one."

"I thought the boomers were leaving for California today."

LeRoy nodded. "Their transfer was delayed for some reason, so they're here at least another week. Take advantage of that. I'm sure Mr. Payne would tell you the same thing."

"I'll be fine. Stop worrying over me like a mother hen."

His friend laughed. "Well, have it your way. Guess I'd best get back to work."

"Owen," Gary Ragsdale called, entering the shop, "I brought over that case of stays you ordered."

"Thanks, Gary. I appreciate you being so quick about it."

"No problem. What are you looking for now?"

"A couple of the tubes we had stored over here."

"Do you need help?"

Owen glanced at Gary. "No, I think I've got it. I just have to get a ladder. The tubes are up there." He pointed to the shelves before grabbing the nearest ladder and maneuvering it into place. It bumped into the shelving unit, so Owen adjusted it and started to climb.

"Watch out. I think you might have a problem with those iron sheets," Gary said, pointing up at the stack above the ladder.

Owen hadn't seen anything amiss but glanced upward just as the entire thing came crashing down, sending parts from other shelves in one direction and then another. He ducked to avoid being hit, but his foot slipped off the rung, and he went flailing to the floor as debris rained down upon him.

"We need some help over here!" Gary hollered.

Several men, including LeRoy, came running. Gary was already assessing the situation.

"We need to get these iron pieces off the top first, and then we can move the sheets. Owen's beneath those. He fell off the ladder, so he's most likely hurt."

He directed one person after another, teaming up several men to move the larger pieces. It wasn't long before a new voice joined the group.

"Looks like you're doing a good job, Ragsdale," Mr. Payne told Gary. "Go get the doctor," Mr. Payne told one of the other men.

Gary hadn't realized the department supervisor was there. He was much too concerned about Owen's condition. He didn't know how any of them would manage to console Susanna if something happened to Owen.

Gary gave Payne a nod and then went back to work clearing the debris. Owen moaned as they removed the last piece, an iron bar that probably weighed forty pounds.

"You're bleeding," Gary told him. "Don't try to get to your feet. Just sit up, and we'll see how bad it is."

Gary took out a handkerchief and wiped the blood from Owen's forehead. "There's a pretty nasty gash along your hairline." He put pressure on the wound with his left hand while holding the back of Owen's head with his right. He soon realized his right hand was wet. "Looks like you have another wound on the back." Gary pulled his hand away, but he couldn't see very well because Owen's hair was matted with blood. "Does someone have another handkerchief?"

Mr. Payne was quick to provide one, and Gary placed it against the back of Owen's head and resumed holding pressure.

When the doctor arrived, Gary stepped aside. The doctor directed the men to bring a stretcher and take Owen to the little company hospital. Owen insisted he could walk, but when he got to his feet, he wasn't at all steady and gave up the fight.

"You did a good job, Gary. You took charge and got things organized. I'm impressed with you a little more each day," Mr. Payne declared.

Gary wasn't used to anyone's praise. He felt his face flush. "Thank you, sir." He wasn't sure what else he could say.

"Keep up the good work, son. I believe you're going to go far."

A swell of pride caused Gary to straighten his stance. He watched Mr. Payne walk away. The supervisor couldn't possibly know how much his words had meant to Gary, but sometimes a person just needed to hear that they were of value—that they were serving a purpose.

⁓

Susanna had never been to Owen's house before. It was a small place in a row of connected houses for company workers. They varied in size but weren't much to look at. The renters relied on the outdoor pump for water and privies in the back.

She found his home and knocked on the door. LeRoy had already told her what happened. He'd come to her directly after work. Susanna had been horrified to hear the news and wanted to go immediately to see Owen, but LeRoy suggested, since Owen was back from the hospital, that she wait until Gary could accompany her for the sake of her reputation. Most of the company places housed only men, but there were a few families here and there. Still, LeRoy thought it better for her to have an escort. He had to return home to Lia and the boys but offered to take her the next day. Susanna didn't want to wait that long.

She got directions to the place, telling LeRoy she wasn't sure Gary had ever been there. Then, once LeRoy had gone, she pulled on her shawl and told her father she'd be back as soon as possible. She wasn't concerned with what people thought. She needed to see Owen for herself.

She knocked on Owen's door and wasn't surprised when he opened it himself. His head was bandaged, but his eyes were clear.

She gave a nod. "I heard you were in an accident and decided to come see for myself."

"I'm fine. Not to worry."

"I'm not worried, I just needed to see for myself that you were all right." She remained outside on the top step. "Does it hurt?"

"Some. The doctor gave me something for the pain, but I didn't like the way it made me light-headed, so I stopped taking it."

"It could be you're light-headed from getting knocked to the ground. LeRoy said not only were you hit in the head by some piece of iron, but you also hit your head on the concrete floor."

"Yeah. I always have to do it big when I do something. I have stitches in the front and the back." He grinned. "You wanna come in?"

"Want to? Yes. Will I? No. I don't want to get folks talking." She glanced down the row of houses. A bunch of children were playing in the sandy dirt in front of the house three doors down. One was pouring sand over the top of another, who squealed in protest. She smiled as they scattered and ran from the angry child. It reminded her of Emilio and John playing with their cousins.

"I'm sure Father would allow you to take Gary's old room at the house. I could take care of you there."

"I'm fine. Really. Doc said I couldn't work for a couple of days, but otherwise I should be fine." He reached out and touched her cheek. "Thank you for caring."

She frowned. "We really should get married."

He laughed. "Yes, we really should."

23

You look so much better, Mother." Susanna placed a lunch tray on her mother's lap. "In just a week's time you look more like yourself."

"I feel better. My lungs are finally free of that heavy feeling." Mother drew the napkin across her body and glanced at the choices. "This looks good."

"It's roasted pig that has been shredded into smaller pieces and mixed with seasonings and a special sauce that Lia's father created. I have to admit, I ate a large helping. If it's too spicy, I can get you something else, but I think you're going to like it. There's a piece of fresh bread and butter to eat with it. And for dessert, a nice egg custard that Mrs. Lewis dropped off."

"Those women from the church have

been so generous to us. I honestly don't know what to say. I've never met people like these."

"That's because you only knew higher society folks. I find that people who don't have to worry about having the best of things are content to have things that matter. These folks are that way. I've come to really enjoy them, and I know you will too." Susanna sat down and picked up the quilt square she was working on. "And they've taught me to quilt. I never knew I'd enjoy it so much."

"I'm impressed," Mother said, noting the piece. "It will make a beautiful quilt."

"You could learn too," Susanna encouraged. "I find it peaceful to do when nothing else is going on. I can sew and talk at the same time. When we get together on quilt day, we have such lively conversations, and I learn so much about the area and how to do things. I'm learning how to make a concoction that will help rid us of spiders at the hotel."

"I would like to know that as well. One for the spiders, as well as the other pests that tend to come into the house, would be wonderful."

Susanna nodded and refocused on her square. They sat in silence while her mother ate and Susanna sewed. It was so different from the past that Susanna couldn't help but ponder what the future would hold for them. Could they somehow have a close relationship? Could she trust her mother's change to include a love like Lia and her mother shared?

"You know, when I visited the ranch owned by Lia's father, I was amazed to see a side of family life that I didn't know existed. There were generations of people together in one place, including extended family members, and it was unlike anything I'd ever experienced."

"I can imagine. When I was very young, before my father settled on politics for his livelihood, we had an extensive family. Both sets of grandparents were alive, as well as some of my great-grandparents. There were cousins and aunts and uncles. We all lived fairly close together outside of Topeka. Most of them were farmers. One was a dairyman—my uncle Pete." Mother smiled. "He once taught me to milk a cow."

"Mother! I had no idea you knew how to milk a cow." Susanna grinned. She could see the amusement in her mother's expression. It was so strange after her years of snobbery and closed-off emotions.

Mother nodded. "I was quite good at it." She sampled another bite of the pork. "This is excellent. We often had pig roasts when I was young. Nothing smelled quite so wonderful." She met Susanna's gaze. "But so much changed when my father went into politics."

"How so?"

"He wanted to appeal to the elite. He knew he needed their money because he had his eye on being president one day."

"President?" Susanna couldn't imagine having a grandfather who was President of the United States.

"Yes. He had it all planned out. He would start with smaller offices and eventually become governor of the state. From there, he figured the presidency would be a simple thing if he had the right financial backers. By the time things became serious and he was actually running for governor, he decided I should marry into a wealthy family who would then be obligated to help him with his dream."

"So Father was chosen."

"Not so much chosen as appointed. My father put out word that he was looking for a man to marry me—an arrangement that would benefit both families. He would use his power to benefit those who were a part of his family. The Ragsdales were just one of several interested parties. I was basically sold to the highest bidder."

"Oh, Mother, that's terrible. I never knew this. I knew it was an arranged marriage, but I thought it was also for love."

"No, I hated having no say. I didn't love

your father. I wanted to make him pay. The early years of our marriage were sheer misery, I'm sorry to say. In fact, I'm so ashamed now to admit the woman I was then that it pains me to tell you about those years."

"You don't have to." Susanna looked at her mother. "I would never demand that from you. We all make mistakes and do and say things we regret. I wouldn't ask you to relive that for all the world."

"But there's something in my changed heart that requires it of me. I can't even explain it, but I feel that I owe it to you to tell you everything. A confession of sorts, I suppose. You see, I've never loved you as I should have. You were my firstborn and such a sweet baby, but I could not appreciate it. I was so full of hate and bitterness. The only thing that ever made me happy were the expensive things your father would do for me or give me, and even then the pleasure was short-lived.

"Part of our agreement was that I would give him a son, and he would bathe me in jewels and give me a beautiful house in a stylish part of town. I figured on only having one child, so when you were born a girl, I was devastated. For years afterwards, I refused your father's advances, but finally I realized I had to try to give him a son. Thankfully, Gary was born. You were nearly six. I rejoiced because I knew my duties were complete. I wanted no more of your father or, sadly, any of you. You only represented to me the arrangement my father had made."

"Did your mother not try to intercede for you?"

"No. Not even once. She loved my father and believed that it was a wife's role to be obedient, even when she didn't agree with his choices. The whole family was that way. It was part of their Christian beliefs, and I suppose that is why I was never fond of God or the church. I thought it was horrible that I should be sent away to marry a man I didn't love—one who didn't love me. And all because of my father's political ambitions and God's will. . . . Well, it was too much for me."

"That is terrible. I'm so sorry."

"I'm the one who is sorry. My anger and bitterness robbed me of having a relationship with you and Gary. I left you to the capable hands of the nanny and went about the business of showing off my new clothes and jewels, of making sure we were seen at all the right parties and political gatherings. My father died the year he ran for governor of Kansas. The doctor said he had a massive heart attack. I remember looking at the other people in the room and declaring that couldn't possibly be the cause of death because my father had no heart." She shook her head. "I was terrible. My mother was so broken by his passing, and I was no comfort to her. I was her only child, and all I could do was make the situation worse. I'm so ashamed." Tears came to her eyes.

"But you were hurt by what they'd done. While it wasn't right to hurt them in return, perhaps it does afford you a little grace for your actions—and understanding."

"Mother died shortly after Father. We never resolved my feelings. My grandparents and great-grandparents of course were dead by then, and much of the extended family had gone their own ways. I wasn't close to any of them at that point. I felt abandoned and betrayed by them all." She dabbed her eyes with her napkin. "I only tell you this because my hard heart did not come about without reason. Whether you see it as a reason worthy of my actions or not, I cannot say, but I want you to know that I regret the woman I was."

Susanna reached out and touched her mother's arm. "I believe you. I can see that you are a changed person."

"But we've lost all of those years."

"Then we must make the best of the ones we still have," Susanna said, smiling. "We must do whatever is necessary to know each other and love each other. I intend to marry

Owen and give him as many children as God deems. I want them to have a grandmother who loves them. I want a family that rallies around one another and can be counted on in times of trouble."

"I never offered you comfort after Mark died." Her mother's expression was miserable. "I don't know how I could have been so heartless. Oh, Susanna, I am so sorry. Please forgive me. How your heart must have hurt. I know how much you loved him. I was so jealous of your relationship with him. Even of the one you shared with your in-laws. I was so self-focused and mean-spirited."

"Mother, you were very broken. You endured much of your own grief. Being used in such a way was abominable. How unloved you must have felt, but now you know that isn't the case. Father loves you quite dearly."

"I know, and the truth of that only shames me all the more. He was always good to me. He knew I was unhappy and never pushed me to accept my situation." She smiled. "Maybe he should have. I know he didn't deserve what he got in me as a wife. All this time, while I was ill, I just kept thinking about it. What a terrible wife I've been. How I've humbled and berated him, and he's just taken it all in stride." She sniffed back tears. "Can God truly change me?"

"He already has, Mother. The old you would never have made such a confession. You are a new creation in Christ. Your way of looking at life and the people around you can be totally transformed. Yield it all to Him, and you'll be surprised at what can happen."

"I hope you're right. I know I don't deserve for any of you to forgive me."

"But we do. I'm confident that Father and Gary both feel as I do." Susanna had never known such joy. Was God truly giving her the family she longed for?

"But what about the women at church? I haven't been very kind, and they've done so much. Will they forgive my snobbish ways?"

"I have a feeling they will. Why don't we host a tea once you're up and about?"

"A tea? For the women of the church?"

Susanna took her mother's hand. "Yes. Let's host a tea, and you can speak directly to them. I believe your testimony would go a long way toward encouraging their forgiveness. I believe it will do their hearts good."

"But how embarrassing." Mother drew a deep breath. "I suppose I deserve much worse than embarrassment."

"I don't think you will be embarrassed for long. I believe you will receive complete love and forgiveness. In fact, I'm sure of it."

Two weeks later, after Gladys Ragsdale was completely recovered, she hosted a tea for the Methodist church ladies. The women arrived with smiles and comments of joy at seeing that she was back on her feet again.

Susanna watched this from the kitchen where she and Lia were putting the final touches on the last of the delicacies they'd created for the party. Lia carried the plate out to the table, and Susanna brought the cream and sugar for the tea.

"It's so good to see you, Susanna. When are you and Owen getting married?" Sylvia Payne asked.

"We settled on the eighth of October."

"That's in less than two weeks. Goodness, I need to get busy," the older woman replied.

Susanna laughed. "I'm not sure what you must busy yourself with, but it's going to be a very simple affair. We'll marry right after the church service, and then there's to be a covered-dish dinner. Pastor Lewis said he'd announce it next Sunday."

"I'm sure it will be a grand affair, even if you're not having a fancy wedding." Sylvia beamed at Susanna. "I'll be there quite happily. My husband and I have long wanted to see Owen settled with someone, and you are the perfect choice."

"Well, thank you. I'm glad you think so. Owen is definitely my perfect choice."

The ladies took their seats, and Susanna watched as her mother, ever the capable hostess, took over.

"Ladies, if I might have your attention for a few moments," Mother announced.

Everyone went quiet.

"First, I want to thank you for coming here today. I want to thank all of you for your kindness during my illness. The fact that you kept my family fed and checked in on me touched my heart in a way I can't quite explain." She bit her lip and for a moment looked as if she might cry.

Susanna whispered a prayer for her mother. She knew her confession would not be easy. Mother had made many of these women feel less than important, and now she would have to face up to her deeds.

"I didn't deserve your kindness. We all know this. I've treated you very poorly. As I recently explained to my daughter, I've been a hard and bitter woman all of my adult life, and I'm deeply ashamed of the things I've done. Without having God in my heart, I had little use for anyone, but especially people I perceived as useless to benefitting me. That was an attitude taught to me by my father, but I should never have adopted it. I should have found value in each person, especially when offered kindness and love.

"But you see, I didn't understand what love was. Love was so foreign to me by the time I grew up. I had known great love as a child, but my father made it clear that things had changed when I became a young woman. He had changed, and with that, the entire family changed, and love became almost unwelcome in our home."

Susanna heard hushed comments of pity and disapproval. She could tell by the expressions on the faces of some of the women that they had gone through similar experiences. Others just offered smiles of kindness and encouragement. They were good women.

"I won't belabor the point," Mother continued, "but I wanted to bring you here to apologize. When I fell ill, it was as if God forced a reckoning in my heart. I was drawn to the memories of times gone by and made to see myself through the eyes of others. I had a great deal of time to ponder the person I had become as I lay fearing my death."

Someone sniffed, and Susanna could see several of the women's eyes dampened with tears.

"I was terrified of leaving this world in that

state of bitter anguish. My daughter helped me find my way to the Savior. Pastor Lewis came later and confirmed the path, and my heart found peace for the very first time."

Susanna felt dampness on her cheeks and realized she was crying. She hadn't expected the tears, but it appeared everyone here shared her heart.

"I ask you to forgive me. The woman I was is no more, and I seek to be a loving child of God." Mother paused and released a breath as if she'd been holding it the entire time.

One by one, the women rose from their chairs to go to Mother. Susanna watched as they embraced her mother and cried in love over the lost being found.

24

How are you feeling?" Susanna asked Owen as he approached the hotel check-in desk.

"Much better. Doc took the stitches out. My hair is starting to grow in over the patch on the back where they shaved my head to put in the stitches. Doc told me I could just wear a cap or hat until it all grew back."

Susanna smiled and motioned for him to turn around. He did, and she noted the spot. Already it was disappearing. "It doesn't look that bad."

"Good enough that you won't be ashamed of me on Sunday?"

"I'll never be ashamed of you, and I would certainly never hold your appearance against you—especially after being injured in an accident."

Owen seemed pleased with her answer

and grinned. "Can you take a walk with me? The day is perfect, the temperature is pleasant, and the there's just enough time to get in a nice walk before sunset."

"I'll let my uncle and father know. I'm sure they can manage things."

She stepped into the back room, where her father and uncle were still talking. Uncle Harrison had arrived an hour earlier by train, and he and Father were still hard at it, discussing the hotel and going over the books.

"Father, Owen has come, and I'd like to take a walk with him."

"By all means," her father replied. "Will you two join us for supper?"

"Of course." She gave them a smile. "I wouldn't want to miss it."

She met Owen at the door and waited as he gallantly opened it for her. They headed down the street to Railroad Avenue and then turned left. Holding hands, they continued their stroll past the depot, then a few tenant houses for railroad officials, and on past the stockyards.

The river had returned to its normal levels, and there was no longer a threat of flooding, much to the relief of everyone in town. Everything seemed picturesque and lovely—like something from a landscape painting or perhaps even one of the Santa Fe's new calendars. Later the saloons would be full of railroad men drinking and playing pool, and the dance halls would sport music and dance, but right now everything was quiet.

"I like this time of day. The men have gotten off work and are busy cleaning up or eating dinner, so they aren't being rowdy yet." Susanna squeezed Owen's hand. "I was actually surprised to see you so soon—and cleaned up too."

"Mr. Payne and the boys insisted I leave early since we're getting married Sunday. They wanted to host a bachelor party for me tonight, but I told them no. I want to be clearheaded and without bruises or cuts for my wedding. So I left early and went home to clean up and finish packing. Are we still moving everything tomorrow?"

"Yes. Gary said he's made some new friends at the shop and invited them to come and help. It's not like there's that much to be moved around, but it's nice that he has decent friends. He's happier than I've ever seen him. Who knew manual labor could give him such a sense of joy?"

"Working hard and having something to show for it makes a man feel alive," Owen replied. "Everybody needs a reason to live, and Gary was going through life without purpose. He's a valuable worker now that we've found what he's good at. I've never seen anyone able to keep track of the details like he does. And, of course, he saved my life—or at least helped me overcome my humiliation."

She laughed and squeezed his hand. "Just don't play blackjack with him. Apparently, he can remember every card that's been played and estimate his chances."

"That doesn't surprise me. He knows where every part is and how many we have. Mr. Payne says he's going to promote Gary to assistant manager of the department."

"That's wonderful. I know it will please him and give a boost to his confidence."

They walked in silence for several blocks, then turned away from the river and started back toward town.

"Has your uncle decided what he's going to do with your mother and father yet?" Owen asked.

"No. I think he's just as dumbfounded by the changes as we are. I know he'll want them to prove themselves over time, but knowing how God has dealt with the two of them is impressive enough to know the change is real. Father confessed everything to Uncle Harrison. Told him about the fire and taking the hotel money. Told him about nearly wagering my house. Everything. He even told him some things I didn't know about. Mostly thoughts and feelings he'd had, but things I hadn't expected."

"Maybe now your uncle will be able to teach your father what he needs to know."

Susanna had prayed so hard that would be the case. "My mother wants us to all be close and have a family like the Mendozas'. Lia suggested we come to the ranch for Thanksgiving. She said her parents encouraged her to invite us all. I thought it sounded like fun."

"I'd like that very much. Anytime we go to the ranch, I enjoy myself."

"I think I'm going to enjoy just about any place so long as you are there." Susanna's voice was soft and full of love.

"I still can't get over the change in you, Herbert. A part of me wants to find fault and prove it's not true, but at every turn you seem completely changed."

"I suppose only time will really set your mind at ease," Herbert replied. He had known his brother would be hard to convince.

"Again, your reply only shows your sincerity. Tell me, what are your thoughts about the future?"

"Well, tomorrow we're moving into the hotel, as I told you. Susanna and Owen will move their things to the house, where they will live. Except for tomorrow evening, when Owen is staying with his boss. Minding all the proprieties for appearance's sake. Gary will stay at the house with Susanna." Herbert smiled. "Susanna is a very respectable young woman. I'm proud to be her father."

"You should be. She is a gem."

Herbert nodded. "Gladys and I talked through this. Susanna has been teaching her how to clean the rooms. We're not sure the laundry is something Gladys can manage, but Susanna said for the time being she would come and get the laundry each morning, then bring it back in the afternoon. While she's on her honeymoon, Tina will manage it alone."

"I think that sounds remarkable, given your wife would take to her bed anytime someone even suggested she do something resembling work."

"Gladys has changed even more than I have, if that's possible. Nearly dying completely altered her heart. She has spent hours talking to me in the evening, something we've never done before. She always despised me too much to want to spend time with me." Herbert smiled. "I can hardly say what this change has done for my spirit."

"I had no idea, Herbert. I knew she never wanted the marriage to begin with, but she convinced all of us that she was a dutiful and at least cooperative wife."

Herbert shook his head. "There was never a moment's peace between us. She hated her father for forcing her to marry me for money and decided that if money was all that mattered, then she would spend as much of it as possible. Do you know, the other day she actually offered all of her jewelry to me, suggesting we sell it and pay Susanna back for what she's spent on us?"

"That is transformation," Harrison said, looking amazed.

"I had to confess to her that much of what she thought to be valuable gemstones were nothing more than paste. I had already sold many of the jewels when I made some of my final investments. I'm so ashamed of the deception, but you know what? She told me it was immaterial—that she could not hold it against me when I had so much I could lay at her doorstep." Herbert looked at his brother. "It's like the scales have fallen from our eyes. How could I have been so blind—so caught up in risking everything? How does a man get that lost?"

Harrison looked at the cup of coffee Herbert had served him earlier. It had no doubt gone cold, but it didn't seem important. "I went through a time when making money was all that mattered to me," Harrison admitted. "I've never faulted you for wanting to make your own fortune. Only that you wouldn't listen to wiser men. The love of money has definitely been the cause of many troubles in our family. Thankfully, my dear wife has always been a sensible woman. She took me aside and told me that nothing mattered to her as much as our life together. She told me she would follow me to a shack in the mountains if it meant we could live together in peace and harmony. She said my constant worry about the financial world—the stocks and investments, the madness of it all—was what worried her. She didn't care if we lost it all tomorrow as long as we had each other. That truly amazed me, and I started to see that the money was changing me.

"I wanted so much for my family. It wasn't about doing better than my neighbors or impressing the world," Harrison said in a thoughtful manner. "It was always about impressing her. And to learn that she didn't care one whit about any of it made me realize my priorities were skewed."

"And now I see that for myself," Herbert replied.

"But it wasn't all your fault," Harrison surprised him by saying. "You were a pawn in our father's game. His desire for political power made him forget the importance of marrying for love. He didn't even remember that his own marriage was a love match—not an arrangement. He should have known better. What he created in you, because of his desire for power, was his own fault. I never quite saw it myself until now."

Herbert nodded and poured himself another cup of coffee. "Do you suppose he figured that out, and that's why he tolerated so much of my nonsense?"

"It could be. I suppose that makes more sense than believing him to be unreasonably tolerant. Maybe guilt is why he allowed you so much leeway, while at the same time safeguarding a portion of your inheritance."

"I wish I could have done well—impressed him as you did." Herbert felt a rush of regret. "That's really all I wanted to do. Impress the two of you. You were both so competent, so good at what you did. People respected you and looked to you for help. How I envied that. With every success you made, I envied it all the more. Then I would try my hand at something and fail and feel all the worse." He shook his head. "Frankly, I'm glad to let it all go."

"What are you saying?"

"My plan is to be a successful innkeeper. I will manage this hotel for you and live modestly and make a new start in my marriage. I am forsaking all of my interests elsewhere. Even the investment I made with the hotel money, which, of course, is failing miserably after what looked to be a tremendous start."

"So you plan to stay on and run the hotel?" Harrison's tone betrayed his disbelief.

"I do." Herbert looked his brother in the eye. "I can do this. I can make you proud and make this hotel a success."

"I must say, I never expected this. I figured you'd tell me how you'd changed and expect me to move you to California and set you up in a grand home with servants and luxury."

"No. Not at all. I want you to take whatever is left of my inheritance and invest it wisely. I place my trust in your abilities. I wouldn't mind discussing what's happening from time to time, but for now, I know you are far more knowledgeable and will do right by me."

Harrison just stared at him, and Herbert refocused on his coffee. He had never thought he could come to this point himself. It was little wonder that his brother was stunned into silence by his declaration.

A smile touched his lips. He had managed to render Harrison speechless. That had never happened before. All this time, it just took telling the truth and acknowledging his brother's abilities. Who knew?

The move the next day went off without a hitch. Susanna was surprised when Lia and LeRoy came to the house with several crates of tiles. Her uncle and father had arranged for them, along with the labor to install them, as a wedding gift. Susanna was so touched that she couldn't help but weep.

"It's perfect timing," Lia pointed out. "You and Owen will be heading to the mountains right after the wedding, so the house will be empty. They'll have everything set in place and ready for you when you return in a week."

Susanna hugged Lia, dampening her friend's blouse with tears. "I don't know what to say but thank you. I love those tiles. I even told Owen that I wanted to spend some money and replace the tile floor in the house."

"There are also tiles for the kitchen. We will be able to cover the counters and part of the wall. I think you'll be more than pleased when you return. Oh, and John wants you to know that he helped decorate some of the tiles that will be put in your kitchen."

"How wonderful. I'll be sure to thank him tomorrow after the wedding. And I'll write a letter of gratitude to your family right away."

"Or just thank them in person when we go to the ranch for Thanksgiving," Owen said.

"Yes. Won't that be wonderful? And Mother and Father and Gary have all agreed to come as well. I think it will do them a world of good. They're only going for the day, but I know they'll enjoy themselves immensely."

"They can always come back for visits," Lia said, smiling. "My family loves to have visitors at the ranch. My father always says, '*Cuanto más mejor.*' The more the better."

"The more the merrier," LeRoy added.

25

Amen," Pastor Lewis said, ending the Sunday morning service. He raised his head and smiled at the congregation. "Most of you are aware that we are now going to have a wedding ceremony for Susanna Ragsdale Jenkins and Owen Turner. Afterwards there will be a covered-dish luncheon, and if you forgot to bring something, don't worry about it. There's plenty to go around. The ladies of the church always seem to know what to make and how much," he said with a chuckle. "Susanna and Owen, if you would come forward now with your witnesses, we will begin."

The organist played softly as Susanna and Owen came to stand in front of Pastor Lewis. Lia stood with Susanna, and LeRoy with Owen.

"Folks, we are here to join Susanna and Owen in holy matrimony. These are two people who have proven to use great sense in their lives, and I've no doubt the good Lord has brought them together for the purpose of matrimony." He smiled down on both of them.

"Owen, will you have this woman to be your wife, to live together in holy marriage? Will you love her, comfort her, honor, and keep her in sickness and in health, and, forsaking all others, be faithful to her so long as you both shall live?"

Gazing at Susanna, Owen grinned. "I will."

"And Susanna, will you have this man to be your husband, to live together in holy marriage? Will you love him, comfort him, honor, and keep him in sickness and in health, and, forsaking all others, be faithful to him so long as you both shall live?"

Susanna couldn't help remembering her first wedding. It had been so lavish and beautiful. Her mother had insisted on fine Belgian lace for her veil, and her gown had been crafted from the best satin available. Now she stood here in a simple gown of pale blue. Nothing special, no expensive jewelry like her mother had insisted she borrow and wear when she married Mark.

Pastor Lewis leaned forward and whispered, "This is the part where you say, 'I will.'"

Susanna flushed and glanced at Owen, who had a questioning look on his face. She laughed nervously. "I will."

Pastor Lewis looked out at the congregation and wiped his forehead with the back of his hand. "Whew, glad we got that part figured out."

The people laughed, and Pastor Lewis continued. "Owen, repeat after me. 'In the name of God and in commitment to Him and to you . . .'"

Owen took Susanna's hands and repeated the words, looking at her with such tenderness that Susanna thought she might burst into tears.

The pastor continued, and Owen repeated, "'I, Owen, take you, Susanna, to be my lawfully wedded wife.'"

"'To have and to hold from this day forward, for better, for worse, for richer, for poorer, in sickness and in health, to love and to cherish, until we are parted by death. This is my solemn vow.'"

Owen repeated the words, and this time Susanna couldn't hold back her tears. As Owen slipped the ring on her finger, she did her best to control her emotions, knowing it was now her turn to repeat the same vows. Fortunately, she was able to do this without stumbling over the words as she had feared.

"This is my solemn vow," she murmured and dabbed her eyes with the borrowed handkerchief she'd gotten from Mrs. Lewis.

They had agreed it was much too dangerous for Owen to wear a wedding ring, given his job, so they merely joined hands again and looked at the pastor.

"Let us pray," the pastor said, reaching out to lay his hands on their shoulders. "Father, we seek a blessing for this couple, Owen and Susanna. You know them to be your children, Lord, and now they have pledged before You and this congregation to be faithful in marriage to one another. We pray strength and encouragement for them and ask for prosperity, health, and understanding for each. In Jesus' name, amen."

"Amen!" the congregation said in enthusiastic unison.

The pastor grinned and stepped back. "I now pronounce that they be man and wife. Owen, you may kiss your bride."

Susanna anticipated a quick peck, but instead Owen pulled her into his arms and kissed her for what seemed like much too long for a church kiss. When he pulled away, she was weak in the knees and had to fight against looking stunned.

The congregation cheered, and immediately the organ struck up.

"Well, we've done it," Owen whispered in her ear.

She nodded, regaining her composure. "There's no doubt of that."

He laughed and pulled her close as others came forward to congratulate them.

The weather was beautiful and made for the perfect lawn picnic after the wedding. Several chairs had been brought out for the elderly who couldn't sit on the ground, but most of the other families set up blankets on the grass so they could talk and visit with everyone at once.

Owen and Susanna had been given a special table and chairs near the food tables so that as people passed by, they could greet the newly married couple and offer gifts or comments. Given the congregation's generosity, Owen was glad someone had suggested positioning a wagon nearby for the gifts.

Mr. and Mrs. Payne came by after many of the others had gotten their food and presented the couple with their gift. Owen was deeply touched when Mrs. Payne pointed to her husband's full arms.

"We ladies made you a wedding-ring quilt. I had the task of finishing up the binding and wasn't sure I'd be able to get it done in time, but here it is."

Mr. Payne began to unfold it, so Owen jumped to his feet and helped him hold it up to show off the fine workmanship.

Susanna examined the piece in awe. "This is so beautiful," she said, tracing the stitches the women had quilted. The colors of the rings were varied against the white background, and Owen had never seen a finer quilt.

"Thank you so much," Susanna said, her tears streaming again.

The day had been precious to both of them, but Owen couldn't help wondering if her emotions had more to do with memories of her first husband than with him. He frowned and hid his face as he helped Mr. Payne refold the quilt.

Did she miss Mark? Had the ceremony stirred up old feelings? Owen had never really considered if Susanna had truly finished mourning for her first husband. She seemed happy enough, but was that just an act?

For the first time since he'd asked her to marry him, Owen had doubts. What if she saw Mark when she kissed him? What if she dreamed of it being Mark's arms that held her? Owen didn't want a ghost to be a part of his marriage.

He reclaimed his seat beside Susanna.

Why hadn't he thought to talk about these things in more detail before the wedding?

As the celebration wound down, Owen was still considering these things. He wanted to be happy and unencumbered by the past. He had fought through his own past feelings of inadequacy, but this was something new.

"It's time you two get over to the train depot. That southbound freight will be here in about ten minutes," LeRoy announced.

Owen got to his feet and extended his hand to Susanna. She studied his face for a moment but got up without question. Her parents and brother came to bid them farewell, and Owen forced a smile.

"You don't worry about a thing," her father said. "We'll have Gary live at the house while you're gone."

There had been several burglaries of late, and Susanna had commented the day before about her worries for the property.

"Thank you, Father." Susanna kissed him on the cheek. "And you too, Mother." She embraced and kissed her mother before turning to Gary.

Owen didn't hear what she said to her brother because Mr. Ragsdale had taken hold of his arm and was talking about his joy that Susanna had found someone to love again.

"You are very welcome in this family—

although," Mr. Ragsdale said, lowering his voice, "you know we aren't without our troubles."

Owen nodded. "We all have them." He hoped Susanna's love for Mark wasn't going to be one of them. He really should have talked to her about all of this.

Lia and LeRoy, along with the boys, hugged them and wished them well. They walked with Owen and Susanna to the depot and waited with them as the freight crept into the station.

"Sorry we couldn't get you a passenger train," LeRoy said.

"I've resolved that matter," Uncle Harrison said, smiling. He motioned to the back of the train. "They're going to attach my private car and then leave it at the Socorro station to be brought back with the next train." From Socorro, Owen and Susanna would take the spur line into the mountains toward Magdalena.

"The engineer knows to stop at 982.9," LeRoy added. "That's where they'll load your horses and supplies for when you head up to the cabin."

Owen nodded, recognizing the mile marker for the Mendoza ranch. "Please thank your father for his generous loan of the horses." Owen had been so blessed by the way people helped him plan their wedding trip.

"And Lia, thank your mother," Susanna added, "and grandmother and all of them for the food and things we needed to take with us. I'm sure I forgot to thank them after the wedding."

"It's not a problem. They know that your minds are on each other."

It didn't take long to add Harrison Ragsdale's private car to the train, and before he knew it, Owen was sitting in the regal furnishings with Susanna at his side.

"Goodness, that was exhausting, and we still have so far to go," she said, leaning against him. "What an adventure."

He didn't say anything. He still wanted very much to reassure himself that the past was behind them. But how could he ask that now?

"What's wrong?" Susanna said.

"Huh?" He looked at her. "What do you mean? Nothing's wrong." That was a lie, and he immediately felt a prick of conscience. "Well, not really wrong."

She turned to face him, her expression loving. "Tell me what's bothering you."

He nodded. "I . . . it's just that . . . well, I never thought to discuss Mark."

"Mark? My Mark?"

"Yeah, that's the problem. Is he still . . . your Mark?" Owen knew he sounded rather pathetic.

Susanna's face lit up with understanding. "Oh, Owen. He will always be my first husband, but if you think he's going to be the third member of our marriage, you are greatly mistaken."

Owen released the breath he'd been holding. "It's just that I know you two had a great love. You had a long time together as friends."

"Yes, we had that," she said, emphasizing the word *had*. "What we had is in the past. Mark was an important part of that time in my life, but you are my focus for the present and the future. I love you, Owen. You are my life and love and all that I desire."

He pulled her into his arms, his apprehension falling away. She was his. All his.

"I love you too, Susanna. You are everything to me—my very heart."

She lifted her lips to his.

Epilogue

MARCH 1901

Oh goodness, this house is hardly big enough for all of us," Mother declared as they gathered around the dinner table in Susanna and Owen's home. She reached out her arms. "Let me hold the baby."

Susanna handed her son to her mother and smiled at the way Mother—Grandmama, now—took to the infant.

"He looks a lot like you did, but there's an equal amount of Owen as a babe."

"You don't know what Owen looked like as a baby," Gary said, rolling his eyes.

"Well, if a feature isn't from Susanna, it has to be from Owen," Mother countered. She fussed over the blanket, and the baby watched her with bright blue eyes. "He's so attentive. You were like that, Susanna."

It was hard to imagine that her mother even knew such things, given their long discussion about her mother's aversion to parenthood. Still, Susanna was delighted to find her parents so caught up in the life of their grandchild.

Lia and LeRoy took their seats on the far side of the table with Emilio and John seated between them. Lia's large abdomen reminded everyone that she would very soon deliver another child. Susanna was so happy to know they would have children close in age. She hoped Lia's child would be a girl with Lia's beautiful features. Then maybe one day her son would fall in love with Lia's daughter, and they could truly be family.

As if they needed that kind of connection to make them so. In every way that mattered, Lia and Susanna were sisters.

Beside Lia, a new member of their entourage sat. Carmelita Mendoza had caught Gary's eye at that first shared Thanksgiving at the ranch. The two were now engaged, and plans for a summer wedding were the constant topic of conversation whenever the families gathered. There was no doubt their families would be forever united.

"I'd like to offer a blessing," Owen said, getting to his feet.

Everyone went silent, even the children.

Susanna bowed her head, but she kept her eyes open. She watched her mother with the newborn and smiled at the changes that had made life so much better.

"Father," Owen began, seeming to read Susanna's thoughts, "we thank You for Your many blessings. We thank You for the success of the hotel and of Mother and Father Ragsdale's management of it. We thank You for Gary and Carmelita's engagement and Lia and LeRoy's new little one who will soon join us, and for their boys, Emilio and John. I thank You personally for the safe deliverance of my son, Michael James, and for my wife's recovery. Lord, You have given us all so many blessings, and we are grateful. Bless this food, we pray, in Jesus' name, amen." He looked at the people gathered. "Let's eat."

They dug in, and when Michael began to fuss, Mother passed him back to Susanna so she could nurse him.

"You never said where you got the names for the baby," Gary said, surprising Susanna as she started to leave the room. "Is there some relative named Michael James?"

She glanced down at her son and then at the others. "There's no one we know with those names, and that was our point. A new start—with nothing from the past. Michael is the future." She smiled and headed to the bedroom to feed her baby.

She and Owen had nothing but hope for the new life they had together with their child. God had mended the past, with all of its problems and heartaches, and blessed the future with His promises. There would no doubt be difficulties, but Susanna knew they would never face them alone.

Tracie Peterson is the award-winning author of over one hundred novels, both historical and contemporary. She is often referred to as the "Queen of Historical Christian Fiction," and her avid research resonates in her stories, as seen in her bestselling HEIRS OF MONTANA and ALASKAN QUEST series. Tracie considers her writing a ministry for God to share the Gospel and biblical application. She and her family make their home in Montana. Visit her website at www.traciepeterson.com or on Facebook at www.facebook.com/AuthorTraciePeterson.

Sign Up for Tracie's Newsletter

Keep up to date with Tracie's news on book releases and events by signing up for her email list at traciepeterson.com.

More from Tracie Peterson

Fulfilling a promise to her dying mother, Elise Wright watches over her father as cook on his Great Lakes schooner. But the behavior of a new sailor unsettles her and first mate Nick Clark, who secretly begins investigating. When tragedy strikes, Nick and Elise must rely on their faith and each other as they confront their greatest fears.

Waiting on Love • LADIES OF THE LAKE

You May Also Like . . .

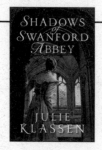

In pursuit of an author who could help get her brother published, Rebecca Lane stays at Swanford Abbey, a grand hotel rumored to be haunted. It is there she encounters Sir Frederick—the man who broke her heart. When a mysterious death occurs, Rebecca is one of the suspects, and Frederick is torn between his feelings for her and his search for the truth.

Shadows of Swanford Abbey by Julie Klassen
julieklassen.com

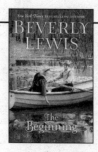

Susie Mast's Old Order life has been shaped more by tragedy than by her own choices. But when she decides to stop waiting on her childhood friend and accept another young man's invitation, she soon realizes her mistake. Will family secrets and missed opportunities dim Susie's hopes for the future? Or is what seems like the end only the beginning?

The Beginning by Beverly Lewis
beverlylewis.com

◊ BETHANYHOUSE